FILLET MIGNON

A Mrs. Millet & Mrs. Hark Mystery

by
Margaret Searles

wp

Wrinklers Press
McKinleyville, California

FILLET MIGNON

Queries regarding rights and permissions should be addressed to:
Wrinklers Press
P.O. Box 2745
McKinleyville, CA 95519-2745.

First paperback printing, 2006

Fillet Mignon / by Margaret Searles
ISBN: 0-9768976-2-8

Cover Art by Ardy Scott
Caricatoon of Margaret Searles by James Oddie

PRINTED IN THE UNITED STATES OF AMERICA.

DEDICATION

For my buddies in the Central Coast Chapter of Sisters in Crime and, as always, for my family. Can't tell you how much your support and encouragement mean to me.

OTHER BOOKS IN THE MRS. MILLET & MRS. HARK MYSTERY SERIES:

TERLINGUA ALE

They winter in a Texas RV park on the Rio Grande. Missing beauty washed up by flash flood, raft trip, catfish fry, two mind-boggling Texas funerals and plenty of the local brew.

DEVONSHIRE CREAM

Tour of West Country England marred by death of harmless (or is he?) postal clerk. Big-time jewel thieves, gorgeous tour guide in peril, lots of delicious Devonshire Cream.

CAST OF CHARACTERS

Margaret Millet... Strange messages on her answering machine shatter her peace of mind.

Judith Hark... Determined seeker of fair play.

Willy Hark... Font of good sense and Mrs. Hark's devoted husband.

Cassandra Gates... So young, so black, so missing. Does she know too much about some dangerous people?

Mbyrna Gates... Don't call her Myrna; it's Oom-burn-a. Cassandra gives her more anxiety than her other four children combined.

Clark Atherton... Scholar, teacher and business man. A little old for Cassandra, but willing to wait.

Venus Valentine... Into Yoga, Goddesses, and the Temple of Repose. Romance could change her way of life.

Julius Portera... Manages BFK Restaurant Supply, employs Cassandra and longs for Venus Valentine.

Glenda Ravenet... Cassandra's Supervisor at BFK believes in getting ahead.

Darlene Evans... Receptionist. One person at the BFK office and another at the Temple of Repose.

Jason Evans... Darlene's brother. A joyful spirit, he shuns the world of fakery and games.

Frank Slee... BFK's sales manager really moves that Filet Mignon.

Darius Clumber... Delivery driver for BFK—until someone shortens his career.

Chief Marion Belgrave... of the Gambol Beach Police. All Cop, he is still rotund but has outgrown his High School nickname, "Marion the Librarian."

Chapter 1
Mrs. Millet: Where Is Cassandra Gates

"Good grief," Margaret Millet muttered to herself. Bad enough that the telephone company hadn't saved her old number while she was gone, but whose number had they given her, anyway? She rewound the tape in her answering machine and listened to the messages again.

"Cassandra Gates, please call this number in regard to your auto loan," the first message began. In the second message, a squeaky, young-girl voice implored, "Cassy, for the love of Isis, (Isis? It sounded like Isis.) get yourself back in here—Julius is interviewing people for your job! He reeely means it this time!" A slammed receiver, a silence, an ear-piercing beep.

Then the third message. "Cassandra, this is Mother. You sound awful—are you sick? That man called me again. I'm scared. I've changed my phone number. Please come to see me—I don't want to give the new number over the phone."

After that the tape recorded one hang-up after another. Margaret fast-forwarded to the end this time, to make sure. Then she pushed the "erase" key and started to rewind. And stopped. "Oh, bother! It's none of my business," she fumed. All the same, she replaced the tape with a new one and saved the messages. Then she listened to her own recording. Why didn't people realize she wasn't Cassandra Gates?

"You have reached 473-2348. Sorry I can't come to the phone right now. Please leave a message. Wait for the beep!" Recorded at the tail-end of a bad cold, her voice sounded low and raspy, not her normal, clear enunciation. Did Cassandra Gates sound like that? Maybe, if she had a cold.

A few days earlier, Margaret Millet had returned to her California home, a studio apartment (converted garage) behind her daughter's house in Gambol Beach. Like the robins, she migrated semi-annually; north in the spring to Brinyside, Oregon where she owned four tiny beach cabins and rented them to summer vacationers, and south in the fall, back to Gambol Beach. This year she had been away from April to November, having taken a trip after the summer season was over. Almost seven months. Too long, it seemed, for the telephone company.

When she called to reinstate her phone, the service representative said, "I'm sorry, your old number is no longer available. We can only reserve a number for six months. I'm sure they told you..."

"Oh no! What a nuisance! I'll have to notify everyone I know." Margaret's old phone number was 639-3696. The lucky numbers in her life always seemed to have sixes in them; her 1966 divorce, her all-time favorite residence, a trailer in Space 66, Malibu Cove, and her first rental property, a duplex numbered 664 and 666 on Branch Street in Santa Porta. The old telephone number with all those sixes had seemed particularly serendipitous. She hated to lose it.

"Well, what number can I have?" she asked.

"I can give you 473-2348."

"Not even the same prefix! What happened to 639?"

"It's filled up. All the new numbers start with 473. We can activate that by noon on Monday, Mrs. Millet. Is that satisfactory?"

Margaret grudgingly submitted. No use taking on the telephone company. Save your energies for things you can do something about, she told herself. This is not one of them.

Then the new number brought these messages from someone else's life...this someone called Cassandra Gates. Why? Why had Cassandra's telephone been disconnected? Why was she not going to work? making her car payments? keeping in touch with her mother? And the mother said, "That man called me again. I'm scared." She sounded scared, too.

Margaret slipped the message tape into the top drawer of her bureau. True, it was none of her business, but if the girl were actually missing....

Glancing at her wall clock, she saw it was nearly four; time for tea. She added bottled water to the kettle and turned on the burner. Gambol Beach tap water wasn't fit to drink, being extremely hard and when used to make tea, an iridescent rainbow floated on top. Oil. Not surprising, since the water came from the rocky hills back of Gambol Beach, land scabbed with pumping oil wells.

Setting her mug on the end table, Margaret eased her short, dumpy form into the rattan armchair. She slid small, white-socked feet out of the canvas shoes she habitually wore and propped them on the ottoman, then took a luxurious sip of tea, hot and strong with a dollop of milk to smooth it out. Relax. After all, the previous user of her new telephone number might have good reason to disappear. This generation had its problems, to be sure. When Margaret was a girl things were easier, not to mention safer. She remembered her first job at the bus depot and the move from her parents' farm to her own apartment in town, when she was still a junior in high school. That had been perfectly safe back in Til-lamook, Oregon, where—and when—she grew up.

In the midst of these memories, the phone jangled and Margaret flinched, nearly spilling her tea. She sighed, clambered out of the chair and stilled the noise on the third ring. "Hello?"

"About time—where the hell have you been?" The caller hissed over a back-babble of talk and clattering dishes. Was he calling from a restaurant? Before Margaret could speak, he went on, "I told you, nothing un-usual! Go to work, keep your mouth shut, don't make any waves, or your old lady gets it. That's no joke, I'm not laughing, you little bitch. Don't think you can hide; you're too dumb."

Outrageous! Margaret gasped, unable to choose from the replies that tumbled into her brain. While she dith-ered, the caller hung up.

Too late to even say "Who are you?" Or ala Lily Tomlin, "This is not the party to whom you are speaking!" And she could have added, "Don't threaten me, you bully!" And "Cassandra Gates may be smarter than you think; you can't find her, can you?" All these choice retorts went to waste, unexpressed.

The man who had frightened Cassandra's mother? It must be! What a foul-mouthed, hateful brute! Furious, Margaret shook her close-cropped gray and beige head and chugged the last of her tea. She couldn't let this pass. No man should berate an unknown young woman (obvi-ously in difficulties), call her vulgar names and threaten harm to her mother—not in Margaret Millet's hearing.

She wrote the man's words on her telephone pad, to the best of her memory. Then she called her friend, Judy Hark.

"Judy, I'm sorry to call so early—I just had to!" Judy

Hark's friends, the thoughtful ones at least, did not call her in the afternoon. Her husband Willy liked his nap, so he could watch the late television shows at night.

"What's the matter—can't you come to Yoga class to-morrow?"

"No, it's not that. I've just had the strangest phone call..."

"Just a minute, let me stir my stew." Judy put the phone down with a bump, followed by sounds of pot lids and stirring spoons. "There, I turned it off. Tell."

Margaret told, in detail, about the messages for Cassandra Gates. "And now this *man*—he must be the one who threatened her mother—he whispered! A loud, nasty *whisper!* So I couldn't tell much by his voice, except he sounded crude and vulgar."

"That poor girl. Any idea who she is?"

"Not the foggiest," Margaret said. "Do you know anybody named Julius who owns a business?"

"The employer. Sorry, it doesn't ring any bells. What about the car payment? Didn't you say they gave a phone number?"

"Yes, but I doubt if they'd tell me anything personal about her. Let me look in the book—maybe her address is listed." Margaret tucked the phone against her shoulder and opened the fat Santa Porta County telephone book. "No. Her name is here all right, and my new phone number, with no address."

"That's no help. Listen, I've got an idea. Stay right there; I'm coming over. Just let me put the stew in a casserole so it can finish cooking in the oven. 'Bye."

Good. Judy had thought of something. The Harks lived three miles away, on the inland side of Gambol Beach. She could be here in fifteen minutes, even allowing for the casserole. Full of energy, Margaret cleared an untidy mess of papers off the table, shelved three books, hung up the jacket she had tossed on the bed, and put out a clean guest towel in the bathroom. Judy Hark was a neat, elegant woman in both housekeeping and dress, and Margaret respected that, even though such things mattered little to her, personally.

"Play the first part again; I didn't quite catch that number," Judy said. She perched on the secretary chair at Margaret's all-purpose table, pen poised over the telephone pad. She looked like a secretary of the most superior sort—auburn hair styled in a French twist, make-up perfect, her fashionable vest and trousers set off by a ruffled shirt—her standard state; she hadn't had time to do more than doff her apron and touch up her lipstick before driving over. Straight backed, tall and slender, she leaned forward, crossed her feet at the ankles and slipped one heel out of its classic spectator pump.

Margaret re-played the tape at a higher volume. Judy didn't like to admit it, but her hearing wasn't as good as it once had been.

Judy noted the finance company's number, jotted a few words on the left side of the pad and looked up, her blue eyes meeting Margaret's gray ones with a twinkle. "Okay, I've got it. Just listen."

She dialed. "Good afternoon. This is the Credit Manager at Mayfair Lumber in Santa Porta. You're carrying an auto contract for a...let's see...a Cassandra Gates. May I speak to your Credit Manager or Supervisor about this? Thank you, I'll hold."

Margaret grinned. What technique! Judy had been a full-charge bookkeeper and office manager in her working days, and her voice still carried authority. Judy winked and Margaret stifled a giggle.

"That's right, Cassandra Gates. Could you verify her employment? BFK Restaurant Supply, yes, that's what we show, too. We're having a little problem—do you show any personal or family references? Oh, a co-signer? Clark Atherton, at 475 Mabel, Santa Porta. Thank you. Is there a phone number? Yes, fine. This should help... You are? No, we haven't been able to reach her either, at least not this week. I've called several times. Yes, I'll let you know. Not at all—it's the least I can do. Thank *you*! Goodbye; we'll be in touch."

Margaret shook her head in admiration. "What a bill collector you'd make, Judy! That was terrific!"

"Nothing to it if you know how. Actually, Ardis Johnson is the Credit Manager at Mayfair Lumber. She's been there ever since I retired. I took a chance—that woman might have known her from the Credit Managers Association or somewhere—but she didn't, thank goodness."

Judy had written "BFK Rest. Sup." and the name, address, and telephone number of the co-signer on the pad. "The finance company has been trying to reach Cassandra for two weeks, both at home and at work. The girl is definitely missing. And considering that man's threat—what did he say?" She referred to Margaret's notes. "'...don't make any waves or your old lady gets it.' Don't you think we should call the police?"

"You may be right," Margaret agreed.

"No, I'm not a relative; I only inherited her telephone number. Sergeant, there must be something you can do. This girl's mother may be in real danger—that man sounded nasty and sincere, believe me. Can't you at least call the company Cassandra Gates works for and get her mother's name? She should be warned..."

Margaret's face flushed an angry red as the smooth, professional voice repeated all the reasons why the police could not take action. No one had filed a missing person report. The anonymous telephone threat was just that—anonymous—and had not been recorded, so it was hearsay, as well. The police department was very sorry, there was nothing they could do unless a relative of Cassandra Gates...Yes, Mrs. Millet could write it all down in a letter to the Chief of Police. That would be fine. The act of a good citizen.

Margaret slammed down the receiver. "And don't think I won't write to the Chief," she sputtered, "at the very least."

"Be careful, Margaret. You don't want to meet that 'don't make waves' man. And you won't go nosing around alone? Take me with you." Judy's face puckered with concern.

"You'd better go take your casserole out of the oven," Margaret snapped, still scowling. Then her face softened and she smiled at her friend. "Don't worry. I wouldn't dream of doing anything without you. I'll write the letter and tomorrow, after Yoga class...We'll see. There must be something we can do."

After Judy departed, Margaret did indeed write to the Chief of Police. She wrote on her computer, letting herself go, releasing her anger at the Gambol Beach Police Department and the Sergeant who had taken her call. "Just like a bunch of regulation bound, bureaucratic men!" she wrote. "If women ran the law-enforcement in Gambol Beach, you'd see some changes! Crimes would be prevented, not just punished..." Margaret Millet was sure the male dominated world could be greatly improved if women had more control.

Her anger expressed, she blessed the lap-top computer that allowed her to edit the hot, passionate phrases down to a cool and factual version. This she saved on disk, printing two copies, one to send and the other for a file folder labeled "Cassandra Gates." The notes she and Judy had made and the tape from the answering machine were added to the file.

Depleted by her efforts, Margaret wanted her supper. She cooked as little as possible, usually preparing a large pot of food to be eaten daily until it was gone. This evening she re-heated chili made with plenty of chili powder, shredded tri-tip beef, and Santa Maria poquito beans cooked all together, California style.

Was it the spicy chili that kept her awake until the wee hours? Or the anxious voice in her brain that kept saying, over and over, "You must find Cassandra Gates...find her... What's happened to her? Where is Cassandra Gates?"

Chapter 2
Mrs. Millet: Cousins

Margaret Millet opened her eyes to two cross beams and the ceiling above them, painted her favorite shade of light butter-yellow. Home. How good it was to be home, the long drive down the coast highway behind her, the Oregon cabins rented for the winter and producing enough money to live on, if she was careful, until spring.

Light streamed through the skylight, laughing at the "room-darkening" window shades. Even in November, Gambol Beach was blessed with sunshine.

Something was wrong, though—some alarming fly struggled in her ointment pot—oh, yes. Cassandra Gates. And Cassandra's frightened mother, whoever she might be.

Margaret turned on her side, elbowed herself vertical and slid her feet into scuffs to protect them from the beautiful, but cold tile floor. The garage's concrete floor had been too uneven for vinyl and her carpenter suggested carpet with thick padding, but Margaret chose unglazed Spanish pavers. This close to the beach (three blocks), carpeting collected sand and fleas—besides, the tile set off the hand-braided rugs she had inherited from her mother, their soft colors a constant remembrance.

The main room of her granny-pad stood open to the raised ceiling. She had constructed the narrow bed herself, a sturdy plywood platform topped by a pair of cot-size mattresses. In the daytime, a Mexican blanket and cushions converted it to a comfortable couch. A closet with mirrored doors reflected the room, doubling its size to the eye. Three side-walls accommodated her furnishings, everything scaled to fit, with a compact kitchen on the fourth.

Margaret pulled on a robe, turned up the thermostat and toddled to the bathroom, a lean-to addition behind the kitchen. It housed a set of Maytag laundry machines in addition to the usual bathroom fixtures. Or unusual— Margaret liked real baths, not showers. "Who wants to stand on one foot to wash the other?" She had installed an old fashioned claw-foot bath tub, its outside enameled a happy shade of blue.

After her usual breakfast (granola, banana and milk), Margaret sipped strong tea and opened the file folder labeled "Cassandra Gates." She turned on her computer and transcribed the recorded messages, playing the tape over and over to be sure of the exact words. She described the voices, too, as accurately as possible; female, young, anxious, squeaky; female, older, frightened. The young one had definitely said, "...for the love of Isis." Wasn't Isis some sort of goddess? She resorted to her copy of Bulfinch's Mythology and read, "Plutarch considers Isis to be the earth, the feminine part of nature, while Diodorus says the Egyptians, considering the earth to be the parent of all things born, called her Mother." Well, well. Had goddesses invaded modern slang? A question for Venus Valentine, the instructor of her Yoga class.

One copy of the transcript joined the now cool and sanitary letter to Chief Marion Belgrave of the Gambol Beach Police. Another went in the "Cassandra Gates" file folder.

The tape itself should be...preserved? Past experiences had made Margaret cautious. This audio tape, the only real backing for her letter to Chief Belgrave, should be kept safe. Ridiculous though it seemed, she wrapped the tape in waxed paper, packed it in the box from a bar of soap and re-sealed the box with glue. She placed it next to an identical soap box in the bathroom cupboard, smiling at herself as she did so. Now remember where you put it, Margaret. And hurry up or you'll be late for class.

"Yoga for Seniors" met at the Veteran's Hall every Tuesday at 10:00 A.M., Venus Valentine, Instructor. A leader at the Temple of Repose, Venus was into relaxation, spiritual growth, and definitely, goddesses. Margaret had joined the class because Judy Hark did, after meeting Venus at one of the Historical Society's perpetual potluck dinners. Yoga, besides cultivating serenity and inner peace, turned out to be good exercise. Margaret enjoyed the bits about nature and Planet Earth that Venus worked into her instruction.

The class had begun. In her baggy, rose-colored sweats, Margaret tiptoed into the community room where twenty "senior" women sat on the floor in a circle, taking deep breaths. She slid her mat into an open space and assumed the cross-legged posture. Not that she could sit like the teacher—her knees wouldn't go flat on the floor—but she did her best, considering the age and rigidity of her joints.

"Inhale fully...the abdomen softens...take in all the goodness, receive the energy, breathe out all the things you don't need," Venus said in her musical voice. The tape player on the floor beside her tinkled a soft background of oriental chimes.

"Deeper and fuller, in and out...feel the circle of life." Venus, lean in a tiger-striped leotard, her hair in a dark braid down her back, exuded an aura of peace and serenity. Margaret inhaled deeply and smiled a greeting to Judy, across the room.

"Hands clasped behind the head, IN-hale, pull the elbows toward the sides of the room...release the neck... open out as a flower opening to the sun. Now EX-hale... tilt the body forward...closing in at the close of day." Venus suited action to words.

"Be aware of the sitz bones, lift the spine out of the pelvic basin..." Gradually, the gentle stretching, the tinkling wind-chime music and the hypnotic tranquility of Venus Valentine's voice detached Margaret from her anxieties and floated her off like a raft on a warm, slow river. For an hour she did as she was told without question, curiously part of this circle of crones, all bending their bodies into absurd postures.

Not until the very end of the session, during the "final relaxation," did Margaret's obstreperous sense of humor penetrate her dreamy state. The women lay supine on their mats while Venus chanted, "Relax the cheeks, the jaw, let the tongue relax down onto the lower palate. Let the eyes relax...the eyelids become soft little pillows. Relax the scalp, let the circulation come, let go each follicle of the hair..."

Margaret's unruly brain flashed a picture of all these women relaxing their follicles—and their beauty-shop curls falling off their heads onto the floor. Laughter boiled inside her, but she took herself sternly in hand. She must be serious. It wouldn't do to roll on the floor in giggles.

After class came hugs and gossip, compliments on colorful exercise outfits and invitations to lunch. There was no chance to ask Venus about goddesses—she dashed away, saying she had a counseling appointment at the Temple. The women sifted out to the parking lot singly and in small groups.

"Let's have lunch at Shelley's," Judy said. "Did you write that letter? Do I get to read it?"

"Yes, yes, and yes," Margaret replied. "Can you come to town with me after lunch?" By "town" she meant Santa Porta, a city of 40,000 people, twelve miles inland from Gambol Beach.

"I can. I knew you'd have something figured out."

"The soup and half-sandwich," Judy told the hovering waitress. "Turkey on whole wheat and a cup of chowder."

Shelley's Restaurant, on a busy corner near the pier, sported an outdoor patio with small tables and large potted plants. The ladies chose a corner behind a potted palm. Still dressed for Yoga (not that attire mattered in Gambol Beach), and anxious to discuss Cassandra Gates, they wanted privacy.

"I'll have the chowder too—and a club sandwich," Margaret said.

The waitress scurried away, and Judy got down to business. "Let me see the letter; I can't wait. Why are we going to town?"

Margaret pulled the letter out of her purse and passed it across the table. "I thought we might visit BFK Restaurant Supply, unless you have a better idea. Maybe we can talk to the girl who phoned—and the mother's name and address should be in Cassandra's personnel file. I'm really anxious about her mother."

"How can we get them to tell us, though?"

Margaret made a wry face. "A reasonable lie? Could

we say we're friends from out of town trying to find her? The mother did change her phone number; she said so. I know, we can be cousins—the mother's cousins."

"What if they ask what her name is? It may not be Gates, you know."

"She just re-married and we don't remember? Oh, boy—we'd better try to steer clear of that—get them to tell us the name, somehow."

Judy said, "You're the actress. I'll play along. I can tell you one thing, though—we'll have a better chance if we get there while all the supervisors are still at lunch— while the front desk is covered by some lowly file clerk or receptionist who doesn't know any better."

"What do you mean, I'm the actress? You were the one who got all that info from the finance company," Margaret protested.

"That didn't take acting. Remember the time in England when you pretended to be a writer? Completely convincing. I believed you myself..."

The waitress brought cups of chowder. Margaret inhaled the aroma and smiled. "It worked, didn't it? We learned everything we wanted to know."

"And you can do Cassandra Gates' mother's cousin, just as well." Judy slipped the letter to Chief Belgrave from its envelope and began to eat her chowder.

Margaret opened a packet of oyster crackers. All that Yoga had made her ravenous. She bit into the sandwich with gusto and said no more until the meal and the letter were both ingested.

"Did I leave anything out?"

"No, it's all here. Good job, Margaret. It should make the Chief curious, at the very least."

"Well, it made us curious. You'll notice I told him we

were going to look into this ourselves, since the police are 'unable to act.'"

Judy sniggered. "I noticed. 'We'll keep you informed.' Well, if anything happens, old 'Marion the Librarian' can't say he wasn't warned. That's what the mean ones called him in school. Poor kid, he was fat and saddled with that name. Marion! What kind of parents would do that to a boy?"

"Really? And he went into police work. What a psychiatrist could make of that. How did you know?"

"He was in my son Johnny's class."

"Oh." Margaret pushed her empty plate, a glass plate in the shape of a clam shell, to the edge of the table. "On the other hand, we could try to find Clark Whatsisname, the man who co-signed the auto loan."

"But he's a man. What if he is the one...?"

"The threatening caller. Yes, I thought of that. I could call, but I'm not sure I'd recognize the voice; he whispered, like he was afraid of being overheard, and his normal speaking voice might be quite different."

"Then the employer is the best place to start. You can do it, Margaret. I'm sure you can do it!" Judy rose, the lunch check in her hand. Margaret left a generous tip and followed to pay her share.

They took Judy's car to town, reaching BFK Restaurant Supply at 12:45. "I hope the supervisors take long lunches," Margaret said.

The business occupied a warehouse on Sacramento Road with a large, gravel parking area in front. A truck stood at the loading dock and another truck waited in line, its refrigeration motor roaring.

The office at the other end of the building was quiet enough. The blond receptionist behind a waist-high counter stopped filing her scarlet talons, looked up and batted her false eyelashes as though she needed the practice.

"Can I help you?" she squeaked, the words garbled by a wad of chewing gum shifted from one cheek to the other.

The voice that had begged Cassandra to "get yourself back in here." Margaret smiled warmly and said, "I hope so. We're from out of town and we're looking for a cousin who lives here in Santa Porta. Her daughter works for you—Cassandra Gates. Is Cassandra here today?"

This speech brought totally unexpected results. The girl pushed her chair back from the counter and let out a whinny of laughter. "A cousin!" she shrilled. "No kidding—a cousin!"

Judy gave the girl a frosty stare and said, "Here, now. What's so funny?"

The girl popped her gum and whinnied again. "You reelly don't know, do you. Oh, you're reelly funny! Cousins? I mean, Cassy Gates is black—like totally black—you know, black as a lump of coal!"

Chapter 3
Mrs. Hark: Black and White

J udy Hark wanted to run. Cassandra Gates was black!
Here they were, a pair of Anglo-Saxons, white as they
come, pretending to be her cousins and Cassandra
Gates was black—a member of that legally equal but
often separate, segment of the American population.
Margaret looked equally flabbergasted.

Judy did her best to save the situation. With both eyebrows at maximum lift, she said, "By marriage, of course.
Perhaps you haven't met any of the Caucasian side of
the family."

Margaret nodded vigorously and beamed at the receptionist.

The girl didn't buy it. "Look," she said. "I don't know
what you're trying to pull, but Cassy's not here. I haven't
seen her for two weeks. If you're from a collection agency—where are you from, anyway? The Health Club?" She
eyed Margaret's rose-colored sweats and Judy's lavender nylon exercise suit and let out another whinny. Then
the telephone buzzed, and the girl pivoted to answer.

Judy whispered, "She sounds friendly to Cassy—do
you think we can trust her with the truth?"

"I don't think we have a choice, do you?"

The receptionist transferred the call and turned her
eyes back to the Yoga outfits. "Well? What do you want
with Cassy?"

"You left a message for her, didn't you?" Margaret
asked. "'Get yourself back in here; Julius is interviewing
people for your job,' or something like that."

The girl's jaw dropped, revealing her wad of gum.

"Yes, I did—how did you know?"

Judy said, "The thing is, we do know. And you haven't heard from Cassy since you made that call." A statement, not a question. "We think she may be in trouble, and we're trying to help. Her mother received threatening telephone calls, and changed her phone number."

"Cassandra's telephone has been disconnected," Margaret added. "The telephone company gave me her number. I've been getting Cassy's calls and messages."

"Oh, my Gawd..." The girl understood. Not only that, Judy would have bet she made connections to something she knew. Something alarming. For the first time, she seemed frightened, unsure of herself.

Judy pressed on. "We want to get in touch with Cassandra's mother. She called Cassandra, but didn't leave her new phone number, so we can't call her. We thought you might be able to help."

"I can't tell you anything. I'm sorry, what business is it of yours? No, I couldn't possibly."

Suddenly the front door swung in and the small lobby filled with people. Judy moved aside for a dressed-for-success, middle-aged woman, tall in three inch heels. A square, forceful-looking man in khakis, plaid shirt, and bolo tie, his dark curls clipped close around a bronzed face and a rotund, eager-to-please chap in a plaid suit followed.

The woman said, "Any messages, Darlene?" Then, to Judy, "Are you being helped?"

"Yes, thank you," Judy managed. She muttered into Margaret's ear, "The bosses. Let's get out of here."

While Darlene handed out message slips, they eased back to the door and escaped to Judy's car, parked across the street.

"Good grief," Margaret said.

"Good grief is right. What do we do now?"

"We didn't learn anything, except that Cassandra Gates is black. Do you want to give it up?"

"No!" Judy was indignant. "What has that got to do with it? She's still missing, her mother's still threatened. Why should we give it up?" So far, Judy had been along for the ride, her main purpose to keep Margaret out of trouble; now she felt a new urge to find out what had happened to the missing Cassandra. Surely, Margaret wouldn't drop the entire matter just because...

Margaret would not. "Okay, okay—just checking. I feel exactly the same. We've never talked about this. I mean, a lot of people would say, like Darlene, 'what business is it of ours?' She's black and we're white."

"That makes no difference to me," Judy maintained. "What do we do now? Go mail the letter to Chief Belgrave?"

"I guess. Or drive by Clark Atherton's place? I think Mabel Street is up by the University—have you got a map?"

Judy pulled a Santa Porta map out of her glove box, loosened its complicated folds and spread it out over the steering wheel. Margaret was mistaken; Mabel Street was nowhere near the University. It angled off Johnson Avenue on the near side of town. "No, it's just past the County Hospital, Margaret. We can go up from this side if we take Laurel Boulevard."

Margaret wasn't listening. She pointed and said, "Look!" Darlene pushed through the front door of BFK and trotted toward the cars parked at the side of the building. "She must take her lunch break now."

Judy started her engine. "Let's see where she goes."

Darlene got into a battered red car, some sort of oriental sub-compact, and without looking right or left, drove into the street, tires spitting gravel, raising a cloud of dust. Brakes screeched as a Jeep swerved to avoid her. Judy waited until both vehicles were half a block away, then followed.

Darlene's car clattered across the railroad tracks and turned up Laurel Blvd., followed by the Jeep, still a shield from Darlene's rear view mirror. At the top of the hill, she turned left on Johnson Avenue for a few blocks, then right on Abby Lane, a street marked "DEAD END." Judy passed the turn and stopped on Johnson.

She had watched Darlene's route so intently that she failed to look behind her and when she pulled over, a large delivery truck nearly rear-ended her car. The driver braked, shifted down and passed them at a crawl, stretching across the seat to stare down into her face. The side of the truck bore a garish picture of a filet steak on a smoking platter. A scroll beneath the platter read, "BFK RESTAURANT SUPPLY."

"Well! Where did he come from!" Judy gasped, then added, "Silly question. I see where he came from." The truck did not stop, to her great relief. "Did you see him? He sure seemed interested in us!" She'd had a clear view of the driver's young-old face, pimply skin and the drooping, untrimmed mustache over his leering mouth. Not a face one wanted to see in one's dreams.

Margaret stopped clutching the arm rest. "Do you think he followed us? Or Darlene? Darn, why didn't we get his license number!"

"I'm just glad he kept on going." Judy shuddered and twisted in her seat to look behind them. "Abby Lane. Nice neighborhood. Did Darlene look to you like someone who lives in Abby Lane?"

Margaret shook her head, "Definitely not. Let's walk back and see where she went."

Judy locked the car and they approached Abby Lane, a steep, tree-lined block of tall houses with spectacular views over Poppy Valley. Darlene had parked in a driveway on the far side, three houses in. Judy took Margaret's arm, slowed her to a casual pace, and stopped behind some oleander bushes to inspect the house Darlene had entered. Large, nearly new, sided with redwood and roofed with blue tile, its single pitch roof sections joined at strange angles over the two-story facade. A "modern" house that would look dated in a few years, Judy thought. No accounting for tastes.

They climbed to the top of the one-block street, paused to admire the view, and started back, nervously debating whether or not to approach the house and knock on the door.

"What if that man lives there?" Margaret asked.

"Why didn't we change clothes," Judy countered, realizing as she said it that if they had, they'd have missed Darlene and wouldn't be walking down Abby Lane.

They stopped behind the oleanders again. Across the street, Darlene raced out of the house. She slammed her car door, roared back in reverse, and drove off with a clash of gears, barely hesitating at the Johnson Avenue stop sign before she turned right, out of view.

"How has that girl lived this long!" Margaret said.

"She didn't even glance our way," Judy said. "I don't think she saw us, do you?" She started across the street. They had come this far; they couldn't stop now! "Come on, are you game?"

Margaret was game. The dumpy figure in rose-colored

sweats toddled bravely along behind.

Judy climbed the steps, crossed the broad front deck, and pushed the doorbell. Melodic chimes sounded inside the house.

Margaret caught up. She pointed to a brass plaque mounted on the heavy oak door. It was engraved with a single word: "Gates."

Chapter 4
Mrs. Millet: Homelife

When the door opened, Margaret Millet thought, if Cassy Gates is black as a lump of coal, she didn't get it from her mother—if this is her mother. The woman who stood behind the screen had golden skin and short, dark hair that waved but did not kink. She stood as tall as Judy Hark and wore a modish coral-colored knit suit, padded shoulders tapering to a snug fit at the hips. She looked sturdy, resilient. Young.

"Yes?" the woman said.

"Mrs. Gates?"

"I am. What can I do for you?" The woman's voice was non-committal, not at all like the panicky voice of the answering machine. Could this sophisticate have anything to fear?

Judy stepped in with her customary tact. "I'm Judith Hark and this is my friend, Margaret Millet. We've been trying to find you, as I'm sure Darlene must have told you. In fact," she cleared her throat, "we followed her, you know."

Mrs. Gates inspected her coolly but did not reply.

Margaret said, "I've got Cassandra's old telephone number, and I've been getting strange calls. I...that is, we thought you might want to know...a man who called Cassandra said he knew where her mother lived in a threatening way..." She felt like a babbling fool. This house, this self-possessed black woman—what had she been thinking of to barge into such a situation? Margaret detested bigotry as much as Judy did, but she had lived in the South for three years during her married life (the last three years of her married life, which was no coincidence), and she knew that some black people despised whites in the same unreasoning, indiscriminate way that Klan members despised blacks. That knowledge hadn't changed her mind about fair and equal treatment for all, but it made her cautious. She was perfectly willing to like and befriend anyone who could reciprocate, but...

"Maybe we'd better go." She turned to Judy, hoping to exit gracefully.

"Wait." Mrs. Gates pushed open the screen. "Come in. You're not what I expected. Darlene didn't explain."

Margaret hesitated. Judy gave her a little shove from behind. "Go on, Margaret. It's all right."

They crossed a tiled entry and stepped down into a living room that scarcely seemed to have walls, so huge was the expanse of glass overlooking Poppy Valley.

Not nasty-neat, though. An athletic jacket and a tennis racquet lay on the low, black leather sofa. Two guitars and a set of bongo drums decorated a corner. Pottery sugar and cream containers and two coffee mugs fought for space among the magazines and books on a glass-topped coffee table.

Across the coffee table, a youngish black man perched on the edge of a black leather armchair and held a large black dog by the collar. The dog snarled and showed its fangs. The man looked tense and ready to spring. Cassandra's mother was not unprotected.

"Please sit." Mrs. Gates pushed the tennis racquet aside. "This is our friend, Clark Atherton. And Kwanza. Say hello to the ladies, Kwanza. They are guests." The black lab stopped snarling and pulling against his collar and raised a paw in greeting. The man released him and sat back.

"What a lovely dog," Judy said. "And so beautifully trained."

"Yes, isn't he. Clark, this is Margaret Millet, I think you said? And..."

"Judith Hark."

"Yes, Judith Hark. I'm Mbyrna Gates." She pronounced her name distinctly, Oom-burn-a, as though she expected them to remember it. "Would you like some coffee?"

"Not for me, thank you. We just had lunch," Judy said, sitting on the couch, as requested. Margaret joined her silently, trying to realign her thinking. "Not what I expected," Mrs. Gates had said. Well, she wasn't the only one surprised.

After an awkward pause, Margaret said, "We wanted to find you because of these telephone calls, you see. And because of your call to Cassandra, recorded on my answering machine. You changed your telephone number? but didn't say what the new number was, so I couldn't call you back and...well, we just thought we should find you..." She bumbled to a halt, not knowing how much she should reveal, with Clark Atherton—auto loan co-signer Clark Atherton—present.

Judy asked the basic question. "Has your daughter been in touch? Do you know where she is?"

"My daughter Cassandra, you mean. I have three daughters and two sons." Mbyrna Gates waved a hand toward a row of pictures on the wall.

"Yes, Cassandra!" Margaret snapped. Hadn't the woman been listening? "By the calls I've been getting, all sorts of people are looking for her. It worried us. We thought something might have happened to her."

Mbyrna Gates' calm coated her face like a glaze. She opened her mouth to reply, but Clark Atherton interrupted.

"What did I tell you, Myrna! This whole frightful week I've looked for her! Not a word of warning—she simply vanished!" He rose and paced panther-like to the windows.

Margaret eyed him gratefully. Here was someone who cared, someone worried about the missing Cassandra, someone who would listen to her. His features were aquiline, almost Arabic, but he had blue-black African skin and close-cropped African hair. Although dressed as formally as Cassandra's mother, he was not in the same tidy condition. His tie hung loose and his white shirt gaped open at the neck. His suit jacket lay in a tangle on the back of the chair.

Clark Atherton was not the threatening caller. He spoke educated British English and the accent was natural, not acquired. This man could never have said, "don't make any waves or your old lady gets it."

Mbyrna leaned on the chair arm. Her eyes flickered and then squeezed tight, as though she had opened a door to horrors and slammed it shut again. Absently, she said, "Must you call me Myrna? It's legally Mbyrna now. I can't help it if my mother admired Myrna Loy."

"I say, Mbyrna! Please!" Clark pleaded.

Mbyrna opened her eyes and sighed deeply. "Yes, all right, Clark. We'll hear what they have to say." She turned to the pair on the couch. "No, Judith, we don't know where Cassandra is. Margaret, please tell us what you know."

That was better. Margaret sorted her thoughts and began. "I was concerned about the messages on my answering machine and then a man called while I was at home. I picked up the phone and he said something like 'go to work, don't make any waves, or your old lady gets it,' and he hung up before I could say anything."

Mbyrna turned to Clark. "I told you. He was dreadful."

"Well, I couldn't let that pass. Cassandra's auto loan company left a number, so I—that is, Judy—called them and found out where she works. Then we went to BFK and asked how to find you. Darlene wouldn't tell us, so when she drove off, we followed her. That's how we got here."

"And we called the police," Judy said. "They said a relative would have to file a missing persons report before they could do anything. Have you done that?"

"The Police!" Mbyrna's glossy poise shattered at the word. Tears started and her voice shook. "No! I didn't tell you, Clark, I'm sorry. The man said he was looking for Cassy and he'd better find her, or else he was coming to see me. He said not to call the police if I wanted to see Cassy again! We can't go to the police—we can't!"

Clark sprang to the sofa and put his arm around Mbyrna's shoulders. "Good God, Myrna, why didn't you say? How could you keep that to yourself? I've a right..."

"Sure, shout it from the housetops! Cassandra is missing! Some thug is looking for her! S-strangers off the s-street know more about it than her m-mother does...Oh, where is she? What's happened to her?"

Kwanza raised his muzzle and mourned, "oh-ooo-ooo" in sympathy. Mbyrna pulled his head into her lap and clung to both Clark and the dog. "Oh, Kwanza, you miss her, too."

Margaret exchanged a look with Judy that said "so she's human, after all," and Judy reached over to pat Mbyrna's shoulder. "Hang on, dear. The man hasn't found Cassandra or he wouldn't make these threats. We'll have to find her first, that's all. Here now—Clark? Is there brandy or something?"

There was no brandy, but Clark found a bottle of sherry and poured four glasses. By the time the excellent sherry had been sipped and Mbyrna comforted, the little group stopped being strangers of different races and started over on a new footing of sympathy and understanding. The ladies encouraged Mbyrna to talk, and she seemed glad to express her fears.

Cassandra was only 19, she told them. Mbyrna and her husband, Jefferson, had been deeply disappointed when Cassy dropped out of Junior College and got a job at BFK. She moved out, to share an apartment in Gambol Beach with two other girls. Mbyrna had been to the apartment a few days earlier, but Cassandra's roommates knew nothing. "She just didn't come home one night. Her things are all still there and her car is in the parking lot."

"When did she give up her telephone, do you know? It doesn't seem like they'd give her number to someone else so quickly," Margaret said.

Mbyrna couldn't explain that, except to say Cassandra had never been well-organized, and the telephone company might have cut off her phone because she didn't pay the bill. She often bought clothes first and paid bills later, sometimes borrowing from her parents or Clark Atherton.

"Our other children have never given us any trouble," Mbyrna said. There were two older than Cassy and two younger, one in college, one in law school, and the two younger ones at home, attending the public schools of Santa Porta. She, Mbyrna, held a Masters Degree in African Studies and taught at Cal U.

"And this would happen when Jefferson is away," she

mourned. "He's in South Africa, out in the Townships, observing for the U.N. There's no way I can reach him."

"I say, Mbyrna, you still have me," Clark Atherton pointed out. Clark also taught at Cal-U. Originally from South Africa, Jefferson Gates had sponsored his immigration. "That's how we happened to meet, Cassandra and me. She's very young—but I adore her, don't you know, and I'm willing to wait while she grows up." He stepped to the row of pictures on the wall, lifted one down, and handed it to Margaret.

"Cassandra?"

He nodded. "She was only fifteen when I took this." The enlarged snapshot showed Cassandra in action, playing with Kwanza, the black lab. Her face was so black and her grin so white that Margaret was irresistibly reminded of the pictures, so common during her childhood and so politically incorrect now, of black children eating watermelon.

Silently, she passed the picture to Judy.

"If only she hadn't gotten involved with those people," Mbyrna said. "I took that child to church every Sunday of her life, and the minute she left home, she took up with those people. Goddesses, no less! And pyramids, and all that."

Goddesses? Pyramids? "Do you mean the Temple of Repose?" Margaret asked.

"Yes and it was Darlene who took her there," Mbyrna said. "Darlene lives in Repose; stays with someone who's a member."

"Are they close friends, Cassandra and Darlene?"

"Thick as thieves. They go on Retreats. Why can't the child spend some time with her family? She stays in Repose all weekend sometimes and I can't even call her.

And poor Clark, she neglects him dreadfully."

What we have here is a generation gap, maybe even a chasm, Margaret thought. Her sympathies tended to lie with Cassandra. The middle child in a family of five—make that eight, counting the parents and Clark A.—and all of them planning her life for her. No wonder the kid moved out.

Judy said, "We know one of the leaders at the Temple of Repose. That may be where she's hi—er—staying."

"Do you think so? Could you find out? But why wouldn't she call and let me know?"

"She may be afraid of this man—the one who called you. Do you have any idea who he is?"

"Not at all. Clark?"

"He hasn't called me; how would I know? Mbyrna, are you sure about not telling the police?"

"You didn't hear him—I don't dare. Not until we find Cassandra—find her and make her say what kind of trouble she's in!"

Margaret opened her purse and took out the letter to Chief Belgrave. "I was going to mail this, but I'm glad I waited. It's a signed statement, and we are your witnesses if you need us." She handed it to Mbyrna as a gesture of support. Of course, she still had the copies in her file and on a computer disk at home, not to mention the hidden answering machine tape.

Judy nodded agreement. "Definitely witnesses. And we'll talk to Venus Valentine. I hope that's where Cassandra is. She's perfectly safe if she's at the Temple. Their way of life may seem a little strange, but they are caring, non-violent people. They wouldn't let anyone hurt her."

Mbyrna and Clark were due back at Cal-U. They exhanged telephone numbers and the ladies agreed to call as soon as they had talked to Venus Valentine.

On the way back to Gambol Beach, Margaret said, "Life is full of surprises."

"Cassandra, her family, or her South African boy-friend?"

"All three. Never go by voices on an answering machine, I guess." It wasn't so surprising to learn that Cassandra Gates was black—the shock there had come from being caught in their "cousin" imposture. Mbyrna Gates had certainly been a surprise, though. Educated, sophisticated, a career in Academia—every indication of money and position in Santa Porta society. Well, why not? Come, Margaret, she told herself, what were you expecting, Aunt Jemima?

She shook her head at the folly of pre-conceived ideas and said, "Don't forget I left my truck at Shelley's."

"I haven't. Should I call Venus or will you?"

"Well, you know her better than I do. I do wish we could find out what it's all about and why that nasty type wants to find Cassandra."

"You don't suppose he's just a very unpleasant bill collector, do you, Margaret?"

"No way. There's more to it than that. Who knows what young people get themselves involved in these days?"

Judy promised to call Venus Valentine and report back as soon as possible. Margaret drove back to her granny-pad, weary and confused. Her mind boggled at the situation and its characters. For the time being, she gave up trying to make sense of all she had seen and heard.

Later, having donned blue jeans, a wind-breaker against the ocean breezes, and a straw hat to fend off the California sun, Margaret locked her door and walked inland, toward the Gambol Beach Post Office.

Almost a mile, the hike to the post office should help to clear her brain. Exercise was her excuse for having a P.O. box; her daughter and son-in-law got their mail at the house. Besides the daily walk however, the box was private and in summer, the Post Office forwarded her mail to Oregon promptly and without fail.

She varied her walk to observe the changes in Gambol Beach. New houses were under construction in several locations, packed three or four on one lot in "Planned Unit Developments," or PUDs. All the disadvantages of both home ownership and renting, Margaret thought. Too close together and if you got bad neighbors, you couldn't pick up and move because you owned the house. Nice, big houses, though—stucco with tile roofs, very Californian.

This afternoon she gave the new construction a miss and walked along Ramona, a block north of Grand Avenue, the long commercial street that ended at the beach. There were lovely flower gardens on Ramona and Margaret enjoyed the glowing chrysanthemums.

Ramona still had a stretch of narrow paving with no sidewalks and small, older houses. It was here Margaret came upon another (or was it the same one?) of BFK's delivery vans, complete with the Filet Mignon logo. It was parked tailgate to tailgate with a second, somewhat smaller, truck almost inside of the BFK van. They looked like two mesozoic dinosaurs caught in the act of mating. The smaller truck was a rental, a "U-Haul" truck. Margaret remembered the many times she had rented such a vehicle to move her belongings. In those days, U-Hauls had a spirited slogan painted on them, "Adventures in Moving," but this one bore only a trite line about "comfortable suspension."

Now why was a U-Haul mated to a BFK delivery van? on a back street in Gambol Beach? She saw no one from outside the trucks, but the tramping of heavy shoes and a rumbling sound—a dolly?—were audible as she passed. A load being transferred? Which direction?

Margaret bent over and re-tied the laces of her tennis shoes so she could look back and see the second license plate. Then she turned the corner and stopped to write both license numbers on a scrap of paper from her purse.

Chapter 5
Mrs. Hark: Venus and Julius

At home, Judy Hark found her husband watching Jaques Cousteau on public television. Underwater shots of life in a coral reef.

"Howdy," Willy said.

"Hi. Sorry I've been so long. Margaret and I went to town. Any calls?"

"By the phone. Myrtle Farrini wants you—something about the trunk." Willy settled his bulk in the recliner and sipped from a glass of white wine. What a good secretary, never lost a message. One advantage of a stay-at-home husband.

"The Trunk. Oh dear, I'd better call her." The Trunk (Judy always thought of it capitalized) was the annual fund-raiser for the Santa Porta County Historical Society. Every year, just before Christmas, they raffled off an old-fashioned trunk full of hand-made quilts, household linens, bits of antique glass and china and other valuable items. As Chairperson, Judy was in charge of filling this trunk and selling the raffle tickets. Myrtle Farrini, her chief lieutenant, descended from a pioneer family and was more than slightly jealous of her Chairperson.

Judy picked up the phone, wishing for the umpteenth time that Margaret Millet would join the Historical Society. Margaret didn't lack interest in local history—it was the Society's monthly pot-luck dinner that deterred her. She refused to have anything to do with an organization that continually, as she put it, "did food."

"Hello, Myrtle? Judy. What's the problem? ...They did? But that's good! An exact duplicate? Oh, I see ..." Judy listened to Myrtle's high-pitched account of two identical tea pots donated for the trunk.

"Myrtle, look at it this way—we have a pair, a matched set. Congratulate both of the donors on putting the pair together. It will be all right. I can't talk now; I have to go out again. We can chat tomorrow, okay? I'll call you. 'Bye."

"You're going out again? You just got home," Willy grumbled.

"I know. It's this business of Margaret's—the strange messages she's getting on her answering machine. I told you about it." Judy had no secrets from Willy.

"The missing girl. Have you found her?"

"No, but...I'll tell you after dinner. Right now, I have to go to Repose and talk to Venus Valentine." Judy had decided an unannounced visit would be better than calling Venus on the telephone.

And it was time—past time!—to get out of her exercise suit. She must take a quick shower and change clothes. Casual clothes, her black slacks and a soft top in black, lavender, and cream. Fresh makeup.

"I'm off! Start the potatoes for me if I'm not back by five, will you dear?" Judy kissed Willy's bald spot and set out for Repose.

An Irish poetess and one of America's first women doctors had founded the Colony at Repose, early in the 20th century. They bought 200 acres just south of Gambol Beach that included prime agricultural land, sand dunes, and a lake. They divided the property around the lake into homesites. Members of the colony, mostly Suffragettes from upstate New York with their husbands and families, bought some of the homesites. The Colony kept the others, built houses on them, and leased the houses to members who couldn't afford to buy.

The Colony farmed the agricultural land or leased it to others: Japanese farmers before World War II, then the migrant Mexicans. Vegetables, strawberries and flowers for seed were grown there. The sand dunes between the lake and the ocean had been left wild and the Colony considered them sacred.

The woman doctor built a huge, three-story Edwardian mansion as her home, sanatorium, and guest house. After her death, that structure became "Temple Hall." The Historical Society held its pot-luck dinners there and Judy knew the place and its history well.

Judy passed Temple Hall and drove on to the Repose store. She wasn't sure where to find Venus and the storekeeper could probably tell her.

Repose Store stood at the edge of the farm land, in front of packing sheds where many hands prepared field produce for shipment. Judy often shopped there, as the store carried items unobtainable elsewhere; handcrafted pine needle baskets, exquisite hand-painted greeting cards, dried fruits, preserves, and vegetables fresh from the fields.

"Martha, how are you," Judy greeted the storekeeper.

"Happy and blooming, Judith. How can I help you?"

"I need to find Venus Valentine. Have you seen her this afternoon?"

"You came to the right place. She's in my office, giving a lesson." Martha nodded her head toward a door marked "Private" at the back of the store.

"Giving a lesson?"

"It's a man, the buyer from a wholesaler in town. He buys our vegetables all the time. Now he's thinking of joining the Temple, I guess." Martha grinned. "I'm not sure if its the Temple he likes, or Venus."

"How interesting! How long do you think...?"

"Oh, they've been at it for hours. Should be finished soon. Why don't you have a chair?" Martha waved toward the wicker chairs and tables at one end of the store, a nook where patrons could rest or eat snacks they had purchased.

"Yes, I'll wait."

Other customers claimed Martha's attention and Judy browsed toward the office. She studied the crystal pendants hung on a revolving rack but they interested her less than the sounds coming through the office door. When Venus taught yoga, she projected. Her voice wasn't loud but its clear, melodious tones carried. They were audible now.

"...all nature is good," Venus was saying. "What we do with nature can be good or evil. Fire can warm us, cook our food, or destroy our civilization, depending on how we use it."

The man, darn him, mumbled. Judy couldn't distinguish his words.

Venus answered, "Souls are constantly reincarnated. Our growing human population corresponds to the loss of other life forms. Migrating Passenger Pigeons once darkened the sky, but they are all gone now and the human population of the earth has increased by many millions. Old souls, already human, are reborn until they find the Sunset Path to our long home with the Earth Mother. Physical love should be enjoyed with care and wisdom, or more humans may be alive on the earth than the planet can support."

Another response too low to be heard.

"Earth Mother, the Goddess, has provided everything we need. It is all here in plenty, if wisely used."

This time the man spoke up. "Venus," he said, "Do you have everything you need? Isn't there something lacking in your life? Something a man like me could give you?"

Silence. Venus must have taken time to stare down the audacious questioner. "I am dedicated to the Goddess, Julius. That concludes the lesson for today."

Chairs scraped and Venus swept through the door and brushed past Judy. That investigator's feet stuck to the floor, unable to choose between sprinting after Venus and waiting to see the man come out. "Julius" Venus called him—and Martha said he was a wholesaler's buyer. How many Juliuses could there be who worked for food wholesalers?

Julius had taken the rear exit to the packing sheds. She heard the outside door slam fiercely behind him.

Martha called, "Venus! Someone's waiting to see you." Venus turned.

"It's me, Venus." Judy waved her hand. "Have you got a minute?"

Venus smoothed the hair around her face. "Oh, Mrs. Hark."

More to give Venus time than anything else, Judy said, "How about a drink while we talk?" and fetched two bottles of gin-seng fizz from the cooler.

They sat at a wicker table. Venus had changed her leotard for a soft blouse and calf-length skirt. Her face was flushed almost to beauty. A woman dedicated to the Earth Goddess, no doubt, but to Judy she looked remarkably like a young girl in love. Oh Venus, be careful! This Julius—what kind of man is he? Do black girls hide from him? Does he terrorize their mothers?

Judy said, "I've never had this before," and sipped the gin-seng fizz. "At first taste, I didn't think I liked it, but it's growing on me. Refreshing."

"Yes, it's very good. What did you want to see me about, Judith?"

"It's a long story. I'm looking for a black girl called Cassandra Gates. She's disappeared and her mother is anxious about her. We think she might be staying here in Repose with her friend Darlene."

"Darlene who?"

Judy didn't know Darlene's last name. Silly oversight—she should have asked Mbyrna Gates. "Sorry, I don't know. I forgot to ask; isn't that dumb? Cassandra and Darlene both work at BFK Restaurant Supply in Santa Porta."

Venus frowned. "I know the company; they buy from us. Darlene..."

"Yes, a blonde, false eyelashes, lots of make-up."

"That doesn't sound like a colony member. And this black girl—Cassandra Gates? We often give sanctuary here, you know. Maybe she doesn't want to be found. Can you tell me more about her?"

Sanctuary! Why was Venus so cagey? Judy got a distinct impression of knowledge withheld. Well, she had come to get information, not give it. She thought of the man who had been with Venus in the back office. Julius. If he was that Julius, whatever she told Venus might be passed on—to a man from BFK Restaurant Supply.

"I don't think I can, Venus. If you see Cassandra, you might ask her to call her mother—no, her mother has a new telephone number. Tell her to call the person who co-signed her auto loan, will you?"

"The person who co-signed her auto loan. That's very

obscure, Judith."

"I know, I'm sorry. The story isn't mine to tell. Just give her the message, Venus. And please don't talk about it to anyone. The girl may be in danger."

"Danger! Judith..."

I have said too much, Judy thought. "Or maybe she only thinks so. I don't really know anything except that her mother is anxious about her. Here—if I don't get home to fix dinner, Willy will fire me and get himself another cook!"

Chapter 6
Mrs. Millet: Death and Steaks

DRIVER SLAIN, STEAKS HI-JACKED, screamed the front page of Wednesday morning's Gambol Beach Lighthouse-Courier. "A body found Tuesday night in a campsite at Gambol Beach State Park has been identified as that of Darius Clumber, delivery driver for a local restaurant supply house.

"Clumber's employer, Julius Portera of BFK Restaurant Supply, said a consignment of filet mignon loaded on Clumber's truck failed to reach the consignee, although the truck returned to its usual spot at BFK headquarters in Santa Porta. A full investigation is under way, said Gambol Beach Police Chief Marion Belgrave. See page 3 for related story."

Horrified, Margaret Millet recalled the two trucks she had seen, tail-to-tail, on Ramona Avenue. Had she passed by as robbery—and murder!—were perpetrated? She reached for the telephone.

"Judy, have you seen the paper? This morning's L-C. Listen!" She read the headline and front page story.

"Oh, Margaret! Do you think? Cassandra Gates?"

"That's not all. I may have seen the hi-jacking in progress!" Margaret described the trucks she had seen.

"A U-Haul truck—and you got the license number? Well, you'll have to call the police, no question about it."

"Yes. I'll have to report it. But do I mention Cassandra? There's a killer out there! This may be why she's disappeared; she may have known about the hi-jacking and who is involved. Oh Judy, she may have been killed, too! What shall I do?"

"I don't know. I can't think! Let me get my paper; it's still out front. We must call Mbyrna. You do that. I'll read the story and call you back, okay?"

Margaret hung up, deeply shocked and uncertain what to do next. There was murder involved here. From the first hint of the girl's disappearance, this was what she had feared. A living, breathing Cassandra Gates would need food, shelter, clothing, money—and would contact someone she knew to get these things, even if badly frightened and in hiding. A hollow, all-is-lost feeling settled just below Margaret's rib cage. Cassandra... she remembered the picture Clark Atherton had showed her; Cassandra tossing a ball for Kwanza, the black lab. Long beaded corn rows of hair flying about a shiny black face with an impish, irresistible grin. Prancing legs and an agile body twisted in the throw. Cassandra may have been the most troublesome child in the Gates family, but she was lovable, Margaret thought. To lose such a child to murder—what if her own daughter were missing under these circumstances? How would she feel?

Yes, she must call Mbyrna Gates, but it was early, only 7:00 A.M. Margaret still wore her robe and slippers, one slipper damp from the wet grass where her paper had been thrown. Why couldn't that boy hit the driveway, anyway? The automatic sprinklers her son-in-law had installed in the front yard came on at 3:00 A.M., and her morning newspaper got wet every time it missed the pavement.

She rose and put the kettle on for another cup of tea, always a comfort, then separated the damp sheets of newspaper with care. She'd read the story on page 3 before she called. Maybe Mbyrna would see the paper and call her.

FOUL PLAY SUSPECTED IN DRIVER'S DEATH, the caption

read. "The body of Darius Clumber, a Santa Porta resident, was found Tuesday evening at Gambol Beach State Park. Gambol Beach Police have not released the cause of death pending autopsy results, but Ivan Stroud, the camper from Bakersfield who found the body, said Clumber had been shot, probably with a small caliber hand-gun. 'There was a neat little hole right between his eyes,' Stroud said.

"Clumber came to Santa Porta from Los Angeles two years ago. He was originally from Arkansas, according to his landlady, Mrs. Rose Aurora. A bachelor, he rented a studio apartment behind her house on Sander Street. 'He was an excellent tenant,' Aurora said, 'He spent some time at the Partitimer Bar, but he never brought the party home.' A champion dart thrower, Clumber's trophies were on display in his room. Aurora said, 'It's just awful. Why would anyone kill Doofus Clumber? I can't believe it.'"

A photograph accompanied the story: Darius Clumber in front of a dart board, receiving a trophy from a mini-skirted girl. His fatuous grin revealed a gap, two teeth wide, in the side of his upper jaw. A Dangerous Dan mustache hid his upper lip and grew to his chin on both sides. The girl's smile was rueful, like she'd just had her bottom pinched and was trying to be a good sport for the camera.

Margaret's teakettle grumbled to a boil. She made tea in her largest mug, the one decorated with white seagulls and the words "BRINYSIDE, OREGON" and let it steep while she stacked her breakfast dishes in the sink and wiped off the table. As she discarded the tea bag, the telephone rang. Judy had read her newspaper.

"Margaret, that's the man! That Darius Clum—whatever his name is—he's the one! I'd know that face anywhere. He was driving the truck that almost rear-ended us, up on Johnson Avenue!"

Margaret thought a moment and said, "There aren't any restaurants up that way, are there? He must have followed us because we followed Darlene. He could even have been in the building at BFK and heard us ask about Cassandra!"

"And he could have known that Cassandra's mother lives up there. I'll never forget how he looked at me as he drove past! Do you suppose he was the threatening telephone caller?"

"No way to tell, now he's dead."

"Have you called Mbyrna? Or the Police?"

"Not yet. Just screwing up my courage over a cup of tea. I will though, right away."

"Okay. I'll get off the phone."

One of the younger Gates children answered. "Mom's not taking calls," she said. "She's in bed and says she's not talking to anybody. Unless Dad calls. That's what she said. Or Cassy."

"This is Margaret Millet. Will you tell her? She may want to talk to me. Just ask her if she wants to talk to Margaret Millet. Please."

"MO-OM! It's MARGARET MIL—LET!" A pause. "She says no. Bye!" A click in Margaret's ear, followed by the dial tone.

Mbyrna Gates has seen the newspaper, Margaret thought, and this is her head-in-sand response. Or rather, head-under-the-covers. Understandable, but not helpful. And of course, Mbyrna didn't know Margaret had seen the two trucks in Gambol Beach.

Neither did the police. Margaret looked up the non-emergency number and called the Gambol Beach Police

Department. A familiar voice answered; the same Desk Sergeant who had taken her previous call, when she reported Cassandra missing.

"I'd like to talk to someone about the hi-jack and murder case," Margaret said in her most reasonable tones.

"Name?"

"Margaret Millet."

Was that a snort? The Sergeant asked for her address and telephone number and then said, "And what did you wish to report, dear?"

Dear? Margaret stiffened and clenched her jaws to keep from screaming in the man's ear. "I saw a truck with the BFK Restaurant Supply logo parked tailgate to tailgate with a U-Haul truck yesterday afternoon. I couldn't see inside, but I could hear sounds that suggested cargo was being transferred from one to the other. I have both license numbers." Just the facts.

"I see. Anything else?"

Not when and where did this happen? or what are the license numbers? just, "Anything else?" Good grief!

"That's it," she said. Catch her telling this booby anything else!

"Thank you for calling. We always appreciate help from the citizens, Ms.—ah—Millet."

Well, she had done her duty. And been snubbed on all sides by people who thought she had nothing to offer. She finished her tea, rinsed out the mug and dressed in jeans and a roomy sweatshirt. A walk on the beach was always good medicine; she'd have one before reporting these rejections to Judy Hark.

Afterward, she estimated that ten minutes elapsed between her phone call and the appearance of the blue and white Gambol Beach Police car at the street, its rack lights flashing.

A uniformed officer got out and approached her. "Margaret Millet?"

Mrs. Millet nodded. "Yes?" She could see curtains twitch across the street and behind her, the front door of her daughter's house opened and Laura, still in a housecoat, called, "Mom? What's going on?"

Margaret ignored the interruption.

"Could you come down to the station, Ms. Millet? Chief Belgrave would like to talk to you—about your call this morning."

Well! Maybe the police weren't such dolts after all. "Of course. Just let me get my purse and tell my daughter I'm not being arrested."

Chief Marion Belgrave rose politely behind his desk and indicated an armless, leatherette chair in front of it. "Thank you for coming, Mrs. Millet." The Chief had just turned fifty; Margaret had seen the write-up of his birthday party in the paper. All the local politicians had attended. No longer a fat school boy, his class A uniform was a triumph of tailoring, emphasizing his massive shoulders and de-emphasizing his equally massive belly and hips. No neck and his head seemed small for his body, with thin, close-cropped hair and a short, aggressive beard. Yes, he would wear a beard. Margaret disliked and distrusted beards. The only man she knew who seemed natural and unaffected in a beard was her son-in-law, Tiny, a gentle giant with skin too sensitive to shave.

The Chief's office reeked of cigars. Behind smoke-stained mini-blinds, its windows overlooked one of the loveliest ocean views in the world; white breakers crashing on the golden curve of Gambol Beach, all the way from the Avila lighthouse to Point Sal.

Margaret sat on the hard, slippery chair, folded her hands and waited for the Chief to speak. The police-woman who had shown her in took a seat slightly be-hind her and said, "Tape recorder, Sir?" At the Chief's nod, she reached past Margaret's shoulder and pushed a button. The machine on the desk hummed softly.

"Now then, Mrs. Millet, please tell me about these trucks you saw. Start at the beginning and just tell me exactly what you saw, in your own words."

Start at the beginning? That would be the messages for Cassandra Gates on her answering machine.

"Yesterday afternoon," she said, "a little after two, I guess, I walked from my house to the Post Office along Ramona Avenue." Margaret carefully described the trucks with no editorial comment whatever.

"And you wrote down the license numbers? Why was that, Mrs. Millet?"

She had written down the license numbers because of Cassandra Gates, of course. Because of BFK Restaurant Supply and Darlene and being followed up Johnson Ave-nue by a BFK truck and talking to Mbyrna Gates and Clark Atherton.

"It just seemed strange," she said. "Here they are." She opened her purse and took out the crumpled bit of pa-per.

Chief Belgrave handed the paper to the policewoman and said, "Get on that, Elsie." The policewoman went out.

The Chief looked down at the papers on his desk and selected an official looking form. "You made another re-port a few days ago, Mrs. Millet, about a possible disap-pearance. Would you like to tell me about that?"

Margaret took a deep breath. Here it came. So tell. Stick to the facts and let him make of them what he will. "Yes," she said. "I was away all summer and when I got home I couldn't get my old telephone number back. The phone company gave me a new one..."

Under Chief Belgrave's skillful questioning, she revealed much more than the facts. His favorite question, "Why was that, Mrs. Millet?" was hard to answer with facts.

An hour later Margaret felt as though every cubic centimeter of her brain had been sieved through a fine mesh and every seed of information it contained strained out. "Marion the Librarian" was good at his work. He could now catalog most of what she knew, felt and imagined about Cassandra Gates and BFK Restaurant Supply.

The same pleasant officer took her home in the same police car, but left its rack lights off for the return trip. She thanked him for the ride and got out quickly, hoping to make it through the carport to her granny pad without encountering her family. They should have gone to work by now, but you never knew.

No luck. The back yard gate clanged with a characteristic clang no matter how quietly one tried to close it. Laura was still at home and must have been listening for the sound. She bustled out of her back door, dressed for work and carrying a briefcase. "Welcome home, Mom! Would you like to tell me what's happening?"

Chapter 7
Mrs. Hark: Apply and Retreat

While Margaret Millet endured what she later described as one of the worst mornings of her life, Judy Hark reacted to the murder news in a different way. Or rather, didn't "react." One always had a choice between acting and reacting, she felt, and on the whole, she preferred to act. She feared for Cassandra Gates but she stoutly fought the paralysis of dread. Her buoyant spirit rose up and asked, "So what are you going to do about it?"

The police were at last on the scene. They would investigate the murder of Darius Clumber far more efficiently than a private citizen could. Would they make the connection that now seemed so obvious and look for Cassandra? Somebody should do so! There were still places where she and Margaret could inquire; BFK Restaurant Supply and The Temple of Repose, for starters.

She let Willy eat his breakfast (one piece of toast with peanut butter and jam) and start his morning coffee (one cup) before mentioning her latest brainstorm. "About this Cassandra Gates business—you know, Willy, I think Venus Valentine knows more than she lets on."

Willy looked at her with interest. "And?"

"Well, just give me your opinion of this. What if Margaret went on one of Venus's 'Retreats?' I can't do it; Venus knows me too well to think I might be open to this Goddess stuff, but Margaret is such a good actress—and if she spent a weekend at Repose, who knows what she might find out?"

Willy seldom gave snap judgements. He liked to

think things over before expressing an opinion. Now he sipped his coffee and gazed out the sliding glass door to the patio. And gazed. And sipped. Judy waited as patiently as she could. The patio was worth gazing at with its jasmine vines, potted orchids and ferns against the high, weathered, redwood fence, but her mind was not on horticulture. She wanted to get Willy into a "yes" frame of mind, because Margaret visiting Repose was only part of her plan.

"You don't suspect Venus Valentine of being involved with the murder, do you?" Willy asked, finally.

"No! Of course not! But I think she might be hiding Cassandra—and might know more than we do about what's going on at BFK."

"BFK?"

"The place where Cassandra works. Or worked. The place that lost the hi-jacked beef. You read the paper..."

"And I heard you tell Margaret you recognized the murdered driver."

"He almost drove into my car. I told you about that."

"Well, it might be okay for Margaret to spend a weekend at Repose. Can't hurt. Might help. And maybe you'd spend a weekend at home if she was 'retreating.'"

"Oh, Willy! That's not worthy of you. Besides, I never stay home. You know that."

"Well, I can hope, can't I?" Willy teased.

Judy chuckled appreciatively. This was the mood she wanted. "And while Margaret investigates at Repose, I'll see if I can't help out at BFK. They must be short-handed with Cassandra gone, and they'll need somebody with office experience to pick up the slack until she comes back or they replace her."

Willy looked at her and pursed his lips. Shaking his head,

he transferred his bulk from the dining room table to his recliner in the living room and fingered the remote until the Today Show blared from the television set.

Judy knew she would hear his thoughts later, after he got them organized. As long as he didn't become alarmed for her safety, he would support her. Willy had shown great interest in Cassandra's disappearance and so far, had approved everything his wife had done. Judy bundled the morning paper into the recycle bag. Keep Willy thinking of the disappearance, not the murder.

At Margaret's granny pad just after lunch, the shades were drawn and Judy's first knocks got no response. "Margaret, are you in there? It's Judy!" Scuffing feet. The bolt drawn.

"Oh, hi Judy. I was lying down. Headache..." Margaret opened the door wide, then dropped a damp wash cloth in the sink. Her face looked drawn and pale.

"I'm sorry. Want me to go away?"

"No...No. Come in, sit down. I should have called you. There's quite a lot to tell. What's that?" She had noticed the file folder Judy carried.

"That's what I came about, but there's no hurry. Have you taken anything?"

"Aspirin. I'm okay. In fact, I feel better just to see you." A little color came to Margaret's face. "How about a cold beer?"

"Best offer I've had today."

They sat at the table and drank Miller High Life out of glass bottles (none of those low-calorie or fake "draft" beers for Margaret) and Margaret described her ghastly morning; the snub by Mbyrna Gates, Chief Belgrave's probing of her brain, and her daughter's questions when she got home. No wonder her head ached, poor thing!

"I know just what you need," Judy said. She lifted a paper from her file folder and passed it over. "You need to go on Retreat."

"What's this? 'Repose Review.' The Temple's publication?"

"Uh-huh. Desk-top publishing; Martha puts it out. I picked it up at the store."

"When you talked to Venus yesterday?" Margaret had, of course, been told about that excursion. "Do you really think she's interested in that Julius, Cassandra's boss?"

"I'm not sure, but he's definitely interested in her. I didn't dare ask much about Cassandra, in case she passed it on to him."

"Yes, we know nothing about him. He might be in the hi-jacking and murder right up to his bolo tie."

"I have ideas about that, too. And maybe you can find out more about him from Venus. And about Cassandra. As I told you, Venus said they often give sanctuary and maybe Cassandra doesn't want to be found." Judy went back to the Repose Review. "Here's the Retreat schedule. The next one starts on Friday."

She explained the rest of her plan. "I want to infiltrate BFK and learn more about Julius and what's going on there. Cassandra may be safe and well or she may be dead—but I'm not giving up. The police will dig into the hi-jacking and the driver's murder in ways we never could, but do they know about Cassandra's visits to Repose?"

"Not from me. It's about the only thing I didn't tell Chief Belgrave; it seemed too far-fetched to mention." Margaret perked up and leaned forward. "So I go to Repose and you apply at BFK." She beamed, her headache apparently forgotten.

"Yes, and I need you to help me update my resume." Judy opened her file folder.

"What about Darlene?" Margaret asked. "What will she do when you turn up as a job applicant?"

"Or when you turn up in Repose, for that matter." Judy had thought about Darlene. "I wish we could talk to her. She might even be willing to introduce me at BFK as someone she knows, someone who can help out while they're short-handed."

"Maybe Mbyrna Gates could fix that with Darlene. I have to tell her that I've spilled the beans, too—if the police haven't been there already," Margaret said.

"Why don't we call Clark Atherton? Maybe he can help."

"Good idea." Margaret produced her "case file" and called Atherton's number. "Mr. Atherton? I'm glad I caught you in. This is Margaret Millet—we met at Mbyrna Gates' house?"

From Margaret's side of the conversation, Judy gathered that Clark Atherton was pleased by their continuing interest and approved of their plans. Margaret said, "Then you'll help us meet with Darlene? Fine. I'll be waiting to hear. Don't mention it, we want to do it!"

She hung up. "He's going over to Mbyrna's house now and he'll try to have Darlene meet us there after work. About 5:30, I expect. He'll call and let us know."

"Good! Now let's get busy on this resume."

Margaret finished her beer and took the dust cover off her laptop computer. "Judy, what would I do without you? I was wretched half an hour ago."

"Nonsense. You always bounce back. I've seen it a hundred times."

At five o'clock the ladies started toward Santa Porta—in Margaret's pickup, since it was her turn to drive. Judy would rather have driven her comfortable sedan, but she understood Margaret's prickly need to avoid sponging. Anyway, the Ranger was all right. It was clean and fairly new, Margaret drove well, and sitting up high in the truck cab gave one an excellent view of the passing scene.

They took the Dolliver Canyon road, shorter and less crowded than the freeway, as they had on their previous visit to BFK and the Gates home. Oil wells and a steam cracking plant were folded into the canyon's hills, but when it opened out to Poppy Valley the hot stink of petroleum gave way to the scents of vineyards. The grapes had been harvested and well-pruned vines were espaliered on posts and wires in long, slope-following rows.

They passed the BFK warehouse in Santa Porta's outskirts and Judy saw that Darlene's car was already gone. Only Company trucks and a blue sedan (a Lincoln or a Cadillac or some other make; they all looked alike these days, round and sleek like fat snakes) remained in the parking lot.

In Abby Lane, Margaret parked at the curb behind Clark Atherton's black sports car. Darlene's red puddle-jumper stood in the driveway.

"Looks like everybody's here," Judy said.

Margaret put a hand to her face. "How can I tell her? About the police, I mean..."

"Mbyrna? Yes, that's going to be tough." Margaret was inclined to blurt out whatever was uppermost in her mind. "First let me talk about our plans—Repose and working at BFK. It will give her something new to think about. The poor woman, she must be frantic if she still hasn't heard from Cassandra."

Clark Atherton opened the door and waved them in, white teeth shining in his ebony face. Kwanza, alert at his side, sniffed the backs of Judy's knees as she stepped down into the living room. Drapes were closed over the panoramic windows and soft lighting made the room look smaller and less spectacular than it had seemed on her earlier visit. Mbyrna Gates, in a flowing red velvet robe, sat curled up at one end of the leather couch with Darlene beside her.

"Come in." Mbyrna beckoned with a limp hand. "Do you have any...any news?" Her voice quavered. Reddened eyes and swollen, mottled cheeks betrayed her emotional state. This was not the cool, capable woman they had first met.

"No, Mbyrna, I'm sorry. We do have some ideas, though. Hello, Darlene. Thanks for coming." Judy took the chair across from Mbyrna and Margaret sat next to Darlene on the couch. Kwanza adopted a sphinx-like pose on the floor at Mbyrna's feet, while Clark hovered and paced, too agitated to sit.

"The police came," Mbyrna wailed. "They said you told them Cassy is missing. How could you?" She looked at Margaret, who ducked back and let Darlene intercept that accusing glare.

So much for the order of business. "Margaret had no choice, Mbyrna," Judy said quickly. "She saw a BFK truck transferring a load. She had to report it. After all, a man has been murdered."

"I'm glad they know about Cassy," Clark broke in. "Maybe they can find her. We haven't gotten anywhere, any of us."

"Not so far, but Margaret and I want to try something."

"Oh, I don't know." Mbyrna pulled a fresh tissue from

a box beside her and wiped her eyes. "You butted in and now we've got the police, and somebody's dead, and Cassy...Oh, I don't think we need any more of your help!"

"Stop it," Clark said. "Mrs. Millet told me what they want to do and I think it's great. So listen."

Before Mbyrna could protest again, Judy plunged ahead. "That's right. The hi-jacking gives us a possible reason for Cassy's disappearance. We think Cassy may have learned who was stealing beef and been told to keep quiet about it. Then she got scared and hid. I want to get into BFK as an office worker and Margaret will go to Repose on one of their Retreats, to see what we can find out."

Darlene said, "But I'm in both of those places. I'm at BFK every day and I take part in all the Retreats. Reely, what could you find out that I don't already know?"

"Darlene!" Mbyrna spoke sharply. "You have told us—you wouldn't hide Cassy and not tell me? Not now, after...."

Although she wore more gaudy makeup than ever, if that was possible, Darlene had lost some of her brassiness. She said, "No! Of course not."

The denial was quick, but half-hearted. Judy remembered her earlier hunch that the girl suppressed something she dared not say. What was she keeping back? "Darlene doesn't do what Cassy did at BFK. And Cassy is the one who has gone into hiding. If I do her job, I may learn what she knew."

Margaret had not spoken since Mbyrna mentioned the police. Now she said, "Believe me, if Judy gets into BFK's books, she will spot any discrepancies."

"That's right," Judy said. "The missing steaks would show in inventory records. If it wasn't just a one-time thing, someone had to be cooking the books."

"Barbecuing them!" Margaret said. "And I can poke around at Repose, too. If I get caught where I shouldn't be, I can say I'm just a stranger and don't know any better. Darlene can't do that."

Darlene nodded reluctantly. "Look, I won't do anything to stop you—but when you come to Repose, I don't know you and you don't know me, okay?" She turned to Judy. "And that goes at BFK, too."

Fair enough. Not the recommendation Judy hoped for, but it would do. "Who do I see when I apply?" she asked.

"The Office Manager, Glenda Ravenet."

"Glenda Ra-ven-et." Judy pulled a note pad out of her purse and wrote the name, then showed it to Darlene. "Is that how she spells it?"

"That's right." The girl took a deep breath and held it until she looked like she might explode. Then she squeezed her gooey, black eyelids shut and blurted, "Reely, why do you want to do it? You're reely taking an awful chance! You may wind up dead—like Doofus Clumber!"

Chapter 8
Mrs. Hark: A Day at BFK

On Friday morning, Judy Hark sat behind the front counter at BFK. I'm too old for first-day-on-the-job jitters, she thought, nervously watching the console telephone buzz and flash. At least she looked the part. Not without effort; her hairdresser had worked late the night before as a special favor and she had chosen her gold suit after trying on half the clothes in her closet.

BFK's office manager had snapped her up, impressed by her resume and easily accepting the story she concocted to explain her application; she had heard about BFK's needs from a friend who knew one of their salesmen. She wasn't sure which salesman.

When Judy had come in a few minutes before eight, the door was unlocked and the reception area empty. The man she had seen on her first visit stuck his head out of a door down the hall, looked her up and down and came forward.

"You must be the new assistant," he said. "I'm Julius Portera, the General Manager."

Then the jitters began. This was the man she wanted to investigate and she should have been braced for their meeting, but his open manner made her feel guilty and sly.

He ran a hand through his crisp, dark curls in a harassed way. "Glenda's not in yet. Let's see—neither is Darlene. Well, you'll have to fill in for her on lunch hours, so you might as well start. Do you know how to manage a multiplex?" He motioned toward the console telephone.

Judy took a deep breath and offered her hand. "Yes, I

do. Judy Hark. Where do I put my coat?"

Julius' handshake was brief but firm. He led her down the hall behind the reception area. His office door stood open and as they passed, Mrs. Hark got a fleeting impression of tight quarters, dazzling light from a tall window and a desk whose surface resembled the wreckage after a typhoon.

In all, six offices opened off the hall, three on each side. At the far end, they entered a room about twelve feet square, equipped with an old-fashioned formica and chrome table and chairs, a refrigerator from the same era, a modern coffee maker and a microwave oven. In one corner, coat hangers hung on a "closet organizer" and a door opened to the toilet and wash basin, both less than clean.

"The warehouse is back there." Julius waved to a half-open door at the back of the lunch room. "This place is mostly warehouse. Office space isn't a big priority with the owners." He grinned and Judy realized for the first time what a good looking man he was. She'd have given both of those donated tea pots to know for sure if he was the Julius who asked Venus Valentine, "Do you have everything you need?"

Back at the reception counter, he showed her the list of extension numbers and she quickly mastered the hold buttons and transfer of calls; nothing she hadn't done before, many times.

Now it was eight-twenty and Judy had her jitters more or less under control. Two phone calls had come in for Frank Slee in the Sales Department, extension 77. The partitions were thin and she located the sales office by the bellowing, jolly voice that answered the calls.

She had stowed her purse under the front counter.

Just as she bent over to get a breath mint from it, the front door flew inward and heels clattered on the vinyl flooring. Judy's head connected with the counter and she winced with pain. Darlene, unable to stop her head-long rush, collided with Judy's elbow and sent the roll of mints flying.

"Oh! You're here!" Darlene gasped. "Where's Glenda?"

Not a word of apology for the collision—these young girls. "She hasn't come in yet." Judy rubbed her head and suppressed the urge to add, Aren't you lucky? She wanted to make friends with Darlene if she could.

"Good. Who told you to sit here?"

"Mr. Portera showed me around. He said I'd have to fill in on the phones when you were out, so I might as well start."

"Oh." Darlene's face softened. "Well, if Julius says so..."

She doesn't like it, but if Julius says so, it's fine, Judy thought. Interesting. She rose to pick up the package of mints and Darlene plunked herself down in the receptionist's chair.

"Well, I've got all these sales orders to type before nine, so you'll just have to wait for Glenda. She doesn't like—uh, her office is locked. You can wait in the lunch room. Back there." She waved one hand, reached into her "In" basket with the other and pulled out a fistful of papers.

"You do have a lot to do, don't you. Can I bring you a cup of coffee?" Honey catcheth more flies....

The coffee maker was the automatic drip kind and a glass pot full of fresh brew steamed on the bottom burner. Judy wondered who had prepared it. Would Julius Portera make his own coffee? Maybe. More likely the salesman, Frank Slee. She remembered from her earlier visit, how he held the door for the others and looked anxious to please.

She found cream (half and half) in the refrigerator and poured some into two styrofoam cups. A heaping tea-spoon of sugar in one, per Darlene's instructions, then the fragrant coffee. A sip from the cream-only cup. Deli-cious. Well, yes, a restaurant supply business should use good coffee. She carried the two cups carefully back to the reception desk and drew up a second chair. "I hope you like the way I fixed it."

Darlene took a sip. "Yeah, it's fine." A deeper swallow. "Boy, I reely need it. Thanks."

Civility coming to the surface. Some people do need that first cup of coffee in the morning. "I'm glad we're alone for a few minutes, Darlene. Will you be at the Re-treat this weekend? Margaret is all signed up, so you'll see her there."

Darlene's rush to work still showed. Her flashy clothes (were skirts really being worn that short?) had been thrown on any old way. She'd taken time to paint her face, though. Under glittering blue eyelids she batted her false lashes. "I don't talk about Repose when I'm here. I don't even think about Repose. And I don't think about here when I'm there. They're reely separate things. I keep 'em separate."

"Yes, I see." Drink some more civility, Darlene. Judy drank her own coffee and tried again. "Did you know that driver very well? Darius Clumber?"

"As well as anybody who works here, I guess. Wasn't reely my type, but he liked to come in and kid around. You know, thought he was reely God's gift..."

"How did he get along with Cassandra?"

"He didn't. Called her Tar Baby. She hated him."

Darlene twirled an order form into her typewriter and

looked at a scrawly hand-written sheet beside it. Her stiff shoulders and bent head said "let me alone" plainer than words.

'She hated him.' Past tense. Of course, Darius Clumber is dead, but the way she said it—does Darlene think Cassy is dead, too?

A possible motive for killing Darius Clumber. Cassy Gates had been missing for over two weeks now. If she was dead and Clumber knew who killed her, he might have been killed to keep him quiet. The meat theft might have been a diversion, to obscure the real reason for his murder. Or was the hi-jacking a one-time thing, a coincidence that had nothing to do with Cassy's disappearance? Judy Hark didn't believe in coincidence. Somehow, Cassy's absence, the hi-jacking and the driver's murder were all connected, she was sure.

At 8:45, Glenda Ravenet came in the back way, through the lunch room. She unlocked the office opposite Julius Portera's, left her briefcase, coat and purse inside, and came out to greet Judy, who rose to face her.

"Good morning. Has Darlene helped you get started?"

No apology for lateness. Judy took in the well cut suit, the gold earrings and matching lapel pin, the tall shoes of polished calf. In her forties, probably went to a fitness center regularly; no sag, no bag. Capable, not pretty. Except—what was it? The appraisal was mutual, but Glenda Ravenet never met her eyes.

"Good morning, Mrs. Ravenet."

"Oh, call me Glenda. We're very informal here." Glenda led her down the hall. "Here we are. Take this desk, where I can talk to you from next door."

There were two desks in this office. The one indicated

faced a connecting door to Glenda's office and guarded a bank of file cabinets along the wall behind it. The other provided a work surface for the copy machine. The room had no windows. A rack of bare florescents glared from the ceiling.

"The thing that needs doing the worst is inventory," Glenda said. "Cassy always entered incoming stock and I just haven't had time to keep it up. We have an inventory program in our computer and we compare that with physical inventory at the end of the month."

Judy sat at the desk. The computer was a newer version of the one she had used at the lumber company just before she retired. She knew how to turn it on, so she did. A menu appeared on the screen, and she used the arrow keys to select INVENTORY.

"I can see I won't have to give you much instruction," Glenda said.

"Well, every program is different. You'll need to take me through it, of course." One thing about bookkeeping, if you understood the principles, you could understand the method, even on a computer.

"Of course." Glenda took folders of packing slips from one of the files and began to instruct her new hire in the BFK inventory system. After half an hour, she left Judy to the job, went into her own office and shut the door.

Judy sighed. How much easier bookkeeping was before computers were invented, she thought. The old-fashioned peg board system was quick, easy and accurate, with no expensive machines, "programs," or down time for repairs. Of course it required a bookkeeper with legible handwriting and the ability to add and subtract, skills our huge, assembly-line schools seemed unable to teach these days.

She sorted the packing slips by company and entered the incoming stock to its proper inventory categories. Pork Rib, Prime, 57 pounds @ $1.47. Chicken, fryer, grade AA, 78 pounds @ $0.57. Beef filet...

Beef filet. Filet Mignon, the trademark of BFK. Here she was, right inside that operation, actually sitting at Cassandra Gates' desk.

Judy completed the entry except for pressing the "enter" key so she could resume work quickly if someone looked in. Quietly, she slid the drawers out and snooped through the desk. If she got caught with a drawer open? She was looking for staples. She emptied the stapler and left it gaping on the desktop to authenticate that story.

The desk had been thoroughly cleaned out. What a pity. The drawers held only office supplies; pencils, ballpoint pens, a wooden ruler with a metal edge, a staple puller, push pins, paper clips and a round box of "tacky finger," pungent and pink. A few empty file folders in the file drawer at the bottom.

The top-center drawer held a box of staples and a thick clump of rubber bands. Was that what kept it from closing completely? Judy took out the rubber bands and tried again. Again the drawer stopped short. Something wedged behind it? It gave when pushed, then sprang back, still not flush.

No room is private that contains a copy machine. Just as Judy was about to pull the desk drawer out and look behind it, a beefy man in a denim jacket walked in.

"They told me the copy machine was in the middle office—yeah, there it is. Do you know how to work it?" He flourished a sheet of paper.

Judy copied his bill of lading. "I'm new here. Judy Hark. Who are you?"

"Oh, me too. Mike. Truck driver."

A man of few words. Darius Clumber's replacement? Mike took his paperwork and made off. He was followed by other copiers. Darlene dashed in and out, Glenda Ravenet copied account cards, even Julius Portera came in, asked how she was getting along, and copied a letter with a vivid red letterhead. Judy took a firm grip on her curiosity and entered inventory to the computer.

Just before noon, she heard Frank Slee come out of his office, slide along the hall and tap on Glenda's door. He said, "How's about lunch?" loud and clear, before his voice dropped to a mutter. Glenda said, "Be right with you," then muttered back. Why didn't they speak up? She could only catch a few words. Then Glenda came close to the connecting door and said, "Not now, not with the police all over the place."

Slee muttered again and Glenda said, "You'll get it, you'll get it. But we can't..." before her voice faded and the door to the hall opened and closed. They were off to lunch, it seemed, and without a word of instruction as to her own lunch hour or anything else. How inconsiderate.

A few minutes later, Darlene bounced in. "I go to lunch at 12:30, didn't Glenda tell you? You should have gone at 11:30."

"I don't mind. There's an awful lot of work to catch up. Could you bring me a sandwich?" On Judy's first visit to BFK, Darlene had been in the office at 12:45—perhaps that was due to Cassandra's absence.

Darlene agreed to bring a sandwich. She was positively cheerful about it. Judy gave her some money. The best way to be liked was to let people help you, preferably with something they could feel superior about. She must ask Darlene for help with the filing system.

Judy's purse was still under the front counter—how careless to forget it. She renewed her lipstick.

Julius Portera left his office. "Are they going to unchain you and let you out for lunch?" He laughed.

Judy warmed to him. He seemed young for his job, early forties she thought. She liked his neat but casual clothes, so appropriate to the warehouse setting. The sharp creases in his khaki pants and the crisp collar of his plaid shirt said somebody took good care of him. His face, a little too round to be handsome, was tan, smooth shaven and kind. She smiled. "Darlene will bring me a sandwich."

"I'm sorry. She could have let you go now, since it's your first day."

"I don't mind." Judy screwed up her courage. "It must be a big responsibility, running a company like this. Do you buy meats and produce locally, or just from the big wholesalers?"

"We do buy locally, as much as we can. You'll see invoices from a number of local suppliers."

Actually she hadn't, so far. But maybe it was safe to say she had..."I noticed some vegetables from Repose Produce. Those should be nice and fresh."

"Oh yes, we buy a lot from Repose. Their produce is the best."

Drat the man! Did she have to put the very name in his mouth? "Do you know Venus Valentine? I take her Yoga class every week, or did until I got this job."

Ah, that did it. Julius sat on the extra chair and smiled a warm, shy smile. "Yes, I know Venus. She's wonderful, isn't she? Not like anyone else. She lives her philosophy."

Yes, this was Venus Valentine's Julius. He was yearning

to talk about her and delighted to meet someone who knew her. Judy felt a twinge of guilt when he said, "She told me once that the Passenger Pigeons are all gone and people get thicker and thicker—I wish you could have heard her explain it." She had heard that explanation but couldn't say so.

Was he aware that Darlene lived at Repose? Several things he said suggested he was not and Judy didn't mention it. She listened, agreed over and over that Venus was wonderful in many ways, and asked encouraging questions whenever the flow lessened.

"I study and read everything I can find," Julius said at last. "A lot of it I don't understand, but she helps me. Have you ever been on one of their Retreats? There's one this weekend, but what with our problems and the Police, I can't get away."

So much sympathy was established between them that Mrs. Hark felt she could ask about the hi-jacking and murder, and even Cassandra's disappearance. Then the telephone rang and Julius rose. "If that's for me, I'm out to lunch!" He bolted out the front door.

The phone call was for him. She took the message, "Call Burkart ASAP," and put it in the mail slot labeled "Julius." Glenda had told her that BFK stood for Burkart, Flannery and King, the owner/partners. The caller was that Burkart.

The mail came while Judy covered the front desk. Glenda had explained the sorting procedure. Letters addressed to individuals went in the labeled mail slots and the rest came to her, Glenda, unopened. Most of the mail was obviously invoices and statements. These might be of interest to her investigation, so Judy made a list of the companies who sent them for later reference.

Glenda came back from lunch and took the mail from her slot. She leafed through the company mail, took out one envelope and handed the others back. "There are a couple of accounts I handle myself. You can open the rest and put the invoices in alphabetical order."

When Darlene brought Judy's turkey-on-rye, she ate it in the lunch room, enjoying the chance to relax for half an hour. This time she remembered to take her purse.

That afternoon, Judy completed the current inventory and graduated to Accounts Payable, another backlogged task. Glenda had said, "There are a couple of accounts I handle myself." She consulted her list and decided Glenda had kept the envelope from Wineena Packing Inc. Why was that account special? Maybe...she tried all the ways she knew to bring up the account on the computer, without success. Wineena Packing was not listed.

Glenda left the connecting door open, so there was no chance to pull out the desk drawer. Frank Slee discovered her presence, after which he frequently interrupted her work with requests for items from the files.

By five o'clock, Judy was exhausted. Her neck and back ached and her eyes would barely focus from looking into the computer screen. The stack of invoices had been diminished, but not conquered.

Glenda walked in, purse in hand, coat over her arm. "Any chance you could come in for a few hours tomorrow, Judy? You're doing so well! If we could just get everything caught up..."

Willy wouldn't like it and neither would Myrtle Farrini, who would have to find somebody else to help her sell chances on The Trunk. The latter thought made Judy smile and say, "I think so. Is the office open on Saturday?

Will I be able to get in?"

"Oh yes. Come in through the warehouse. There's always somebody there. I'll give you the key to this office."

Glenda departed and the building gradually hushed to an after-hours quiet. Judy eased out the center drawer and placed it on top of Cassandra's desk. Peering into the narrow cavity, she could just see a small, flat something, jammed into one corner at the back. Could she reach it? She knelt on the floor and put her right arm in up to the shoulder. Yes, her fingers just brushed the thing. A grainy feel of plastic. A corner. Painfully, she wedged her arm farther in (her shoulder would be one purple bruise tomorrow) and grasped it between thumb and forefinger. She pulled gently and felt it budge, come unstuck. She got a better grip and pulled it out. A tiny black-covered book—a pocket address book? A miniature notebook?

Julius Portera's door opened across the hall. Judy dropped the crushed and dented object into her purse and quickly slid the drawer back into the desk. Time to go home.

Chapter 9
Mrs. Millet: Welcome to Repose

Friday afternoon while Judy Hark entered data and "looked for staples," Margaret Millet packed her weekend satchel with blue jeans, t-shirts, underwear, a set of sweats to sleep in, and enough ankle sox for three days. For the reception that evening, she'd wear the red boucle pullover and navy pants she had bought for her end-of-summer trip, but she wasn't going to dress up all weekend. Let's see...calcium tablets, the chewable kind (she hated swallowing pills) and vitamin C, ditto. Unguentine antiseptic salve for sunburn, scratches and insect bites (Original Formula; she had no use for the "new and improved" version). A can of bandages, a paperback mystery, a wad of facial tissues, a box of granola bars for energy. That should do it.

As she zipped the bag, Margaret remembered her old peacock-blue caftan—a gorgeous garment left over from career days in Los Angeles. It might be nice for lounging in the cabin she was to share with three other, so far unknown, retreaters. Bother! Laura had borrowed the caftan when she and Tiny went to the Ironworkers' convention, and hadn't brought it back. Well, Laura would soon be home from work.

"Come on in, Mom. How about a drink?" Laura seemed glad to see her mother—unusually so, in fact. Maybe she felt guilty about her nosiness when the police car came. Laura ran her own bookkeeping and consulting business and worked hard. No wonder she liked her evening cocktail.

"Thanks, Honey, but make it a light one. I'm going away for the weekend. Don't want to start out tiddley..."

Laura grinned, tucked her long, brown hair behind her ears, and led the way to the kitchen where she mixed bourbon and Coke, her "house drink."

Margaret sat at the kitchen table and got to the point. "That's why I need my caftan. The blue one you borrowed."

"Hey, haven't I...? No, guess not. I know—I washed it. Almost all the stain came out, too. I'll get it for you." Laura dashed to the back bedroom and returned with the caftan over her arm. "I love these colors. Thanks for letting me take it. It was tomato sauce but you can hardly see it. It came out really well. What's this about going away?"

Margaret lifted an eyebrow. "I'm going to the Temple of Repose, on Retreat. I expect to learn all about the Earth Goddess."

"Oh, Mom, not you! You aren't serious?"

"I'm perfectly serious. Just you remember our pact." When Margaret moved into her granny pad, she and Laura shook hands on a solemn non-interference pact, agreeing never, never to meddle in each other's lives just because they lived on the same city lot. That hadn't stopped Laura from asking questions when the police showed up, but Margaret might have asked questions too, in that case. As a general rule, she and Laura both observed their agreement.

"Well, Mo-om, first policemen, now Goddesses?"

Margaret couldn't truthfully say the two were not related, so she smiled, sipped her drink and inspected the caftan, now folded in her lap. Laura was right; the stain hardly showed. The fabric shimmered like a peacock's feather and the stain could have been part of the print. She remembered the German engineer she had worn it for when she was a chemist in Los Angeles. How long ago. A wonder the caftan hadn't disintegrated, like the love affair.

"A caftan never goes out of style," she said. "And don't worry, I haven't lost my mental balance. This visit is pure research."

Margaret turned her pickup onto Highway One and wondered how Judy Hark's first day on her new job had gone. "I asked Glenda Ravenet why the previous person left, just to see what she'd say," Judy had reported after her interview the day before. "She got all red in the face and said Cassy was a flighty black kid, 'their token of equal opportunity,' who took off without giving notice and left her to do all the work. The racial prejudice was obvious."

While it wasn't fair to blame Cassandra's disappearance or her flightiness (and the child's own mother considered her flighty) on her race, one could understand the office manager's annoyance. Anyway, Judy was in at the BFK office. I just hope I can do my part, Margaret thought.

Somehow, as she neared Repose, she felt closer to the solution, closer to finding Cassy. Was she here, somewhere in the 200 acres that surrounded the Temple? Cassy had visited Repose often, according to Mbyrna. Had she explored the settlement for hiding places? Or the dunes—could shelter still be found there? During the 1930s Depression, people lived in the dunes, constructing shacks from driftwood and scrap materials and eating Pismo clams from the beach and vegetables pilfered from nearby truck gardens. If Cassandra was still alive...no, don't say "if." Just think how many good hiding places there must be in Repose.

Many, many, hiding places; that was the rub. In one weekend, how could she find them all? Impossible. Well, approach it logically. Assume Cassy, hiding in Repose. What about food? She would have to come out for food, probably at night. She might raid the kitchen at Temple Hall. Or try to get into the store. Or one of the private homes? No, too risky. Unless she had help. If someone carried food to her, she could be anywhere, stay hidden all the time.

Okay, then look for someone carrying food. Darlene? No. In the face of Mbyrna's heartbreak, Darlene simply couldn't have kept such a secret. She knew something, though; Judy was right about that. Perhaps she had merely seen or heard something odd, out of the ordinary, something she didn't understand. Darlene wasn't as silly and featherbrained as her bleach and face-paint suggested, either—look how quickly she contacted Mbyrna Gates when Judy and I came around asking questions. One important step at Repose will be to get closer to Darlene, to find out what is on her mind.

What about Venus? A possibility, definitely. If Venus thought hiding Cassy was the right thing to do, she'd do it.

Near the appointed time, 7:00 P.M., the Retreaters gathered on the second floor of Temple Hall, in the huge pillared room that had once been the sanitarium. The first time she saw this room, Margaret imagined white hospital beds along the walls, with the tall screened windows open to the ocean breezes. Tuberculosis—a common disease in the early years of the century—and in those days the only treatment was bed rest, good food, and good air for damaged lungs to breathe.

No white beds now. Instead, perhaps fifty people milled about. Roughly 80 per cent were women, Margaret estimated, mostly quite young or elders like herself. Perhaps mid-aged women were too busy to meditate for a weekend. Several of the men looked fortyish, though, and were casually dressed, not a suit in the lot. Even a couple of over-age hippies in sandals and beards.

Some of these people stood in small, clamorous groups and others sat in the rows of folding chairs that faced a raised platform at one end of the Hall. An oak lectern stood on the platform, flanked by a piano and a potted palm. In front of the lectern, a basket of chrysanthemums glowed bronze and purple.

Just inside the entry arch, Margaret checked in for her sleeping cabin. "Sycamore," she said firmly when offered a choice of cabins named Sycamore, Eucalyptus, and Monterey Pine. She hoped the name indicated the kind of trees around the cabin. Eucalyptus trees smelled wonderful and Monterey Pines whispered in the ocean breeze, but deep-rooted sycamores wouldn't fall on your roof in a storm. Margaret had once battled a Municipal Tree Committee for permission to remove an 85-foot Monterey Pine, well past its normal 50-year life span, that threatened to smash people or property no matter which way it fell. In the process, she developed a strong prejudice against Monterey Pines.

She accepted a brochure and a neatly sketched map of Repose. Wouldn't you know it? She had selected the cabin farthest from Temple Hall. "Sycamore" stood well out along a path labeled "to Willow Grove and Shrine." Oh, well, she had only her small satchel (still in the pickup at the moment) to carry.

Her eyes searched the crowd, but saw no familiar face. The din hurt her ears and she lingered near the staircase, wondering if she could go back down and wait outside until things quieted down.

Then Venus Valentine swept up the stairs in a long white robe, her lithe body erect, head high, dark hair unbraided, hanging thick and wavy down her back. She looks marvelous, Margaret thought. Why had she ever seemed plain? True, her features did not conform to the common ideal and she wore no make-up, no jewelry except a crystal pendant, but her mouth was generous, her eyes wide-set under a truly noble brow. A Goddess, indeed.

Three women in long calico dresses and a tall young man in jeans and a Hawaiian shirt followed Venus up the stairs. Venus stopped on the top landing and surveyed the noisy Retreaters. A few people noticed her and stopped talking. Like a wave, their silence spread through the crowd until the hall was still and everyone turned to face Venus and her party. Was this what was meant by an aura?

In silence, Venus moved forward through the hall, her white robe swishing with each stride. She mounted the platform and stopped at the lectern. Her entourage arranged themselves in the chairs behind her.

"Please be seated," Venus said in clear, sweet tones. The crowd hurried to do her bidding. Margaret picked a seat on the aisle in the back row, where she could see everybody and everything.

Venus waited patiently until they settled before she spoke again. "Welcome. We're delighted to see so many of you for this weekend Retreat. We hope you will relax and meditate, calm your minds and open them for new teaching about our planet and the life path.

"I am Venus Valentine, your keynote speaker this evening. I'm going to talk to you about why we are here, we who belong to the Temple of Repose, and about our aims, our goals, our hopes for the future.

"First, let me introduce the Counselors for the four discussion groups at our Retreat. You are free to attend as many sessions as you like, all of them, some of them, or none, just as you choose. If you want to spend the weekend quietly in your cabin or hiking in the dunes, by all means do so. The group discussions can help you only if you willingly participate and keep an open mind."

Margaret liked this approach. She had half expected to encounter brain-washing techniques instead of this laid-back, "let them do as they will" attitude. It was all so pleasant she had to sit up and remind herself sharply that she was here to investigate, not to take a vacation.

"Tomorrow morning," Venus said, "Urania will lead a group discussion on Rituals and How They Empower Us."

The first of the calico set, a tall, older woman with a shock of lovely white hair, rose to polite applause.

Venus continued, "As you will see by the schedule in your brochure, we meet for lunch tomorrow at Willow Grove, near the Shrine of the Dunes. The location is marked on your maps."

And so on. After the picnic lunch, Euterpe, young and slender, would help people create their own special songs. Sunday morning the young man in the flowered shirt (Venus introduced him as Jason) would teach the lore of pyramids, crystals, and gemstones.

The names! Straight out of Greek Mythology—or was it Roman or Egyptian? Margaret longed for her copy of

Bulfinch so she could look them up. Surely Euterpe was one of the muses? And Urania suggested astronomy and the stars. Jason? Of course, the Golden Fleece. Jason had freckles, sandy hair, and a face full of laughter. Margaret liked him on sight.

"Finally," Venus said, "on Sunday afternoon, Thalia will discuss the three aspects of woman as defined under Isis; the Maiden, the Lover/Mother and the Wise Woman or Crone. We especially recommend this session for men who want to understand women—and for women who want to understand themselves."

Thalia took her long calico skirt in both hands and swept a graceful curtsey. As she rose, she looked directly at Margaret and with a jolt, Margaret realized who she was. Almost unrecognizable, but not quite. What a transformation! Clean face, a soft scarf over her brassy hair, the calico granny-dress, Indian moccasins instead of high heels; all the same, Thalia was Darlene!

Chapter 10
Mrs. Millet: A Bag of Pennies

Refreshments were served after Venus Valentine's keynote speech. Margaret ate a fudge brownie, sipped fruit punch and took a turn around the hall, speaking and nodding to those who greeted her. Venus was the magnetic center of a crowd of well-wishers who wanted to ask questions, compliment her on the speech or just get closer to her person. No chance for a word there. And no sign of Darlene/Thalia, who must have slipped out right after Venus concluded her message.

Margaret decided not to linger. She had investigations to pursue. She wanted to find the kitchen and larder—sources of food. A woman with a tray of cookies came through a door at one side of the speakers' platform and Margaret stood aside to let her pass. "Can I get to the parking lot this way?" she asked.

The woman nodded and smiled. "Go right through the kitchen." Exactly what Margaret had in mind. She went down the way the woman had come up—a back stairway, narrow and dim, with a sharp turn halfway down.

The old-fashioned kitchen was large and well equipped. In passing, Margaret noted the restaurant-size stove and refrigerator, a freezer and a dishwasher. The cook, in a stained wrap-around apron, directed two underlings who fetched and carried from the adjoining pantry. Anyone looking for food could surely find it here.

Margaret breezed through. "Excuse me, please." She mounted three steps to a narrow entryway, pushed open the back door and crossed a gravel driveway to the brightly lit parking lot. After collecting her satchel from the pickup, she studied the map for the route to Sycamore Cabin.

A high fog had drifted up from the sea. Once away from the parking area, only a few footlights lit the path marked "To Willow Grove and Shrine" on her map. The lights intensified the woodsy darkness on both sides. Perhaps a dozen cabins lurked in the trees around Temple Hall. The nearer ones were close together, in view of each other and the central building. Farther out, the cabins were more widely separated, with Sycamore the most distant. The cabin names were carved into thick boards, mounted on posts beside the path.

As her satchel got heavier, Margaret reflected on the vagaries of chance and the influence of past experience. If she hadn't had problems with a Monterey Pine tree she might have chosen a cabin near Temple Hall, handy to the parking lot and in calling distance from its neighbors. On the bright side, her nocturnal investigations might be easier from the more private location. A lot depended on her cabin mates—would they sleep soundly? Or would they want to sit up and talk?

She passed Walnut, then Persimmon, without encountering a soul. For the moment, the grounds about Temple Hall seemed deserted. Ah, here was Sycamore on a little mound of its own amid tall trees and shadowy bushes. A yellow bug light glowed above the door. The low-roofed cabin had redwood siding, aged black, and looked remarkably like a "Tourist Court" cabin from the 1930's. Come to think of it, it could have been built in that period.

The door was not locked. In fact, it was not lockable from the outside. It's wooden latch made Margaret think of the wolf's words in Little Red Riding Hood; "Then lift the latch and come in, my dear." Inside, a block of wood mounted on the jamb could be pivoted to prevent entrance.

An ancient rotary switch turned on the ceiling light. The far set of bunks, upper and lower, had already been claim-staked by suitcases. She heaved her satchel onto the remaining lower and rubbed her aching wrist, hoping her cabinmates would all, at least, be female. These days, even college dormitories were co-ed and in a place called the Temple of Repose one didn't know what to expect.

The toilet and wash basin were in a private cubby large enough for changing clothes—good. The shower stall was separate and had its own door. Indoor-outdoor carpeting covered the floor and Margaret was pleased to note that she could walk on it without making a sound. The heavy redwood door, however, creaked. She opened and closed it several times, found the exact spot where it gave tongue and tried lifting its weight. It only creaked more loudly. Maybe if she pushed downward... yes, that was better. Still there, but the sound shouldn't wake a sleeper if she was careful.

A vase of asters adorned the table. A jug of drinking water and a package of paper cups stood on the counter. A compact refrigerator purred under the counter. All the comforts of home.

Margaret secured the door and changed into her dark gray sweats. She pulled on her caftan over the sweats and took toothbrush and wash cloth into the toilet cubicle.

Someone tapped on the door while her mouth was full of toothpaste. "Just a minute," she burbled, spitting and wiping her mouth. As she put out a hand to release the wooden block, the tapping turned to pounding.

That annoyed her, so she stopped short and said, "Who's there?"

"Is this Sycamore Cabin?" a shrill voice demanded. Someone who didn't believe in signs.

Margaret opened the door and laughed. "That's the password. Enter at your own risk."

A tiny woman wrenched a suitcase almost as big as herself over the sill. Why did people bring so much stuff, just for a weekend? If the bag hadn't had wheels, she would have needed a barrow to get it down the path.

"Cozy, if primitive." The woman looked around the cabin. "Hope I'm in time to get a lower bunk...Oh, oh..."

"Sorry. First come, first served." Margaret wasn't about to give up her lower bunk; she'd never get outside from the upper without waking somebody.

"I'm Madge, Madge Barnstable. Be a sport. I'm afraid of heights."

Madge Barnstable seemed mighty used to getting her own way. Ordinarily, Margaret would have yielded, but not tonight. She pushed her satchel over and sat on the disputed bunk. "I'm Margaret Millet. The bathroom and shower are both free, if you want to beat the rush." Deliberately, she pulled a paperback out of her satchel and curled up, head propped in one hand, to read it. Never mind the tingle of toothpaste in her mouth, she could rinse it later, after this territorial matter was settled.

Voices called outside, a head poked through the door, a foot nudged Madge's suitcase out of the way and two women entered. They were both white-haired, sixtyish, and built like Abbott and Costello, respectively. It was quite impossible to imagine the heavy one climbing into an upper bunk.

The skinny one called out, "Any poker players in here?

Let's have a game!"

My sainted Aunt Matilda, poker players! At a Retreat? And the all-night kind if ever I saw them. What shall I do?

She put on a discouraging, wet-blanket face and tried. "I came here to meditate. This is supposed to be a Retreat." She laid her head on the pillow and shut her eyes.

"Oh, what a party pooper! You play poker, don't you?" This to Madge, who put out her hand and said, "Madge Barnstable. Indeed I do, and I'll play anybody in this room for a lower bunk—but first I want to use the bathroom."

Abbott and Costello turned out to be Esther and Louise. Costello/Louise brought in grocery bags full of pretzels, potato chips, onion dip and Mexican beer. She put the beer in the refrigerator, opened and started on the pretzels and took her turn in the bathroom when it came. In half an hour the three of them were wearing pajamas and robes, the table had been pulled to the middle of the room, and the cards stood ready for use.

Madge repeated her challenge and Margaret realized it might be her only hope of avoiding an all night session. She had been a good poker player in her youth (most of her college textbooks were purchased with poker winnings) and one of the few things she missed from married life was the occasional Saturday night Poker Party. She sat up and changed her face to "interested."

"Poker's not much of a game with only three people," Louise coaxed.

Esther said, "That's an awfully pretty caftan. Why don't you bring it up here where we can see it? You're not going to get any sleep, anyway."

"But I haven't played in years," Margaret said. "I've forgotten how!"

"You never forget how to play poker. It's like riding a bicycle."

"I'm really tired...and I can't afford it..."

"We play for pennies, nickel limit. Esther, where's the penny bag?"

Margaret allowed herself to be persuaded. "Well, okay, on one condition," she bargained. "We set a time to quit right now and go to bed when it comes, no matter who is winning."

"One o'clock," Madge said.

"Midnight."

"All right, twelve-thirty." A triumphant grin split Madge's face. "And whichever of us—you and me that is—wins the most money, gets the bottom bunk. You're my witnesses, girls. Cut for deal."

Margaret eyed the bunk wistfully. "It's a good bunk." Then she muttered, "High card, pair, two pairs, three of a kind, straight, flush, full house, four of a kind, straight flush. Luck be a lady tonight."

Each player bought 100 pennies from Esther's bag and stacked them on the table in ten cent stacks. From their conversation, Margaret decided that Esther and Louise must have more money than sense. They talked about weekend tours and overnight theater trips, always with their cards and bag of pennies along. They also played Bingo at the Senior Center and sometimes pumped the slot machines at the Santa Ynez Indian Casino. They showed no particular interest in systems of belief—a Repose Retreat was just another excursion.

Their poker was, to say the least, optimistic. Esther, the skinny one, liked seven card stud and was sure the next card would complete her flush. Louise like games with wild cards; "baseball," and "the King with the axe."

For Margaret, taking their money was a matter of "folding" when she didn't have the cards and raising when she did.

Tiny Madge, so short her chin almost rested on the table, got good cards and played like she intended to sleep in that lower bunk. At twelve-thirty, her penny piles were slightly taller than Margaret's.

"Last hand!" Margaret dealt, so the game was five-card draw. She eyed her hand—a single ace and four odd cards that added up to nothing. The others drew cards, sorted them, and bet around the table. Margaret remembered those long-ago Saturday night poker parties of her married life and a useful technique she had developed then. Would it still work? After an entire evening of never betting unless she had a good hand, she would—bluff. Just once.

She let a tiny smile lurk in her poker face and raised. Another round, a second nickel raise.

"Oh, what's the use," Esther grumbled. "You're too lucky for me!" She threw in her cards.

Louise, a follower by nature, bet once more and tossed a pair of aces, face up, on the table. "These haven't got a chance, have they?"

Margaret let her smile deepen and looked at Madge.

"What ya got that's so great?" Madge said, putting out her nickel. Margaret held her breath—if Madge merely called, she was sunk!

"Come on Madge, stay with me. I love taking your money."

Madge raised, and looked at her penny piles. "I can still beat you, even if you take this pot," she said, expecting Margaret to call and scoop up her winnings.

Margaret raised.

Madge recounted her pennies and grudgingly threw in her cards. "This could go on all night. Okay, let's see what you've got."

"You folded; I don't have to show," Margaret said, gathering up the pot. When the pennies were stacked, she had six cents more than Madge. Enough to retain her sleeping place.

Esther and Louise had drunk three beers each and were soon snoring, but Madge rolled and turned and moaned in the upper bunk like a spoiled child put down for a nap. Maybe she did have a fear of heights, being built so close to the ground. Finally Margaret got up, took one of the blankets off her bunk (she was too warm anyway) and made a fat roll of it. "Madge," she whispered, "this will make you feel safer up there." She placed the rolled blanket as a barrier along the edge of Madge's bunk. Madge turned on her side and put a hand on the roll. She said nothing, but her fears must have eased—or she finally gave up trying to get Margaret to switch bunks. Ten minutes later Madge lay still, her breathing deep and even.

Margaret lay still too, eyelids heavy, body and mind exhausted after the long, tense, exciting day. It would be so easy to drop off, to leave detecting until tomorrow. So easy...

Margaret's eyes flew open. Her heart thumped in panic. She had overslept and was late for something important! Where was she? Oh yes, Repose; the search for Cassandra Gates. How could she have fallen asleep? And what had awakened her? Something...An owl hooted outside the cabin. Was that it? No, not the owl, someone singing. A light tenor voice, drifting past the cabin. She caught snatches of the song. " ...sunny days I thought would never end...find a friend..."

That melody! He was singing "I've Seen Fire and I've Seen Rain." Margaret had seen fire and rain too, and known the pain of losing someone. She thought again of the man for whom she had worn the blue caftan and remembered how the song expressed it; "But I always thought I'd see you, again." She waited for the words, but the singer had passed out of hearing.

Could this be the food provider for Cassy Gates? Margaret eased out of the bunk and felt for her shoes. Ah, there they were, with her watch inside the left one. Five minutes past two. Don't stumble over anything—and remember the door creaks.

Chapter 11
Mrs. Millet: Shrine of the Dunes

The fog had blown away and a half-moon hung over the trees. Margaret saw that Sycamore Cabin did have a massive old sycamore tree nearby, its autumn foliage silver in the moonlight. A bougainvillea vine, surely as old as the tree, flowered up through its branches. The landscape of a dream. Was she awake? Was it real? She turned into the sea breeze and strolled like a sleep-walker, inhaling honeysuckle and pine and eucalyptus—and that sandy beach tang known to ocean lovers everywhere.

If the singer was Cassandra's food provider, was he going toward her or coming away? If going, she was hidden in the dunes. If coming away, she was somewhere in the colony, perhaps in Temple Hall itself. What a lot of ifs!

She walked on to the willow grove on the banks of a trickling stream where picnic tables and benches were scattered among the trees. Inside the dark grove, the open path caught enough moonlight so she could see her way. She drifted on, camouflaged by the shadows and her gray sweats. Would she come upon the singer? Was Cassandra hidden in the grove? She looked for possible shelters, but saw none.

On the far side, the willow grove opened onto the dunes, mountains of sand that constantly blew and shifted. Although the sea was a quarter-mile away, echoes of pounding surf came to her ears. And something nearer; a rhythmic, throbbing sound, soft as a heartbeat.

The "Shrine of the Dunes" must be out there. Pagan

rites performed under the moon? Was some worship of Isis under way? Some sacrifice to the Goddess? Things she had heard about cults and black magic flickered through Margaret's mind—until common sense intervened. Venus Valentine was no cultist, at least not one of those. And could someone who sang about fire and rain be on his way to a sacrificial rite? Not likely.

The throbbing sound was closer now, right on the other side of this dune. She climbed to the top, her feet sinking in the dry sand with each step, then dropped to her knees and peered over.

That must be the shrine, that open structure about the size of a small tool shed. Wooden columns and cross beams supported its tile roof. The back was enclosed, and the sides sheltered from the wind by a wooden fence.

In deep shadow before the shrine, someone sat cross-legged, gently thumping on a set of bongo drums. She could make out a bent head and the white splotches of a flowered Hawaiian shirt. Jason, the young man from the reception. He lifted his face to the stars and sang:

"She sashays with a dancer's grace,
My Nubian Princess
The Fairies and Elves designed her face,
My Nubian Princess
Her eye is a dark, sparkling gem,
Her smile is the essence of fem,
I adore her! I live for her!
My Nubian Princess!"

Margaret backed down to the path and slipped around the dune, listening with delight. The voice a melodic tenor, the song a serenade, a fitting part of this dream-like night. Without thinking (why does one do things in a dream?), she clapped her hands. "Lovely," she said, "just lovely!" advancing into the moonlight so Jason could see her. "Please don't stop."

Jason's grin flashed white in the shadows. He did not seem surprised. "Thank you. Would you like to hear it again?"

"Yes, please." Margaret sat on the slope of the dune and emptied the sand from her shoes. This time, when he got to the last line he sang, "My darling Cassandra, My Nubian Princess."

Cassandra! Margaret spoke very quietly, very gently. "I'm looking for Cassandra. Have you seen her?"

To the tune of "Who is Sylvia," Jason sang, "Who is Cassy? Where is she? Cassandra is a dream..." Then he broke off and said, "Why are you looking for Cassandra?"

Margaret moved closer with one hand out, much the way she would have approached a strange cat she wanted to pet.

"Her friends are worried. Is she safe?"

"Her friends. And did you come from the friend who wants to amputate her beautiful childhood and turn her into a Professor's Wife?"

"No—but I've met him. Her mother is terribly worried and afraid. A man has been killed, you know..." She carefully kept her voice neutral. This lad would not be influenced by the pain of his elders.

"She only wanted to be free," Jason said.

"Can you tell me about it? Is she all right?"

"She was fine when last I saw her."

Margaret knelt quite close to him now, and the moonlight glinted through his long, sandy lashes as he looked into her eyes.

"When was that?" she breathed.

"Before the friend came poking around. He scared her away. She wouldn't stay with us any more." He started to hum his tune again, "My Nubian Princess." He was entirely too serene, too relaxed, to be true. Could he have smoked a little pot for inspiration? Strange cats were not usually so willing to be petted.

"I haven't met Cassandra, you know, only seen her picture. Tell me about her." If she could stop asking questions —What were the right questions, anyway?—and start him talking...

"Tell you about Cassandra." Jason tilted his head and smiled in a dreamy way, seeming to sort through memories that pleased him.

"My little sister brought me Cassandra." Jason thumped the bongo drums for emphasis. "All dressed in gay garments, like a well-wrapped present, she was. My poor little sister does that too—the gaudy garments, I mean. She can't free herself. Goes into the maelstrom every day and slaves to pay for things she doesn't need. But Cassandra! I taught her to milk my goats. We picked peas and dug potatoes together. She sat at the feet of Venus with me and she was happy. Until her Friend came poking around." He gave the bongos another thump.

Then Jason embarked on a philosophical discourse so logical and well worked out that Margaret was almost converted. She decided he was not, after all, under the influence of drugs—unless the idea of living in harmony with man and nature was a drug. Jason seemed to be beyond the anxieties and fears that plague us, half-way to some Nirvana where mundane things mattered not at all. He was fond of Cassandra but worshiped Venus Valentine and quoted from her teachings to illustrate his beliefs. If Cassandra had disappeared, he said, she was only retreating from the world's difficulties and would return in her own good time.

"But a man has been murdered—a man Cassandra knew through her job. It's possible that Cassandra has been killed as well." Margaret was pricked by Jason's impenetrable calm.

"No. Oh no. Cassandra is alive. I would know if that vital spirit had gone to her long home. Cassandra is still with us." This positive statement was followed by a flurry of drumming and more philosophy.

Jason didn't seem to feel it, but the cool ocean breeze blew right through Margaret's sweats. Shivering, she listened and interposed an occasional query as facts emerged from Jason's theories.

Darlene was Jason's "little sister." Jason lived in a trailer behind the house Darlene rented from the colony. They were semi-vegetarians, except for dairy products (goat) and shell fish (Pismo clams) and he cultivated a garden, tightly fenced to keep out the milk goats. In essence, he provided food and Darlene paid the rent and bought clothing and other essentials.

"Although plenty of clothes are available for people who understand their real needs. Thalia doesn't need the things Darlene wears to the office." Jason spoke of Darlene and Thalia as two people, one who lived in the outside world and one who belonged to the Temple of Repose, as indeed seemed to be the case.

Would managing without Darlene's income be as easy as Jason believed? Maybe. He was enormously appealing, with his sandy hair and smiling face. He fit her favorite definition of a gentleman: A Gentle Man. Margaret felt that someone would always be happy to look after

Jason—she might enjoy the job herself.

Unlike most people, when Jason finished his discourse, he stopped talking.

Margaret made no effort to start him again. She was cold. The dream had run its course; she was wide awake and had plenty to think about. "If you see Cassandra, tell her she is loved and missed at home and her mother needs her." She left him there, thumping his miniature drums and singing to the stars.

On the way back to Sycamore Cabin, brisk walking warmed Margaret's limbs and invigorated her mind. She believed what Jason had told her; Cassandra had been at Darlene's house (or Jason's trailer?) and gone. This explained Darlene's evasions. Also his words rang true when he spoke of the "friend" poking around—Clark Atherton, of course. Now why had Clark A. not mentioned visiting Repose?

And where was Cassandra now? Jason thought she was still alive. He spoke as though he knew and perhaps he did. Margaret's fears receded and she was heartened, believing more than ever that Cassandra must still be hidden somewhere in Repose. She did not stop at Sycamore Cabin. Instead, she broke into a jog-trot that brought her quickly to Temple Hall, the best place for a refugee to find food and drink.

She made a circuit around the hall, keeping to the shadows, watching for anyone abroad in the night. She peered into windows as she went and tried each door to see if she could enter.

It was darker now. The moon was low in the West and would soon drop behind the fog bank that stood offshore. Floodlights still blazed in the parking lot, costing Margaret her night vision. She turned the corner back into darkness and stood still until she could see again. Ah, the back door. Locked like the others. Holding one hand to the glass she peered in but could see nothing. She remembered the narrow entryway and steps to the kitchen, the place where food was kept.

It was very late. If Cassandra had access to the building, she could have visited the kitchen earlier. Margaret decided to stay a while and watch, anyway. She perched on a low retaining wall under a lemon tree.

Time passed slowly, as it does when one waits. Two of Repose's owls conversed sleepily back and forth. To whoo? asked the first owl. Who-o-o-o, replied the second. All questions, no answers, just like Cassandra's disappearance.

Then a dim light flashed—from inside the building! Margaret pressed her face to the door-glass. In the kitchen, out of her view, the light came on again, stayed on for fully half a minute, and then blinked off. Someone had opened the refrigerator.

Margaret backed away and watched from the shadows, hoping the food bandit would slip out the back door.

No luck. The refrigerator opener must have gone another way. Finally she gave it up and started back to her cabin, berating herself for standing there like a ninny. Why hadn't she run around the building to check the other exits?

Chapter 12
Mrs. Hark: Saturday Overtime

Judy Hark munched her breakfast toast and wondered how she could survive until Monday without talking to Margaret Millet about her experiences at BFK. Then the telephone rang—Margaret.

"You heard my thoughts! Where are you?"

"At the Repose store—the pay phone outside. Judy, I've so much to tell you!"

"Me too, but I'm going in to BFK. Glenda asked me to work this morning."

"We have to meet. Wait 'til I tell you about Darlene! And her brother, Jason—and Clark Atherton hasn't leveled with us, either—how late will you work?"

"Just until noon. Can you get away? I don't think I should show up at Repose, do you?"

"I don't want to miss the picnic in Willow Grove—I might get a chance to talk to Darlene. Can you come to my place about two? If I'm not there, use your key. I'll come as soon as I can."

Judy cleared away the breakfast dishes and saw Willy settled comfortably before the television set. At the last possible moment she called Myrtle Farrini and dealt with her other obligation, the Historical Society Trunk.

"Myrtle? Judy Hark. Sorry to call you so early..."

"Oh, Judy, I was just going to call you! Do we really need to wear our costumes today? Mine's not washable, you know, I have to have it cleaned every time. Couldn't we..."

"That's what I called about. I can't make it, Myrtle."

"Can't make it! What's wrong?" Myrtle gasped. "Is Willy

sick? For heaven's sake, Judy, what's happened?"

"Willy's fine. I'm doing some bookkeeping for a company in town, today. You'll have to call somebody else. How about Betty? And do wear your costume. You know how it tickles people to see us in our long dresses and fancy hats."

"But the cleaning bills...I thought..."

"Well then, don't. I'm sorry, Myrtle, I have to go or I'll be late." Judy terminated the phone call to a background of chortles from Willy.

"There won't be many raffle tickets sold today," Willy commented.

"I can't be in two places at once. They'll just have to get along without me." Judy felt guilty enough without Willy rubbing it in. She was the faithful, willing horse in the Historical Society—couldn't remember when she had last begged off. Well, it would do them good. They counted on her far too heavily. Any of the others could have made excuses without a qualm; they did it all the time.

"Bye, Willy. Not sure when I'll be home, but I'll call you. Your lunch is in the fridge."

On the way to town, Judy mulled over the things she and Margaret should discuss. The little black book she had found in Cassandra's desk, for starters. What a disappointment it had been, when she finally inspected it! She hadn't waited to get home, but pulled off the road at a convenience store and pried open its crushed pages. She could have cried—it made no sense at all. Letters and numbers that could have been written in Sanskrit for all she could make of them. The tiny book held perhaps thirty pages, half of them blank, some with only a few characters, some packed from top to bottom and edge to edge. There was no identifying name, no way even to be sure the book was Cassandra's, as she had never seen Cassandra's penmanship.

Wait, there was an idea. There must be samples of Cassandra's writing in the BFK files.

Cheered by the thought, Judy pressed down on the gas pedal and sped toward town.

As instructed, she used the warehouse entrance. Two men stood just inside, talking. One wore a shop coat and a knit cap (the warehouse was completely unheated), the other, a man with oriental features, wore a rumpled gray suit. Judy smiled and brushed by them.

"Just a minute." The man in the cap turned to the other. "This lady works in the office, I think."

The Oriental man bent his head. "Detective Louis Soong, Santa Porta Police Department, Ma'am."

"Judy Hark. How can I help you, officer?"

"Detective, Ma'am, investigating the disappearance of Cassandra Gates. Just a few questions. Is there somewhere we can talk?"

"Yes, of course. This way." Judy led him through the lunch room and unlocked her office. She dropped her purse on the desk and sat behind it.

Detective Soong took the extra chair and opened his notebook. "Your full name, please—and what is your position with BFK Restaurant Supply?"

"Judith Hark. I'm just temporary, filling in until Cassandra Gates comes back—or is permanently replaced."

"And your regular occupation?"

"I'm retired."

"Why are you working on a Saturday, Ms. Hark? Isn't the office closed on Saturdays?"

"Mrs. Hark. The Office Manager asked me to work

today. Things have gotten behind."

"That would be—ah—Glenda Ravenet." The detective checked his notes. "And Darlene Evans, will she be in today?"

"I don't know, but Darlene and Glenda can tell you more about Cassandra Gates than I can, I'm sure." If they would, Judy thought, if only they would. And Darlene's last name is Evans. She tucked that bit of information away for future reference.

"I see. Do you know Cassandra Gates at all?"

"We've never met." Judy hesitated. She hated to cut short the chance to learn something. "I have met her mother, though and I've heard about her disappearance. You've talked to Mrs. Gates, I suppose."

Louis Soong's face was small and pointy as to chin and nose. The eyes folded in above the high cheekbones were small as well, but sharply focused, analytical. He pursed his lips and flipped to another page in his notebook. "When and how did you meet Mrs. Gates?"

"Quite recently. Through a friend."

Detective Soong read from his notebook, "'These two old white ladies came to the house and one of them said she was getting Cassandra's telephone calls.' Is that someone you know?"

Well! "White ladies" she could tolerate, just, but she never considered herself old. Inside, she wasn't a day over 35. Experienced, yes. Mature. But not old. Judy felt tweaked.

"I can't believe Mbyrna Gates said that. Not 'these two old white ladies.' She's a cultured, educated woman. She wouldn't say 'old white ladies' any more than she'd say 'middle-aged Chinaman.'" Rude, but he started it.

"Mrs. Hark, I was born right here in Santa Porta. My family..."

"I'm aware of your family. Ah Soong would be your grandfather, I expect." Ah Soong of the famous shop, Ah Soong's, where exquisite pieces of carved ivory and jade could be purchased by discriminating collectors. The Soongs were part of Santa Porta's history and owned a good deal of property in the old Chinatown district and elsewhere.

Detective Soong made a little bow. "Yes, he is. But we digress, Mrs. Hark. About your meeting with Mrs. Gates..."

"Margaret Millet and I called on Mrs. Gates because of the telephone messages. Margaret reported all this to Chief Marion Belgrave in Gambol Beach. I trust you and he are sharing information." What was it about Louis Soong that made her tongue so spiteful?

"Certainly." The thrust went home; Soong winced and frowned. His counter-thrust quickly followed. "And is it pure coincidence that you now work at this job, Mrs. Hark? Or are you snooping?"

Judy stared at the man. His lip twitched. Was that a twinkle? A touch of humor beneath the stiff, official manner? She let her shoulders relax, smiled her sweetest, gentlest smile and said, "I'm snooping."

Detective Soong covered his mouth and coughed. He loosened his tie and the collar of his pin-striped shirt gaped open. "I thought that might be the case." He added, "Did I smell coffee when we came through the lunch room? Maybe we could have a cup and talk this over."

Much better. Perhaps he would, after all, tell her something about the investigation. At her best as a hostess, Judy soon had two mugs of coffee on the desk, his laced with the low-cal sweetener he asked for.

Soong made himself as comfortable as the straight

chair allowed. "And what have you learned?" The very question she longed to ask him.

"Well, I've only been here one day. You see, Margaret and I think Cassandra's disappearance may be connected to the hi-jacking. She could have known about the thieves and how they operate. We hope she just got frightened and hid—is hiding—but since the murder..."

"We hope so, too." Soong's face darkened. He didn't sound hopeful. Crime was his daily work.

Judy told him about the accounts Glenda handled separately. "Although there could be special arrangements that make it necessary. I tried to find one vendor in the computer files—Wineena Packing. It wouldn't come up, but we got something from them in the mail. Glenda took that envelope; I didn't get to open it."

"Wineena Packing. How was that spelled?"

Judy spelled it for him. "Of course, it could be a new account, not entered to the computer yet."

"In other words, you have suspicions, but no facts. Nothing that isn't part of a normal business."

Judy admitted it. She told him what she had overheard between Glenda and Frank Slee: "Not with the police all over the place, but you'll get it..." Soong made another note and another unsympathetic comment. "That could have referred to anything that took time. We kept her pretty busy after the murder."

Judy decided to keep the black book to herself, at least for the present. If she gave it to Detective Soong, she'd never see it again and she wanted to show it to Margaret. It might have nothing to do with anything, anyway—and Detective Soong would probably tell her so.

Soong finished his coffee and handed her his business card. "Call me if you learn anything, Mrs. Hark. You are well placed here." He smiled a patronizing smile. "I won't give you away." He walked out of the office, still smiling. Smug. Superior. Quite sure of the silliness of old white ladies. She had done all the informing. Soong could take pride (and probably did) in his ability to take without giving.

At least the police were finally investigating Cassandra's disappearance—and connecting it with events at BFK. As to silliness, time would tell about that.

For the next hour Judy entered accounts-payable data to the computer. The offices were quiet as the moon except for the hum of her machine and the beeps as each entry was accepted into the system. The routine of data entry—call up the account, enter the date, the invoice number, the items purchased, the balancing debit to the proper expense account or "cost of goods sold," close that entry and start another—became rhythmic and soothing. She continued until she had reduced the pile of invoices to three. Then she stopped, as she had done the previous day, at a point where she could quickly finish an entry.

First the copy machine; turn it on to warm up. Then look in the files for some example of Cassandra Gates' handwriting, both letters and numbers. It didn't take long to find invoices with hand written notes on them. "Short 1 case. Don't pay until complete." "Item 3 returned for credit." "Hot file—5% discount, 10 days."

In the customer files, letters were filed with the monthly statements and some had notes in the margins. These notes were signed "Glenda" or just "G," "JP," (Julius Portera, no doubt), or "Frank" and two of them were signed "Cas." The first was short, only two words. "Electronic transfer???" on a letter from the buyer for "Bully

Beef Steak Houses" headquartered in Santa Barbara. Not knowing how long she would be safe from interruption, Mrs. Hark copied the letter quickly, without reading it. The second note was longer. "Can't find the other order she mentions. When shipped? D. Clumber says not on his load." Mrs. Hark copied that letter, too, and then copied samples of handwriting by Glenda Ravenet, Frank Slee, Julius Portera and Darlene Evans (a telephone message stapled to one of the invoices).

Her heart was doing a drum roll under her ribs by the time she closed the last file drawer, folded the copies and got them out of sight in her handbag. Deep breaths. Settle down. Investigating was exciting, wasn't it? And now she could compare the notes with the script in the black book.

What else? She was still alone in the office and should take advantage of it. Glenda Ravenet's office? The "special accounts." Did she dare?

Judy went to the hall door and looked out. Detective Soong had closed the lunch room door behind him. Glenda's office door was shut, as were Julius Portera's and Frank Slee's. The lobby remained dim and silent. She retreated to the door connecting her office and Glenda's. Locked. She eyed the doorknob more closely. No keyhole; a privacy lock, operated by pushing in a button. It locked and opened on Glenda's side.

Unless you knew about sticking something in that little hole, the safety feature that allows parents to rescue children who have locked themselves in bathrooms. It only took Judy a few seconds to straighten a paper clip and poke it into the hole. The latch popped and she opened the door.

Glenda was neat. Her walnut desk was bare except for

the blotter, pen holder and matching accessories. Telephone on the left, note pad beside it, in and out baskets immaculately empty. The locked desk drawers looked capable of keeping secrets.

A two-drawer file stood beside the desk, a shabby, black metal cabinet of the cheapest sort. This was also locked, but Mrs. Hark knew its mechanism of old. A metal plug, pushed in to lock and popped out again by the key. The paper clip wire was too soft to trip it, but the tip of a metal letter opener...there, the plug yielded with a soft thunk.

The top drawer held credit reports and personnel files. She leafed through the latter. Nothing significant, but she might copy the reprimand for "frequent tardiness" in Cassy Gates' file. She also noted Darlene's street address in Repose—she might want that later.

She pulled out the bottom drawer. At first it seemed equally innocuous, filled with computer print-outs for two-thirds of its depth. At the back, three folders without labels stood behind a green, five by eight notebook. Mrs. Hark opened the drawer as far as it would go and crouched to peer into the first folder. She caught her breath when she saw "Wineena P" at the top of a sheet of figures. This was it! Down on her knees, she reached both hands into the drawer, flicking though the papers. Copies. She must make copies.

In the hall, a door slammed. Steps sounded on the vinyl flooring, and someone whistled the opening bars of "Melancholy Baby" in a cheerful, non-melancholy manner.

Judy quickly closed and locked the file. When Julius Portera stuck his head through her office door, she was seated at the computer, entering another invoice.

Chapter 13
Mrs. Millet: Picnic at Willow Grove

After she arranged to meet Judy that afternoon, everything caught up with Margaret Millet. The meeting with Jason in the dunes, the vigil outside the kitchen at Temple Hall, the lack of sleep! and the length of time since her last meal all combined to pull her down. She trudged along the path, longing for food and rest. Could she face a social breakfast and a lecture on "Rituals and How They Empower Us?" No way.

Approaching Temple Hall, Margaret saw light blazing through the back door, where she had caught that dim gleam in the small hours. The cooks were cooking. Maybe she could beg a bagel, take it back to her cabin, eat it, and sleep. Sleep...oh, yes. Margaret's "sleeve of care" was raveled.

She pushed through the door and followed her nose. The scents of bacon and fresh-baked biscuits led to the kitchen, where the cook, a large lady with a bun of iron-gray hair, trod rapidly from stove to counter, assembling trays of food. Youngsters of both sexes, some of them no more than ten or twelve years old, carried the trays upstairs to the main hall.

The cook saw her and stopped in mid-stride. "Hello! Are you lost?" She grinned like she was the last jolly-fat-person in the world and knew it.

"No, just hungry. I didn't sleep very well and I was hoping I could grab a bite and go back to my cabin for a nap before..." Margaret felt as pathetic as she sounded.

"Sure, Retreats can be hard on your sleep. Bet you got stuck with some night owls who wanted to hoot and wouldn't go to bed, di'n't ya? Well, just a sec—got a fresh pan of biscuits coming out—right now!" She opened the oven and grabbed a huge biscuit sheet in her padded mitt, swooped it across the kitchen to the serving table and slammed it down hard, making the biscuits bounce.

"Like bacon? I'll make you a sandwich." She sliced a biscuit and stuffed it with rounds of Canadian bacon. "There, now. That should hold you. I'm making my Chicken Supreme for lunch today, so don't sleep though the picnic." She wrapped the bacon-biscuit in a paper towel and passed it over.

"That's wonderful. Thank you so much. Chicken Supreme sounds wonderful, too." Margaret wanted nothing so much as to take this fragrant morsel to Sycamore Cabin, eat it and collapse into her bunk, but she couldn't waste a jolly cook who liked to talk. "Do you do all the cooking for the Retreats? It must be a lot of work..."

"Of course it's a lot of work, but I can handle it. Just a matter of planning and organization. I have my menus, everything in hand, all going like clockwork—that's the way. Not afraid of a little work. Work is good for the soul." The cook laughed a big, hearty laugh.

"Your food is so good. Is it hard to keep people out of the things you fix ahead of time?"

"Well, now—funny you should mention it. Never had a problem until just lately. And not really a problem now—we've got so much, with all the good things that grow right here in Repose. I'm missing a bowl of tuna-macaroni salad this morning. Made it last night and put it in the fridge, and it's not there now! Don't know what to think! Half a roast chicken disappeared a couple of days ago, too. Expect it's some of these KIDS!" She raised her voice, and her helpers turned to look at her. "Teen-age appetites, you know. Eating to grow, I guess. Sure a nuisance, though. I was going to use that chicken for enchiladas."

Madge, Esther and Louise chattered into Sycamore Cabin like a flock of starlings coming down in a corn-field. "How could you miss it?" Madge shrieked, bend-ing into the bottom bunk and stripping the blanket off Margaret's semi-conscious form. "I'm empowered! I'm empowered! And you, you lazy thing—you slept the whole time? When you could have been cleansing your soul with Rit-chu-als!"

Margaret, startled out of a warm, cozy dream, sat bolt upright and bumped her head, hard, on the under side of the top bunk. She rubbed the spot and grumbled, "Rituals. Isn't there one for letting people sleep?"

"Oh, no," Louise said. "Rituals are for celebrating Life!"

"Did you know that eating together is a ritual?" Esther chimed in. "And games? Even Poker! You won't have a chance tonight. We're all empowered except you."

Tonight. These women were all high and they wanted to play poker again tonight. Margaret stumbled to the bathroom, shaking her head. Once behind the bathroom door, she realized she was still? again? ravenously hun-gry. Sleep had rested her body and thanks to Madge, she was wide awake and needed food. The picnic couldn't happen too soon.

Smoke from charcoal fires and the fragrance of roasting corn and toasting garlic bread wafted through Willow Grove. The jolly cook bent over a grill, turning corn ears in their husks. Picnic tables bore pans of baked chicken, crocks of spicy Mexican beans, bowls of green salad and pasta. Margaret got in line behind her cabin mates and filled a tray, salivating as she went. She did appreciate good cooking—perhaps more than most people, since she so seldom did any herself.

Darlene—no, today she was definitely Thalia, domestic as a pot holder in her calico dress and apron—served the beans.

"My, that looks good." Margaret held her tray in position. "When do you get to eat, Thalia?"

"Oh, hi. Don't worry, I'll get mine."

"I'll save you a seat, right over there." Margaret pointed to a small table at the far edge of the grove. "I talked to Jason last night. Eat with me and I'll tell you about it."

Darlene's eyes widened. "Jason! Wherever..." The line moved and Margaret moved with it. She waved toward her chosen table again and smiled.

It took some maneuvering to avoid her roomies. Madge was especially matey. "Over here, Margaret— we've got the best place," she called, squirming over to make room on the bench. Margaret could hardly turn away, so she carried her tray to their table and made polite chat while her eyes searched the grove for escape.

There. Venus Valentine came into view on the path from the dunes. "There's Venus; I must ask her something. Oh, Venus..."

As Margaret approached with her heaped-up tray, Jason ducked under a willow branch and caught up to Venus from the rear. "Jason, too! Good. Won't you both join me? Is this table okay? I asked, uh, Thalia, to sit here too, as soon as she finishes serving."

Venus eyed Margaret's tray. "Jason, do get us some of this lovely food. You know what I eat."

Jason smiled. "Ah, it's the lady of the dunes." He walked away, whistling "I've Seen Fire and I've Seen Rain," a young man who moved to his own music.

Margaret deposited her tray on the table, then sat and pivoted her feet over the bench. Venus perched on the end of the table like a butterfly ready to flit.

"I've not seen you here before, Mrs. Millet. Is this your first retreat?"

"Yes. I thought your speech last night was just right. Everybody should do what they want to, just relax and rest. It's wonderful to be fed and not have to wash the dishes." She took a bite of chicken. Delicious.

Venus said, "Did you enjoy Urania's talk on Rituals?"

"Ah...um. People really came away empowered! I look forward to creating my own song this afternoon, too." Did Venus know she hadn't made the ritual thing? She added, "And I'm anxious to hear Thalia's talk on the three ages of woman. Did you know Judy Hark is working at BFK, where Thalia works, uh, when she's Darlene?"

That got Venus' attention. "Why, no...I didn't," Venus settled on the bench and turned her golden brown gaze to Margaret.

"Yes. They're short handed. One of their office girls has gone missing; did Thalia tell you?"

"Is that the black girl Mrs. Hark asked me about? I've been meaning to ask Thalia about that, but I haven't had the chance."

"Cassandra Gates. Her mother is most anxious about her, as you can imagine. Especially since one of the BFK drivers was murdered. I'm sure you've heard about that."

"Terrible. The Manager at BFK was supposed to be here this weekend, but he couldn't come because of the investigation. He seemed very upset when he called."

"Really?" Julius Portera coming here? Did Judy know that?

"Yes. I know him quite well, actually. He's one of my students." Venus' voice was cool, but a flush rose in her cheeks.

"Well, he's sure got problems. Cassandra missing, a driver killed and a load of Filet Mignon hi jacked. You're a good judge of people, Venus—what sort of man is he? Do you think he could be mixed up in anything criminal?"

"No! Certainly not!" Venus paused as though realizing such vehemence was not required. In calmer tones she said, "Julius is a good person. There are things he doesn't understand, but he's trying to learn. Money is not the most important thing in his life—and money is the basis of most criminal activity, wouldn't you say?"

"Yes, money—money and power, the 'roots of all evil.'"

Venus went on, "Money and business success can never lead to harmony. I've made it clear to Julius that his life must change before...before..."

"Before you can marry him?"

Venus started, a crimson blush rising to her hairline. Then she let out a gust of laughter. "You take my breath away! Have you been talking to Julius?"

"No. Just a guess. You're a lovely woman, Venus. What man wouldn't want you?"

Venus brushed the compliment aside. "Oneness. I admit I think of it," she mused. "Julius is so alive, so eager to live fully. But my life—could he accept it? You see..."

Margaret could certainly sympathize, having chosen the single life herself after twenty years of marriage. She wanted to continue this fascinating discussion.

Jason approached, bearing two well filled trays. He

placed one before Venus like an offering and then sat opposite her. Evidently, it was better to look upon his deity than to sit beside her.

"Thank you, Jason. What a lot of different things to eat! I must choose carefully to keep my channels open and flowing today." Venus took the chain of her crystal pendant in hand and dangled the glittering crystal over the tray. "Yes, I can feel the flow. The green salad, the fruit cup, macaroni—no, definitely not. Chicken, yes. Garlic bread? Yes...maybe. Beans, no. Pound cake and raspberry sauce, certainly. Our cook puts a lot of love into her cooking. You can feel it, ever so strong."

Was this bright, intelligent woman really going to eat only what her crystal approved? It certainly looked that way. Margaret shook her head and dug into the food on her tray, heedless of the crystal's advice. If only our education system would require a course in physics, she thought, so people could learn how things really work. And every child should read Isaac Asimov's essays on pseudo-science. With these two precautions, superstition—what Asimov called "The Perennial Fringe"—might disappear in a generation!

Her working life had been spent in Los Angeles chemical labs, first on research into materials and manufacturing processes, later (after Nixon nixed the research grants) in the dirty, dangerous, electro plating industry. She had finally escaped, moved to Santa Porta and opened a used book store. During her chemical career, she had seen some furtherance of human knowledge and plenty of harm done to the planet. She liked Jason's philosophy; live simply, do no harm, stay out of the rat-race—but choosing food with a crystal? What about good nutrition? vitamins? minerals? Had two hundred years of food research been done to no purpose?

Although she felt smothered in gullibility, especially after Thalia joined them and performed similar rites, she repressed the scientific lecture and listened.

Venus questioned Jason and Thalia about Cassandra's visit to, and disappearance from, Repose. Jason responded fully and even Thalia seemed less secretive. There would be a good deal to report when she met Judy Hark that afternoon.

Chapter 14
Mrs. Hark: The Black Book

The front house had a closed look and no vehicles occupied the carport; Laura and Tiny must be elsewhere. Judy Hark let herself into Margaret's granny pad, closed the screen and left the door ajar. The autumn day was warm. The air smelled of drying leaves and sunshine.

She filled the kettle, set it on the stove to boil and collapsed into the rattan chair. What a relief to relax! I'm not made for this spying, she thought. It's bad for my blood pressure. She closed her eyes and let her body go completely limp for a few minutes, as Venus always had them do at the end of a Yoga session. She breathed deeply, in and out, in and out. By the time the kettle boiled, her pulse was back to normal and she was ready to pool her supply of facts, conjectures, and suspicions with whatever Margaret brought from Repose. She reached a brown pottery teapot down from the cupboard and rinsed it with boiling water; they would need a full pot of tea.

A few minutes later, Margaret clanged through the gate and came in. "Good! You're here!"

"There you are. I made myself right at home."

"Tea! And how I need it," Margaret said.

Judy poured out and they both sat at the table. "Did anybody see you leave?"

"I don't think so. I signed in at the afternoon session. It was crowded and I managed to slip away while everybody was milling around. Too bad I won't Create my Own Song, though."

"That's a shame. What would your song be like?"

"Oh, I'd sing of my blessings. Think what I've survived! Twenty years of marriage, three years in the South during the worst of the civil rights struggles, sixteen years of driving in Los Angeles traffic...and I did survive and now it's 'home port at last,' right here in Gambol Beach. I know how lucky I am. Hey, I'm here, drinking this fine tea in the best of company." Margaret held up her mug in salute.

"Hmm. The feeling's mutual." Judy acknowledged the compliment with a surge of warm affection for her friend. "So how's the Retreat going? You said you had a lot to tell." A born listener, she liked to hear the other person's news before telling her own.

"Okay, I'll go first." Margaret's descriptions of the assembly at Temple Hall on Friday night and Darlene's transformation to Thalia were deft and succinct. When she got to her cabin-mates and the poker game, it was too funny! And meeting Jason in the dunes—well, some people had all the luck.

"Some people have all the luck. There I was, entering data and scared to death snooping in Glenda Ravenet's office—and harassed by policemen—and you were singing in the moonlight with a handsome young man! What did he say about Cassandra?"

"He thinks she's alive and I think she's still there, somewhere in Repose. She stayed with Darlene until—get this—Clark Atherton showed up in Repose, looking for her!"

"Why didn't Clark tell us he'd been there?" Judy felt betrayed; they had been so open with Clark, he seemed so grateful for their help, and yet he'd kept this to himself!

"I don't know. Cassandra's mother was pretty upset. Maybe he would have told us, but he hadn't told her and didn't want to make things worse."

"And why hadn't he told her? I don't like it," Judy said. "You're right about Mbyrna, though. Repose was really a touchy subject with her."

Margaret described her vigil outside Temple Hall and the light she had glimpsed in the kitchen. "Somebody raided the refrigerator, and it could have been Cassandra. I don't know how she got in and out or where she's hiding, but who else would it be at that hour?"

"I do hope so. If she is still alive—she could probably solve the murder and hi-jacking in a minute, if she'd only come out and tell! Did you get a chance to talk to Darlene?"

"Yes, at the picnic—I ate with her and Venus. Only, like I told you, she's 'Thalia' in Repose—a completely different girl. Venus started to talk about your Julius Portera, too, but then Jason came with the food.

"I told Venus that Cassandra was missing and you were filling in at BFK. Venus asked Jason and Darlene for the full story. Most of it I've already told you, but one thing was new. Darlene said when Cassandra didn't show up for work, Glenda Ravenet made many telephone calls on her private line. Said she could hear her, every fifteen minutes, punching the buttons, waiting and hanging up without speaking. I don't know how she could hear what Glenda was doing inside her office—do you? Anyhow, all those hang-ups on my answering machine may have been Glenda's calls."

"Darlene probably listened in the hall—easy enough, on her way to or from the coffee pot." Judy felt it was now her turn. "Julius Portera talked to me about Venus, too."

"I might have known!" Margaret laughed. "You've got him confiding in you, already."

"That was on Friday, while the others were out to lunch. He thinks she's just wonderful—not like anybody else in the world, he said. If it hadn't been for the murder investigation, he'd have been at the Retreat this weekend."

"Yes, Venus said that, too."

Then Judy told Margaret about Detective Soong and about Glenda saying Frank Slee would get his, but not now. "And I found something in Cassandra's desk—now where did I put my purse?"

The purse turned up in the bathroom. After a little sorting, Judy extracted the battered little book. "Here it is. See what you think."

Margaret took the book between thumb and forefinger. "Did you show this to that detective?"

"No, I didn't. He was so negative—well, I just didn't. Cassy's desk had been cleaned out—nothing left except office supplies—but the center drawer wouldn't quite close and this was why." She rubbed her bruised shoulder, remembering how hard it had been to reach the book and pry it loose.

Margaret turned the blue-lined pages. "Have you studied these Notes? What do you make of them?"

"I haven't had a chance. There are letters and numbers, but I couldn't recognize any words. Some pages are full and some have only a few marks. The writing is Cassandra's. I matched it to samples of her writing in the files. Here, I'll show you." Judy handed over the documents she had copied. "See? On this letter she wrote 'Electronic transfer???' and the capital E has that same squiggle. And these numbers—the 3 and the 5 both have long tails, just like in the book."

"The question marks match, too. Oh, well done!" Margaret lifted the tea pot and refilled their mugs.

Judy read the letter from Bully Beef Steak Houses. "Listen to this. 'We agree to pay cash on delivery to secure the special price of $75 per case.' That is a special price! Good grief, Margaret, a case of twenty-four restaurant-quality steaks sells for $140 and up! I know—I've been entering the invoices all morning."

"Bully Beef Steak Houses." Margaret leafed through the little book. "There, I thought so! This page has "BB" in the top corner. Maybe it's a record of what they bought."

"Let me see that."

"Why 'Electronic transfer,' I wonder?" Margaret passed her the book and picked up the letter.

"That's one way to make payment. It's something I could check, too, if I had access to BFK's bank statements. Maybe Cassy was looking for this payment to show up—and couldn't find it? Because they paid cash to the driver?"

"And he didn't turn it in to the company?"

"Oh, I don't know. They must have some way to check the receipts against what went on the truck. The driver couldn't get away with that."

Judy studied the page headed "BB." The top line started with numbers. 0911. The number for police emergencies, but it could also be a date; September 11. The line read "0911 D 50 7OZFM CH 3750 NoET."

"There seems to be a pattern here," she said. "Those first numbers could be dates—see, the next line starts '0927.' September 11 and then September 27. And the next two lines start with '1005,' then '1018.' October 5 and October 18? If you were used to computers, that's the way you'd write dates, with zeros to make two-digit numbers.

"If only Julius hadn't come in, just when I found those

files in Glenda's desk! I saw a sheet headed 'Wineena P,' and Wineena Packing is the company I told you about that's not in the computer."

"Is one of those pages marked 'WP?'"

Mrs. Hark thumbed eagerly. "Yes! Right here!"

"Let me see. Wow, it's a full one, too."

They could not find meaning in the cryptic notations, but Judy began to have a few glimmers. Some of the letters suggested the wording of invoices and bills of lading, if she could only sort them out. "I'll study these tonight, after dinner."

Before they parted, Margaret copied the marks in the black book, page for page, and added the copies to her file.

"Here, put the handwriting samples in there, too," Judy said. "Hadn't you better get back to Repose?"

"Yes. There'll be a bonfire on the beach tonight and I don't want to miss my dinner, either. The food is great."

"What about tomorrow?"

"Tomorrow...Sunday. Oh yes, Jason's talk on pyramids, crystals and gemstones in the morning and Darlene's seminar on the three stages of woman in the afternoon. Why don't you come for that? It starts at three o'clock, in Temple Hall."

"Three stages of woman?"

"Uh-huh. Virgin, Wife/Mother and Crone."

"And we're the Crones. What a thought."

Margaret said Crones were good—the honored elders of the human race—but Judy didn't like the word in the least. "You needn't become a Crone if you don't let yourself go."

Margaret laughed. "I'm already gone. I'll search for Cassandra's hiding place again tonight, if I survive the poker game."

"I hope you find it—and I refuse to be a Crone," Judy said. "The Historical Society Barbecue is tomorrow, but I'll try to come for Darlene's talk. Julius may be there; he said something about getting to the final session, if he could."

Chapter 15
Mrs. Millet: The Bonfire

Margaret Millet parked her pickup at Repose as the afternoon session in Temple Hall was breaking up. She mingled with the Retreaters and strolled toward Sycamore Cabin, grateful for the late afternoon shade under the trees. It was one of those warm fall days when the sea breeze fails and dry, inland air reaches for the ocean.

In the cabin, she shut herself in the shower stall. The tepid spray felt good. Much as she liked tub baths, a shower did do a better job of rinsing off the soap.

She was washing her hair when she heard someone bang through the cabin door, caroling, "I will never fear the heights, I will soar and climb! I will fill with great delight, and view eternal ti-i-me! la la li, la la lee, la la lo o oh!" Madge had created her song.

Margaret wondered what her own song would have been. Could she sing of joy and contentment? At the moment, she didn't feel contented; she felt frustrated. True, she and Judy were making some headway. Not enough. Not fast enough. She wanted to find that lost black girl, and soon. If she sang what was in her heart, it would come out like the Spike Jones song, "Chloe." "Cassandra...Cassandra..." wailing through the swamps.

Esther and Louise were also in the cabin when Margaret emerged. Louise said, "Next!" and carried her towel and robe into the shower room.

Esther said, "Where were you? Aren't you going to do any of the workshops?"

Margaret ignored her. "Sing it again, Madge. It's a terrific song. Sounds like you've conquered your fear of heights."

Madge sang and Esther repeated her question.

Margaret considered her session with Judy Hark and said, "I meditated."

Supper consisted of cold cuts and salads, since there would be hot dogs and marshmallows at the bonfire. A more perfect evening for the beach could not have been chosen; the fog had moved out to sea and dry, warm air from the east wafted over the dunes.

The bonfire blazed high. Oak and pine limbs burned brightly, with yellow flares from the pitch pockets and pine cones. The fire had been built above the tide line at the end of a gravel road from Repose to the beach. The long sea swells crashed into foam on the sand. A fattening moon hung in the east and a million stars glowed over the sea. The beach and the desert, Margaret thought, the last places where you can see the stars. Everywhere else, they are dimmed by man-made light.

Near the fire, she stopped to watch and let her cabin-mates go ahead. Jason thumped his bongos and Venus played her guitar on the far side of the fire, their faces lit by the leaping flames. Jason, in cut-offs and a denim vest open to his waist, sat lotus-fashion on the sand, his bongos before him. Venus, in a light colored granny dress, perched on a camp stool with her instrument. They sang "My Bonnie Lies Over the Ocean," and the group joined in. "Bring back, Bring back, Oh, bring back my Bonnie to me, to me..."

A man brushed past Margaret, a square, solid looking man in khakis and a plaid shirt. Wasn't that—yes it was. Julius Portera had come for the bonfire.

Margaret sat in the outer fringe of singers and watched

Julius circle the fire. He picked his way among the bodies on the sand and squatted directly behind Venus, his eyes on the long, dark braid down her back. He reached out a hand as though to touch it, then drew it back.

Time passed swiftly and pleasantly. Margaret lifted her voice and sang, basking in the campfire camaraderie. The fire burned to embers, the marshmallow packages and wiener wrappers emptied; the trash cans filled. Esther and Louise offered to share their smuggled beer (alcohol was tabu in Repose), but Margaret shook her head. She wanted to keep her wits about her.

Once she glimpsed a shadowy movement behind the nearest sand dune and wondered who might be lurking out of view—but she didn't investigate. It could have been any one—or two—of the Retreaters. Maybe Retreats were like Camp Meetings, more souls made than saved.

Madge, Esther and Louise showed signs of leaving the party. Couldn't they give up poker for one night? Margaret crawled on hands and knees to the far side of the fire and hid behind the largest back she could find. Her tennis shoes and turned up pant legs filled with sand as she went. She emptied them and retied the shoe laces. The large back covered her long enough—her roomies passed from view on the road back to Repose.

Now, where did Venus go? And Julius? She had watched them all evening (they seemed to thoroughly enjoy each other's company), and the minute she hid behind a back, they disappeared! Unfair.

Jason and two other young fellows smothered the fire with sand. What with the fresh air, the food, and the lack of rest the night before, Margaret was half asleep—might as well head back to the cabin.

She had come by the road, but the path through Willow

Grove—if she could find this end of it—should be a short cut back to Sycamore Cabin. She could look for hiding places, too, in the hitherto unexplored area between the beach and the Shrine of the Dunes. Even if she didn't join the poker game tonight, she doubted if she could wake up later for another moonlight prowl, so if she was to search at all...

Jason didn't take the road—he was striding up the beach, his bongos slung over his shoulder on a strap. He would use the Shrine path, surely. She followed.

Farther up the beach, Jason turned inland. Margaret marked the spot as well as she could. He had just passed that big log. Why hadn't she brought a flashlight? Oh, well, the moon was bright and the path, at least the part of it she had seen, was well defined.

Ten minutes later, she still hadn't found it. Bother. Unless she wanted to wade in soft sand all night, she had better follow her ears back to the ocean and take the gravel road.

Turning toward the muffled roar of the surf, she heard something else. Voices. People.

The sound came from a row of cypress trees above the dunes. She struggled toward them, deep sand impeding her progress and silencing her steps. What a snoop she had become! The possibility that she might find Cassandra overrode her qualms. She would just take a peek.

The cypress trees cast dark shadows on the sheltered hollow beneath them. Margaret flattened her body behind a root and peered over, waiting for her eyes to adjust to the dimness. With the tops of their heads toward her and startlingly close, two people lay on the slope, side by side, their shoulders touching.

Venus said, in her bell like tones, "I'm glad you came

tonight, Julius. I can almost believe you are sincere."

Julius mumbled something that sounded like, "I sincerely adore you," and reached an arm around Venus' shoulder. Why couldn't the man speak up? If everybody spoke as clearly as Venus, a lot of misunderstandings would never happen.

"It's your way of life," Venus said. "I can't ask you give it up, but I could never fit into it."

That's right, Margaret thought. If these two ever get together, one of them will have to change his way of life. And I do mean his; it won't be Venus.

Julius said, "I want to give it up. Truly, I want to live with you, for you, and in the way you want to live. Please, Venus, believe me! I want to take you off the market! I know I have a lot to learn. I'm your pupil; teach me." He gently drew her to him, waited when she held back and then, when she yielded, kissed her passionately and murmured inaudible, but no doubt tender, words into her long, dark braid.

Well! Margaret knew when to leave. This was absolutely none of her business. She started to crawl backward. Wait—a twig cracked. A short distance away, a dark form burst between the trees and ran madly into the dunes. Margaret had not been the only witness to Julius' declaration of love. In the moonlight, she saw long legs in shorts, a tousled head, elbows flailing in a dark jacket. The figure seemed feminine, but she couldn't be sure. She followed cautiously.

The other witness did not go far. Tripped by a root or a pocket in the sand, she (definitely she) fell headlong into the hollow between two dunes. She lay gasping for breath and then beat the sand with her fists and thrashed her legs like she was having a fit. Or a tantrum.

Yes, exactly like a thwarted three-year-old, except the screams were silent, the mouth working without sound. Margaret could see the woman's face now and contorted as it was, she recognized Darlene. Darlene in agony because Julius loved someone else—loved Venus Valentine, the near-goddess, the serene leader, the impossible competition. Oh dear, poor Darlene.

Margaret retreated to the water's edge and walked back to the road on hard sand. It took half an hour to reach Sycamore Cabin, but she needed every minute of it to regain her composure.

The poker game was going strong. Madge said, "Well, here's our lone wolf at last—we were about to send out a search party. Did you enjoy yourself out under the moon? Who with—anybody we know?"

Louise said, "Shame on you, Madge. Mind your own business. Here, Margaret, pull up a chair and I'll deal you in."

Margaret declined to answer questions or take part. She showered off the sand, pulled on her gray sweats, and crawled into her bunk. She would not go out again that night. For one day, at least, she had seen quite enough.

Chapter 16
Mrs. Hark: The Barbecue

Judy Hark and Willy ate their Saturday night dinner from trays in the living room so Willy could watch baseball on TV—the final playoff game for the National League. When she had finished her stuffed pepper, Judy left him to keep track of the hits, runs, and errors and retired to the kitchen to assemble a bowl of potato salad for the Historical Society barbecue the next day.

She peeled and cut up potatoes (cooked the night before), diced celery, sliced green onions, and added chopped pickle, plenty of hard cooked egg and bits of sweet red pepper for color. Then she mixed mayonnaise, mustard and a little pickle juice and stirred the mixture into the vegetables carefully, so the potatoes wouldn't get mushed. A pattern of sliced egg sprinkled with paprika to top off the bowl—there. Worthy of a picture in Gourmet Magazine.

The Historical Society had reserved the pavilion at Gambol Beach State Park for their fund-raising barbecue. Experienced cooks would grill chicken and beef tri-tip, toast buttered garlic bread and heat pots of spicy beans. Judy and other members would bring deserts and salads. At $12 a head, the barbecue should clear a goodly sum.

The fabulous Trunk would also be on display, with all its donated treasures. Judy Hark and Myrtle Farrini, in historic costume, would sell raffle tickets on the Trunk.

Judy tasted her potato salad with satisfaction. When its flavors had blended overnight in the refrigerator, it would do her credit.

Now to re-examine Cassandra Gates' little black book. Yes, Willy was engaged with the ball game, twisting in his chair over the umpire's dubious call. She fetched the book and opened it to the page marked WP.

At 9:30 the next morning, Judy carried the chilled potato salad from her car to the long serving table, already filled with pies, cakes, gelatin desserts, and salads. She stowed the bowl underneath the table, in the shade. When it came to eggs and mayonnaise, one couldn't be too careful.

She looked around her, taking pleasure in the open meadow, the shady trees and the trickling creek that could be viewed from the park pavilion. Gambol Beach State Park lay north of Repose on the long sweep of public beach that ended in cliffs, just past the Gambol Beach Pier. The Park reached inland to Highway 1 and in summer, its shady camp sites were packed with the trailers and RVs of inlanders, escaping the heat of Fresno and Bakersfield. Its eucalyptus and cypress trees had been planted in the rowdy days when big bands played at the Gambol Beach Ballroom and the town's very name was enough to get laughs for radio comedians like Jack Benny and Fibber McGee. The comedians were long gone, but the trees had grown and prospered. No longer crowded this late in the fall, the park was now available to local folk and "snowbirds," the RVers who came down from Canada and the Northwest to escape the winter.

Myrtle Farrini interrupted her reverie. "There you are, Judy!" Myrtle's husband and son had boosted the heavy Trunk onto a nearby picnic table. Myrtle had it open and was pulling out items for display. "I wondered if you'd get here." She showed her tiny, even teeth. Myrtle was in costume today, whether or not she had worn it yesterday. Her ruffled skirt swept the ground and a pink organdy picture hat obstructed her vision in most directions.

Judy readjusted her own hat, an 1890s straw boater with daisies around the crown. "How did you do yesterday, with the downtown merchants?"

"Really well! Oh, we missed you, of course, but we sold lots of tickets."

"How many?"

"Well, I only got the money for three, but lots of people said they were coming to the barbecue and would buy them here. I got these lace doilies—look, real tatted lace!—from Mrs. Morton. She was going to take them to your house, but I said you weren't there and she'd better bring them to me." Myrtle draped the doilies over the edge of the trunk with a self-satisfied smirk.

"Well, good! You didn't need me at all then, did you?" Myrtle shouldn't have let those merchants put her off. She was willing. She was eager. Pity she was so stupid. "Did you wear your costume yesterday?"

"Oh, yes I did. I forgot I was going to wear it today too, so it will need cleaning anyhow. How did your little job go? Listen, My Husband (you could hear the capital letters when Myrtle mentioned her spouse) knows a lot of people. If you and Willy are...you know...feeling the pinch, he could find you a job, easily. You mustn't be afraid to say. What are friends for?" Myrtle was ever so sweet and patronizing.

"Thanks, Myrtle, but Willy and I are just fine. The company had an emergency, and they called on me for help, that's all. One's skills are known in the community, you know." What was it about Myrtle Farrini that made her respond with such a put-down? Judy lifted a hand-painted demitasse cup from the trunk and rearranged Myrtle's higgledy piggledy display so the cup would show to advantage.

By noon, the park overflowed with the citizens of Gambol Beach. The barbecue's purpose, to fund a new edition of THE FACE OF THE CLAM by Luther Whiteman, a famous 1947 best seller about the Great Depression in Gambol Beach, had been well publicized. Judy saw the Mayor and his lady and two of the City Council members joining the queue at the serving table. She hoped Hizzoner liked potato salad.

Ah, the Chief of Police, in dress uniform. Judy rose from her seat beside the Trunk. "Do you mind if I go first, Myrtle? Can I bring you a plate?"

Myrtle lifted the brim of her hat and made a shooing gesture. "Go ahead, Dear. I'm dieting—I'll just have a little green salad later." Good grief—dieting, with all this fancy food prepared?

Chief "Marion the Librarian" Belgrave picked up a paper plate and began to fill it from the bounty on the table. Just one plate; he must have come by himself. Judy fell in behind him and handed him a spoon for the stuffed cabbage balls. "Glad you could make it, Chief Belgrave."

Like most of the local politicians, he knew her from her civic activities. "Ah, Mrs. Hark!" He couldn't shake hands; his were full. "What a spread you people put on! Wonderful. Wonderful." He extended his plate for slices of barbecued tri tip and received a double helping. The server must scale his portions by the size of the recipient. Looking at the Chief's bay window, Judy wondered how much longer his uniform would button.

He scooped up some of Judy's potato salad, already

decimated by those ahead in the line. "Doesn't that look good?"

Mrs. Hark took some herself. A good thing she had saved some for Willy; none of this would survive.

She followed Chief Belgrave around the table and stood at his elbow while he surveyed the crowd for an advantageous seat. She ought to go back to Myrtle and the Trunk, but she hated to miss a chance like this. The Chief might tell her what progress, if any, had been made in investigating Cassandra's disappearance.

"I see a place over there, Chief. Do you mind if I join you?"

What could the man say? "Delighted, Mrs. Hark. Delighted."

They sat together at one side of a small table. The young couple on the other side had eyes only for each other, bless them, so Judy felt she could speak freely.

"How strange," she said. "How strange that here we are, in the same park where a murder victim was found only a few days ago. Here you are, Chief, picnicking on the job, you might say! I hope the case is going well?"

"Don't remind me. It's good to get away from the job when I can. All I want to do is relax and eat some of this fine food." He masticated a large mouthful and washed it down with a swig of coffee.

Judy persisted. "What I really want to ask you about is that missing girl, Cassandra Gates. Did you know I'm doing her job at BFK Restaurant Supply? Just until she comes back—or is replaced, if that happens."

Chief Belgrave's mind connected with a nearly audible click. "Why, yes, Louis Soong sent me a report—and it's you, of course. What do you think of that place?"

"BFK? They're doing a good business. The manager,

Julius Portera, seems capable—a nice person. What I've seen of him, I like. Did you know that Cassandra spent a lot of time here in our neighborhood—at Repose? She was good friends with the BFK receptionist, a girl named Darlene Evans, who lives in Repose."

The Chief chewed thoughtfully, swallowed, and took another mouthful of beans. "Repose, huh. And that truck driver's body turned up in the park—not here in the picnic area, though—way over on the other side, by the creek. Both cases right here in my bailiwick."

"Yes. Maybe they're two pieces of the same case." Was the Chief susceptible to flattery? "If anybody can solve this, I'm sure you can. They both worked for BFK. Cassandra lived in Gambol Beach, didn't she? A shared apartment, her mother said. I'm sure you've talked to her roommates—what do they think happened to her?"

"Lt. Trusco talked to those girls. He didn't get much out of them, except they said the black girl seemed spooked about something before she went missing. I really don't see any connection to the murder, myself. The girl, by all reports, was a typical, scatty teenager—could be a typical runaway. No need to jump to conclusions."

Judy remembered something that had bothered her all along. "And the telephone company disconnected her phone—and gave the number to Margaret Millet. That has always seemed so strange to me, Chief. When was the phone disconnected and why did they give the number to someone else so soon? Am I making sense?"

The Chief looked at her with new interest. "Margaret Millet, yes. Friend of yours? She thinks she saw those steaks being hi-jacked, you know."

Why did he evade her question? "The telephone, Chief. Do you know when Cassandra's phone was shut off?"

"I guess we could find out. I doubt if it's important, but it's a point to check. Might give us an excuse for another visit to the roommates."

A line of people waving money had formed beside the Trunk and Myrtle signaled with both arms, like a drowning swimmer trying to catch the lifeguard's eye. Judy would have to go. "I'll have to go, Chief. Nice talking to you." Would he bother to check with the telephone company? She doubted it. With Chief Belgrave, you could never tell; he didn't give anything away. She had planted the question and that was all she could do.

Cassandra's roommates—was there some way to approach them? Clark Atherton had talked to them during his search for Cassandra, before the murder. Perhaps they would tell a lady of mature years (not a Crone) things they wouldn't tell the police.

Chapter 17
Mrs. Millet: Pyramids, Crystals and Gems

In spite of the passions she had witnessed and the noise of the on-going poker game, Margaret Millet's exhausted body sank into a deep, dreamless slumber, pulling her mind along. When she awoke, the sun hot on her sleeping bag, the cabin was empty except for herself. Good. Her cabin-mates had called her "lone wolf" and that appellation suited her book.

She got to Temple Hall barely in time to pour a cup of coffee, pick up a biscuit and spoon jam and scrambled eggs onto a paper plate before the workers cleared away the food. The eggs were cool, but tasty. Cook's biscuit—well, it might be a long time before she had another chance to eat anything so good. She spread it with strawberry jam and relished the result.

She had chosen a table by one of the long windows looking out over Repose. Another warm, dry day with a rising east wind to push back the ocean air. Trees that grew slantwise from the prevailing westerlies now blew in the opposite direction, shedding leaves and dry needles. Wildfire weather in California. The kind of weather that made people sick, as well, with all manner of colds and viral infections. Margaret's throat already felt a little raw.

She looked at her watch. Almost time for Jason's lecture on Pyramids, Crystals and Gemstones. The Hall would soon fill with "seekers."

She visited the rest room to freshen up, thinking of Jason—such an unusual young man—content, apparently, to live without the things most men strive for, playing and singing as merrily as any grasshopper in this world of worker ants. Would he perish in a cold winter like the grasshopper of the fable? Not likely. Jason wasn't all grasshopper; he worked enough to provide food, clothing and shelter. He simply refused to extend his needs. His definition of success was not based on things accumulated. Maybe this tired old world needed more people like Jason.

What had been his impact on Cassandra Gates? Her family offered a classic example of striving for—and achieving—what the world called success, and Cassandra had found Jason during her own period of teenage rebellion. Then there were his other attributes—that manly body, those long, sandy eyelashes and that sweet smile. What young girl (make that female of any age) wouldn't find him attractive?

So today, Jason would discourse on "Pyramids, Crystals and Gemstones." For seven years after her escape from the industrial chemistry labs of Los Angeles, Margaret had owned and operated a tiny used-book store in Santa Porta where books on these subjects sold very well. She had dipped into them herself, the better to converse with her customers, so she was familiar with the powers attributed to pyramids, crystals, and gemstones by believers in the occult. She did hope Jason wasn't going to talk about "psychic emanations" and "auras." His philosophy on human relations and human needs made beautiful sense and she would be greatly disappointed if he went off into pseudo-science.

In Temple Hall, the long folding tables had been pushed into a semi-circle and an easel-chalkboard erected on the open side. Jason stood before it, looking incredibly young and clean in one of the loose flowered shirts he favored. His jeans fit him neatly. His sandy, shoulder-length hair shone and his suntanned face was freshly shaved. The leather sandals revealed clean feet and trimmed toenails.

The Retreaters ambled into the hall and chose their seats. Margaret sat at the center table where she had a good view of the proceedings.

On the chalkboard behind him, Jason had drawn a hexagon divided into triangles. He now surveyed his audience and said, "Good morning."

Several people responded, "Good morning, Jason," and one man (there was always one!) bellowed out, "Top o' the marnin' to you, Jason!" at full volume. Margaret noticed Esther and Louise just as they saw her. They waved and grinned.

"Today we'll talk about pyramids, crystals, and gem—" Jason began. The main doors flew open and tiny Madge trotted in, plunked three books on the table beside Margaret and wrestled herself up onto a chair. Jason waited until the racket subsided, smiled at Madge and made a fresh start.

"Pyramids, crystals, and gemstones, in that order. Are these things connected? I believe they are. In order to trace that connection, I want to call your attention to a simple geometric figure, the triangle. I've drawn a hexagon cut into triangles here on the board." He backed away to let everyone see the sketch.

"A triangle," Jason said, "is the strongest basic structure known to man. This is because it cannot change its shape. If you attach three straight pieces of rigid material—wood, metal, plastic, anything unbending—firmly together at the ends, the resulting triangle is as strong as the material itself. It may break, if the material is breakable, but its shape cannot be changed. A rectangle will change to a rhomboid under pressure, but a triangle stays a triangle.

"How many have taken a course in Trigonometry? Hands, please."

Margaret put up her hand, as did the man on her right and a few others. She shook her head; what neglect! Everybody should study Trigonometry.

Jason went on, "Trigonometry is the science of measurement based on the triangle. The diameter of the earth was first calculated by Trigonometry. Ships use it to determine their positions on the ocean."

The boisterous one said audibly, "What has that got to do with pyramids and crystals?" He had not raised his hand as a student of Trigonometry, either. Margaret mentally chalked up a third mark against him.

Jason wasted his beautiful smile on the heckler. "I'm coming to that, my friend. Let us first consider the pyramid." He drew a square on the board beside the hexagon. "A pyramid is a three dimensional figure whose base is surmounted by triangles that meet in a single apex at the top. If you look down on it from above, it looks like this." He drew two intersecting lines, dividing the square into four triangles. "While the base of a pyramid can vary, the ancient Egyptians build theirs with square bases and hence, four sides. This type of pyramid is called a tetragonal pyramid—tetra, four sides.

"The Great Pyramids of Egypt were huge structures built of stone and the weight involved was enormous. The pyramid shape, however, is capable of supporting this weight. The stones would literally have to be crushed for the pyramids to fall down and with the largest number of stones—that is, the greatest weight—at the bottom, that is not likely to happen. In fact, it has not happened. The Egyptian pyramids still stand, thousands of years after they were built."

The know-it-all had read the occult books. "The pyramid preserved the mummies; that was why they used it. Decay can't happen inside a pyramid. That's the wonderful thing!"

"There are ongoing experiments to determine the effects on matter placed inside pyramids, that's true. Some people believe we would be happier living in pyramidal houses instead of cubical ones, although personally, I think the narrow overhead would be claustrophobic. It's more natural to nest under a big, open sky, to my way of thinking—a small enclosure on the ground, with room overhead. There is no question that pyramidal houses would be strong, though.

"Buckminster Fuller solved the constriction effect by building with many triangles" (he pointed to the hexagon he had drawn) "expanded into a dome. The geodesic dome is very strong."

Jason had neatly guided the discussion back to architecture. Margaret relaxed—with his capable management, this would not turn into a voodoo session. Or would it?

"Crystals are another matter, however," Jason said. "Crystals have marvelous properties, some of which have been thoroughly studied and scientifically documented. Magnetite and quartz crystals, for example, have surfaces that are sensitive to radio signals on contact with fine wire probes. They were used in an early type of radio receiver called a crystal set. This receiver was simple enough to build at home and lots of people did, before the invention of the vacuum tube. Some crystals are electrical conductors or semi conductors. Some even produce electrical charges under pressure, such as the tourmaline crystals used in pressure gauges.

"If a crystal can receive a man-made signal like radio, might it not also receive natural magnetic emanations? I think it can, but whether the emanations come from the atmosphere, from other matter, or from the humans who study the crystals—that is the part we have not been able to pin down."

Margaret thought of Venus and Darlene dangling their crystals over their food. What Jason said made sense. Perhaps they did feel something—some emanation—from this process. Deciding what to eat based on those feelings, however, still seemed like nonsense.

Margaret couldn't help it; she was impressed by Jason's presentation. She said so to Madge. "I'm impressed."

"Yes, but you're an intellectual," Madge said.

Surprised, Margaret could only answer, "Am I? I'll have to think about that."

Jason went on to discuss the formation of crystals and the fact that most liquids get more dense as they get colder and solidify, with the great exception of water. "Ice is lighter than liquid water, so it floats," Jason said. "This fact is one of the best indications of a higher power in the universe. If ice crystals didn't float, all the life in the rivers and lakes would freeze and die in cold winters."

The most active participant brushed ice crystals aside and said, "Pyramids have to be lined up with the North Pole to work right, don't they?"

Jason sidestepped this. "Well, the North Pole—or rather, the magnetic north, does attract iron; every Boy Scout uses that property in his compass. Magnetic fields exist and so do radiation belts. You may have enough iron in your blood to make you slightly influenced by electromagnetic attractions." He laughed. "And I'm not talking about attraction between man and woman—that's another field entirely. We won't discuss hormones today. Any other questions?" He inspected his audience, person by person. When he looked at Margaret she gave him an unobtrusive "thumbs up." His eyes twinkled and moved on.

"Some of the best known crystals are the gemstones. Their beauty, durability and rarity make them valuable all over the world. Portable wealth! Did you know that most gems are colorless in their pure state? The color in a ruby or a sapphire is caused by impurities included in the stone. Only the diamond is valuable when pure, and even diamonds have added value with color. That's something to ponder."

As he continued, Margaret pondered. Everything Jason said could be verified in her Encyclopedia Britannica. He suggested interesting possibilities, but did not ask them to take a single idea on faith. If he told them anything unconventional, it was simply to keep an open mind, to admit there was a great deal that humans still did not know.

The session broke up in a clamorous whirlpool of excited, gesturing, arguing, human forms. Jason stood at the vortex of this pool and Margaret spun toward its outer edge.

At the head of the broad staircase, she looked back over the room. Only one person remained seated. Darlene, in Thalia garb, still occupied a chair against the back wall. Her body slumped over, her forearms inert on her thighs, she seemed not to know or care that the lecture had ended and she was free to go.

Chapter 18
Mrs. Hark: Retreat Finale

Judy Hark spoke softly into Margaret's ear. "I saw Chief Belgrave at the barbecue. I told him I was working at BFK."

"What did he say?"

"Not much. He said Louis Soong had already reported it to him. Oh—and he said the police talked to Cassandra's roommates, and they said she acted 'spooked,' just before she disappeared. Do you think we should visit them?"

"It's an idea. How well do you know the Chief? I'm surprised he told you that."

"Not very well. I see him at the Historical Society things and his wife is in the Women's Club—she and I are 'hugging acquaintances,' you might say."

Margaret laughed. "Hugging acquaintances? Is that like kissing cousins?"

The double door at the top of the stairs swung open and the retreaters surged into Temple Hall. Margaret said, "They had tables up this morning. Now we're back to rows of chairs, just like the first night."

"Was there a big crowd this morning?" Judy asked.

"No. Not like this."

The Hall rapidly filled. This lecture must be popular, Judy thought. Perhaps non Retreaters also attended, guests invited to this final session, as Margaret had invited her.

Margaret nudged her. "There's Julius. Wait 'til I tell you about the bonfire last night."

Julius wore a glowing face. He hadn't looked that happy at BFK; Repose must agree with him. "Was Julius there—at the bonfire?" Margaret nodded and led the way to seats in the third row. Judy was glad to sit; selling raffle tickets at the barbecue had been an exhausting business.

The platform stayed empty, and by 3:15 the crowd grew restive. A row of women in calico dresses tapped their feet rhythmically on the floor and chanted, "Thal—ya. Thal—ya. Thal—ya."

Judy said, "Darlene was late at BFK, too. She must be one of those people who can't get anywhere on time. Have you seen her this morning?"

"Yes, at the morning session. She looked miserable and I'll tell you why, but I don't want to talk about it here." Margaret was full of secrets today.

A door opened at the rear of the hall and an instant hush greeted Venus Valentine. She wore a knee-length tunic over leotards, her hair braided the way she wore it for Yoga class. Serene as ever, she walked to the platform and smiled on the crowd.

"Good afternoon. How nice to see so many here for the last session of our Retreat." Her smile warmed noticeably when she spotted Julius Portera.

Enthusiastic applause. Venus put a finger to her lips and it stopped as quickly as it had started.

"I'm so sorry Thalia can't be with us today, but something has come up and you will just have to put up with me, instead." Renewed applause showed how much the audience minded that and this time it was harder to quell.

Judy turned to Margaret. "Whatever has happened to Darlene? This is her big scene, isn't it? What do you suppose?"

Margaret shook her head. "Later." What on earth had

happened here since yesterday afternoon? Why did Margaret keep shushing her?

Venus moved behind the podium. She had no notes, no papers of any kind, and must have taken this on with practically no warning. Still, she spoke without hesitation.

"My purpose today is to help you understand the three-fold nature of womankind. I'm glad to see so many men here today—you need to know which phase of womanhood you are dealing with, believe me." Did she say that directly to Julius? He watched her intently, hanging on every word.

"We are told that Isis, the Earth Goddess, has three faces, and three forms of energy correspond to the three phases of a woman's life. These energies are not exclusive—they overlap and all three forms may be developed and used, singly and collectively.

"The first phase is childhood, girlhood, the young virgin seeking to find her own identity. She grows like the waxing moon, absorbing energy from those around her, opening and developing in the morning of her life. She is educated, chooses a career, develops attitudes and attributes she will have all her life long. On the negative side, if her personality is stunted and stops growing during this stage, she may become intensely selfish and egocentric, the sort of woman who is grasping and greedy and never interacts well with others."

Judy allowed a fleeting image of Myrtle Farrini to skip through her mind, grimaced, and banished the thought as snide and unworthy.

"The Virgin phase is the shortest of the three," Venus went on. "Much too short for many girls. They enter Phase Two before establishing their own identity, a grave mistake, because the second phase is one of giving, not taking and it needs all the maturity and skill a woman can muster.

"The second phase is the Wife/Mother, the mature woman who is partner to a man and has young children to guide and care for. At this stage, a woman enjoys warmth and intimacy with her family, a connectedness that comes from filling their needs as no one else can. She gives off energy to those around her, the way a full moon gives light. She creates new life. She is the nurturer, the mother. We find the mother figure in all religions: Isis, the Earth Mother, Mary, Mother of Jesus—our Statue of Liberty is such a mother figure—the Mother of Freedom. These are the positive examples.

"Women, being human, sometimes spoil this stage of their lives by being controlling and over-possessive. They devour their young in an attempt to re-live their own youth. A very difficult phase, it can only be successful if the woman is a whole person within herself and can nurture her family and then let them go, when the proper time arrives."

What true words! Judy thought of her children and grandchildren, all out in the world, living their own lives. She must have done something right. So many kids failed and came dragging back home these days, but not hers. On that score at least, she had every right to feel satisfied.

Venus scanned her audience and looked directly into Judy's eyes. "The final stage of a woman's life can be the most rewarding of all. Nature puts an end to her childbearing years and she takes on the third face of Isis, the Crone, the Wise Woman of the tribe. She no longer absorbs energy from others or gives out energy to them. Instead, she is part of the universal flow, the stream of energy that carries all nature along in the endless cycle of birth, growth, death and rebirth. She has experience, perspective, objectivity. She may be partial to her own grandchildren, but she sees them differently from her children, because she is not the one responsible for their well being.

"If the Crone phase turns out badly, that is a sign that the earlier phases were not successful. We all know old women who are sour on the world and incapable of peace and contentment. We know helpless, dithery old ladies who lean on their husbands and children for everything, making their lives miserable.

"The triumphant Crone is not like that. If she is fortunate in her husband, he appreciates the serenity and wisdom she has acquired and a new companionship grows between them. He makes fewer demands and they enjoy more fellowship, more common interests. If need be, however, the Crone has the strength to stand alone, dependent on no one. She is the calm voice of reason in a crisis, the wise, understanding friend to whom we turn in time of need. It is the evening of her life and she prepares her soul for death and rebirth, the ever revolving cycle."

Judy sat up straight, facing her future. Let them come. She was ready to share the wisdom of a lifetime, to... Maybe this Crone business wasn't so bad after all.

Venus went on to describe a ceremony called "Croning" that celebrated a woman's passage into the post-menopausal state. Instead of grieving for her lost fertility, she and her friends gathered to rejoice in her new energy phase, her new empowerment. It was customary, Venus told them, to bring living plants to this ceremony and start a "Crone Garden" for the honoree.

A lively question period ensued. Margaret pointed out two of the women who shared her cabin. "Esther is the one asking all the questions. As if they cared! They came to have fun and play poker."

"If the seminars were all as interesting as this one, maybe they got something out of it, at that." Judy felt generous and wise.

After answering questions for half an hour, Venus neatly wrapped up the discussion, tied a blue ribbon around it and sent them back into the world with a benediction.

"As you leave Repose to take up your customary lives, let the things you have studied and the fellowship you have shared go with you. Before you say goodbye, take a walk around our grounds, visit Willow Grove and the Shrine of the Dunes again. Let the peace of this place enter your soul and stay with you in your everyday life. We love you all. Come back soon." Venus went to the rear exit, where Julius stood waiting for her.

"Let's do," Margaret said.

"Do what?"

"Walk around the grounds. Have you ever seen the Shrine?"

"No, but I've been in Willow Grove. Yes, I could use a walk, and you can tell me what's been happening! I'm dying to know."

On their way out, Margaret introduced her room-mates, the pair she called "Abbott and Costello" and also Madge, the near-midget with a fear of heights. Judy shared this phobia and had felt a certain sympathy for Madge's battle to gain the bottom bunk. As Madge shook her hand, she said, "I know how you feel about high places."

"Oh, I'm all over that, didn't Margaret tell you? It was the Retreat! You should come to one and get empowered—really, I just sing this song, and it goes away."

She seemed about to sing and Judy wouldn't have minded, but Margaret pulled her away. "I'm so glad for you, Madge. You're a real trooper. Come on, Judy, I'll show you my cabin."

Judy inspected Sycamore Cabin with interest. Maybe she would attend a Retreat some time.

Margaret had already taken her belongings to her truck and the roommates might show up at any moment, so they didn't linger. They needed a private place to talk.

The sun hung low in the sky as they strolled down the path to Willow Grove. Inside the grove, the trees were trimmed like a canopy, so one could walk among the picnic tables. At the outer fringes, the willow branches were interwoven all the way to the ground, forming a tapestry of fine branches and leaves, with openings only where the path came in from Temple Hall and went out toward the Shrine of the Dunes.

"Show me where you sat with Venus and Darlene."

"And Jason. Right over here." Margaret led the way to a table near the shrine path. "Venus came from the Shrine, or that direction, at least."

"And Darlene and Jason?"

"Darlene had been serving food, over there. And Jason—hmm, let me think. Yes, Jason followed Venus but he didn't come along the path. He came through there, though the willows." Margaret pointed to the left of the path, where the branches looked nearly impenetrable. "He clawed his way through that—like he had been following Venus, parallel to the path, but not on it. That's odd, now that I think about it."

Judy said, "Behind those branches he could hide and observe what was going on inside the grove, couldn't he?"

"He sure could."

A clucking covey of Retreaters straggled into the grove, interrupting this exchange. Judy and Margaret moved on toward the Shrine and the sea.

The Shrine of the Dunes also had visitors. Margaret pointed out the spot where Jason had sung in the moonlight. "I want to see where this path goes. After the bonfire last night, I tried to find it from the other end, but I got lost."

Judy followed, looking around her in the last glow of sunlight. The path wove among the dunes, and seemed well traveled. They walked on, and soon she saw a row of cypress trees near the beach. The trees edged a bank above the winter tide line. Beneath them, their needles carpeted the ground and the sand dunes marched toward them from the sea.

"There's where I went wrong," Margaret said. "I didn't go far enough up the beach—got sidetracked into those trees." She looked around on all sides. "This seems safe enough. Let's sit on this log and I'll tell you what I saw."

She told. Judy's romantic nature thrilled to the story. Imagine Julius declaring his love—as Margaret eavesdropped! "I'm happy for them. I watched him while she spoke this afternoon. He just worships her, you can tell."

"Yes, he makes no effort to hide it. And that's what's wrong with Darlene. She overheard that love scene, too." Margaret described the explosion of temper and pain she had witnessed.

"Oh, dear. I noticed that at BFK, but I had no idea—I thought she just had a crush on the boss. The poor thing!"

"That's not all," Margaret said, dryly. "Jason is crazy about Venus. Aren't you glad we're Crones? Those raging hormones are all behind us. They make people do awful things, don't they?"

Chapter 19
Mrs. Millet: The Hiding Place

M argaret Millet sighed. "So the Retreat is over, but I haven't found Cassandra or any real sign of her, except for some food thievery—which may have nothing to do with her, at all. I haven't even found a place where she could hide! Coming here has been an experience all right, but it hasn't helped much."

"Oh Margaret, don't say that! Look how much more we know about Cassandra's life and the people who knew—know her. We should write down every single thing, right away. We aren't through, either—I'm still at BFK and we can visit Cassy's roommates. I want some explanations from Clark Atherton, too. Why..."

They spoke in low tones as they approached Willow Grove. A red glow from the setting sun lit the outer tapestry of branches, reflecting on the fallen leaves and twigs on the ground. "Look," Margaret said. "Where the path enters the grove. There's a trail."

Just before the entrance, a faint track skirted the grove and went up a short rise. In ordinary, overhead sunlight the track would be lost in the shadows, but the rosy sunset rays coming in almost parallel to the earth made it visible.

"Where do you suppose it goes?" Margaret looked around to be sure they were not observed, then started up the track. At the top, she saw a swale below, where the creek soaked its way out of the grove. Tall reeds grew thickly in swampy water. Behind the reeds, half hidden in undergrowth, she glimpsed a pile of driftwood and weathered boards.

"Judy—what's that?"

"Where? Oh—that! I don't know."

They moved closer. The pile looked like a primitive hut with a plywood roof, about the size of a soldier's pup-tent. Margaret stopped and her eyes widened. She whispered, "Wow. Now there's a hiding place! Just what I've been looking for."

"How can we get to it?"

The path veered to the left. Margaret sent her feet down the track, losing sight of the hut behind the reeds. A blackberry briar raked her cheek. She held it aside for Judy and hissed, "Careful. That's a mean one."

Judy took the lead. "It's soft here. Look out." The path sloped steeply down to the swale. "Too wet. We'll have to take off our shoes and socks."

"And wade in that?" Margaret squinted at the murky frog-scum and brown, decaying reeds. A great place for broken bottles, the better to slice up bare feet. "No thanks. There are hummocks—they look used, too." True, the tufts of grass poking up in the swale looked trodden, as though they had been used for stepping stones. They weren't very close together; a long stride would be required.

Margaret backed up three paces and took a run at it. The worst that could happen would be a soaking, and if she spaced her leaps just right—there, she was across, back on firm ground. She waved and Judy gallantly performed the same feat, slipping once, but recovering with only the side of one shoe soiled.

Retreaters on the main path chattered into Willow Grove, out of sight but not out of hearing. The ladies crouched motionless, until they passed. The sun was below the horizon now and the glowing sky began to dim.

"This way," Margaret breathed. Was this Cassandra's hiding place? Were they really going to find her?

She could see the side of the structure now. Its open end must be on her left, where the brush was beaten down. On this side, a narrow log about eight feet long had been used for a foundation—the corpse of some fallen willow tree, half buried in the sandy soil. Tree limbs and driftwood were staked into the ground on both sides of the log and the space between them filled with whatever was handy. Mrs. Millet identified soda cans, bits of plank and 2x4 boards, even the remains of a beach umbrella. The walls might have passed as a heap of flotsam if not for the sloping roof, formed from two weathered, but nearly whole, sheets of plywood, overlapped and weighted with rocks so they wouldn't blow off.

Something protruded from the open end—what was it? Margaret moved closer. "What's that sticking out?"

"A foot! Somebody's asleep in there!"

A foot—well, a shoe at least, presumably filled by a foot. A woman's day-at-the-office shoe, brown calf, with a neat, two-inch heel—surely not the sort of shoe Cassandra Gates would wear out here in the Repose Wetlands. What was such a shoe doing in this primitive, driftwood shelter?

Margaret skirted the hut, keeping behind the reeds and undergrowth until she could see into it. The woman attached to that foot lay in a crazy, unnatural pose, body bent backward, head turned grossly awry, arms outflung. She was asleep, all right. Permanently asleep.

"Judy?" Margaret spoke aloud and abruptly sat on the ground. There was no further need to whisper.

Chapter 20
Mrs. Hark: Found and Lost

"Put your head between your knees, Margaret. Breathe! That's it." Judy Hark didn't feel so good herself, but Margaret looked ready to pass out and this was no place for the meegrims.

Margaret followed instructions. Judy rose and looked around. Nobody in sight. She listened. The breeze had dropped at sundown and all was still except for the gulls, crying themselves home for the night.

She approached the hut and knelt to look inside. Death was unmistakable. "It's Glenda Ravenet." She turned to find Margaret's white face at her shoulder. Judy shut her eyes and forced herself to touch the ankle above the protruding shoe. "Stone Cold."

Then to Margaret, "Are you all right?"

Margaret made a face. Her voice shook as she blurted, "I'm okay. Better than she is."

"What should we do?"

"Get out of here. Call the police. Oh, shit—here we go again." Margaret had used her only four-letter word, a sign of extreme distress.

Judy had felt "this isn't really happening" and now the reality hit her. This body was a former person, somebody she had begun to know, lying dead—violently dead, by the look of it—in this rude hut in the dunes. Glenda Ravenet would never approve another invoice, never sign another check. Nausea rose in her throat. She didn't want to, but a sense of duty made her say, "Shouldn't one of us stay here?"

"Don't be silly," Margaret said, "and don't touch

anything. Let's just look and remember every detail."

A useful thought; Margaret's brain still worked in spite of the shock. Judy did look, making the most of the fading light. She noted the posture of the body, the small bullet hole in Glenda's forehead, the clenched hand that reached outward, a broken nail on the index finger. Glenda's neck might be broken, too, from the way the head lay. Her clothing, a good quality beige pullover and knit pants in a darker tan, seemed only slightly stained and rumpled. There were heel marks outside the hut, probably made by Glenda's shoes, but no other footprints that she could see. "She arrived on her feet, I guess."

"In a book, someone would have walked around in her shoes to make us think that, after she was dead," Margaret read a lot of mysteries.

"It's getting too dark to see. Let's go."

Somehow, they got back across the swale and returned to Willow Grove, now deserted. It was dark under the trees. They passed Sycamore Cabin and reached Temple Hall without encountering a soul. Judy imagined murderers on her heels at every step, and the parking lot lights looked like the pearly gates of salvation. "Where can we find a telephone? Is anyone still at the Hall?"

"The kitchen crew, probably, but I don't know about phones. Let's use the booth by the store."

"Yes," Judy said. "We won't have to talk to anybody that way. Let the police give out the news—or not, as they choose." Their purses were locked in their respective vehicles, so they had no coins, but it didn't matter. Dialing 911 was free.

"Gambol Beach Police Department. What is your emergency?"

"I'd like to report finding a dead body," Judy said.

Two uniformed officers in a police car responded quickly to their call and lit their way with flash lights to Willow Grove and the dim path.

Judy stopped where they had first glimpsed the shelter hut. "It's down there. Give me your light so I can show you." The flashlight was one of those long jobs, nearly a searchlight, but the darkness was complete, the moon had not yet risen and the hut was hard to see. "That's it. That piece of plywood is the roof of a shelter. The body's inside. We recognized her—it's Glenda Ravenet, who works at BFK Restaurant Supply."

The tall, pleasant one was Officer Morton, who had driven Margaret to her interview with Chief Belgrave. "How did you ladies happen to come here?" He flashed his light over the swale.

"Well, it wasn't dark then," Judy answered. "We saw the hut from here and were curious about it."

"We were exploring," Margaret said.

"The Chief's not going to like this." Morton moved down the path. "Probably just sitting down to his Sunday supper."

Too bad, Judy thought. "He ate enough at the barbecue this afternoon; he doesn't need any supper." Chief Belgrave wasn't the only one to have his day ruined.

She showed the officers where to cross the swale and let them do it. "Margaret and I will wait here. We've seen it and we don't need to see it again."

Officer Morton managed the hummocks with considerable grace, but his short, stocky partner didn't bother, he just waded across. Tough. Impervious to water and mud.

It wasn't easy to wait, there in the dark. Margaret stood close beside her and they watched the flashlights jitter and glimmer through the reeds. What were they shouting about? Had they no respect for the dead? The lights came back. Now maybe the police would take over and she and Margaret could go home.

Officer Morton leaped across the bog and shone his flash directly into Judy's face. "Is this your idea of a joke? Don't you know that turning in a false emergency is a crime?"

Margaret cried, "Who's joking? She's dead!"

"You mean the body's not there?" Stunned, Judy remembered the creepy presence she had felt on the way to the telephone; not paranoia after all. Someone had removed Glenda's body while they were calling the police. Someone must have been close by when they found it. Someone might still be watching—a murderer with a gun.

Chapter 21
Mrs. Hark: Focus on Repose

Officer Morton said, "Look here—you two are old enough to know better. First disappearing black girls and now dead bodies—what are you going to report next?"

Thinking a murderer might be nearby, Judy Hark found it hard to be coherent, so it was Margaret who gave convincing details and dragged the officers back to examine the hut. Judy wasn't about to stay alone in the dark, so she went too, leaping over the bog without missing a tussock.

On closer inspection, the officers found splashes of blood both inside and outside the shelter. Several of the heel prints Judy had noticed were still visible, plus marks where something had been dragged out of the hut.

Morton had the grace to apologize. He escorted the ladies back to Repose Store, where he called in from the police car. A few minutes later he told them, "Okay, the Chief's coming out with a search party and a crime scene crew. He says you can go home—but he wants both of you at the station first thing in the morning. Eight o'clock. You just come in and tell him all about it. Can you do that?"

"We'll come." Judy smiled a false, sweet smile. He needn't talk to them as though they were infants.

Margaret looked about to boil over. Judy took her arm and led her up the road toward Temple Hall and their vehicles. "Hurry up. I want to get out of here."

"A false emergency report! The nerve!" Margaret seethed.

"Well, you can't blame them; the body was gone. They

didn't see it like we did. Think about it, Margaret—whoever moved it must have been close by when we found it."

An oncoming car forced them off the road and nearly off the narrow shoulder. Margaret said, "Where would you take a body to get rid of it? A cold body; she had been dead for hours. Why wasn't it moved sooner?"

"Too many people around? Remember, the place was crawling with Retreaters. Maybe the killer—killers?—left it hidden there until they could dig a hole somewhere and then came back for it."

"And then we showed up, before they could move it. I don't know about a hole, though. They could just chuck it in the ocean on the outgoing tide."

"It might come back in. If they wanted the body to disappear, they'd bury it deep." Disappear. Cassy Gates had disappeared. Cassy Gates, who worked at BFK. Was she dead, like Glenda? Like Darius Clumber? Tomorrow she, Judy Hark, was supposed to go back to work at BFK. Was anybody at BFK safe from this murderer?

Judy looked at her watch. Only a little after seven. So much had happened in so short a time. "At least, you don't have to tell your kids about this tonight. I hate to think what Willy will say."

Willy said quite a lot, once he caught his breath and understood what she had told him. At first, he was adamant that Judy should not return to BFK Restaurant Supply. Judy pointed out that no murders had occurred there and he finally agreed to a compromise. She would give notice immediately and stay for a few days while they interviewed and hired her replacement. And Glenda Ravenet's replacement.

The next morning, Willy accompanied Judy to the Police Station. "We'll just let Chief Belgrave know that you are not some lone woman who can be pushed around," he said grimly. He hadn't even turned on the Today Show; he was that upset.

Margaret was waiting for them, with a female police officer. The policewoman hadn't expected Willy and eyed him doubtfully. He stood firm and gave her such a look that she made no protest. At Chief Belgrave's door she rapped, then opened it. "Mrs. Millet and Mrs. Hark, Chief."

"Good Morning, Chief. I think you know my husband."

"Hello, Willy. Good to see you. Do you know something about this business, too?" The Chief spoke affably and seemed glad Willy had come. Perhaps he felt grateful for masculine support.

In an amber glass ashtray on the Chief's desk, a half smoked stogy spiraled smoke into the polluted air. Judy fanned herself with her hand and took the chair farthest from the cigar. Margaret sat in front of the desk. The policewoman scurried to pull up chairs for Willy and herself.

"A bad business." The Chief shook his head. His short, tidy beard scraped audibly on his collar. Someone with no neck shouldn't wear a beard, Judy thought. With his round head and round body, it gave him a shape like Frosty the Snowman.

"We'll wait a few minutes, if you don't mind. Detective Soong is on his way from Santa Porta. He wants to sit in."

Detective Soong got around. He had been at BFK earlier, when Judy called to say she'd be late to work. Julius had said, "It doesn't matter, Mrs. Hark. Nothing's getting done anyway—the place is full of policemen—there's a Detective Soong here in my office. Glenda is missing, he says. Darlene hasn't shown up either." Judy had not told him Glenda was dead. The less said the better, until her body was re-found.

Margaret squirmed on her narrow chair. "I suppose it's too early to tell, but do you think Glenda Ravenet and that truck driver were shot with the same gun?"

"We don't think anything," the Chief said, "but we'll surely check for that possibility."

Only momentarily squelched, Margaret coughed and turned to the policewoman. "Could you open a window, please? I'm a non-smoker."

The policewoman suppressed a grin and Chief Belgrave nodded and grudgingly stumped out his cigar. She opened two windows and the Chief grabbed for his papers as the cross draft sent them flying. Judy took a deep breath. Oxygen.

When Detective Soong joined them, they got down to business. Chief Belgrave activated the tape recorder and the questions began. The police asked some and Margaret and Judy asked some too, after they told their tale of joining the Retreat, exploring Repose, and finding Glenda's body in the shelter hut.

They learned that Glenda Ravenet had last been seen on Saturday afternoon. She lived alone in one of Santa Porta's better condominiums and her neighbors hadn't missed her. They said she was frequently absent overnight. Her car had turned up on a side street in Repose and was being checked for clues. Detective Soong planned to search her condo as soon as he could obtain a warrant.

No bodies or lurking murderers had been found in Repose, but the police would search again, now it was daylight. The "crime scene" hut was sealed off and guarded.

Soong said, "I couldn't get much out of the manager at BFK. Either he doesn't know what's going on, or he knows all about it and isn't telling. What do you think, Mrs. Hark? Have you noticed anything?"

"Nothing that would link him to the murders. I do know that his mind is not on his business. He's very much in love with Venus Valentine, one of the leaders at the Temple of Repose."

"Where you saw Glenda Ravenet's body," Chief Belgrave commented.

Margaret added, "Where Darlene Evans, the BFK receptionist lives. Where Cassandra Gates may be hiding. Where Julius Portera was on Saturday night and Sunday afternoon. He didn't behave in the least like a criminal at the bonfire on Saturday, though. He proposed to Venus and I think she accepted. The man was on cloud nine." Margaret described her eavesdropping in the dunes. "Darlene was the unhappy one, and that seemed to be personal."

"That's right," Judy said. "Darlene has a crush on Julius and seeing him with Venus must have been a blow. But it's Glenda who's been killed, not Venus or Julius. Have you questioned the BFK salesman, Frank Slee?"

Soong nodded. "He was at work this morning and seemed properly shocked to hear that Glenda was missing. That's all we've told them at BFK, Mrs. Hark, and I'd rather you didn't spill the beans."

Judy was glad she hadn't. She agreed to listen, not talk, when she went to work.

Chief Belgrave opened his desk drawer and took out a small plastic bag. "Have you ever seen this, or one like it?" He stretched across the desk to hold the bag under her nose. It contained a small, oval object.

"What is it? Oh, a button?"

"Yes, a button. Color, brown—enameled to represent a football. We found it just outside the—uh—the structure where we didn't find a body."

Judy examined the button closely and passed it to the others, who did likewise. "I don't know. It does look vaguely familiar." Somehow, she associated the football with Frank Slee, but that might be because they had just spoken of him. She couldn't be sure.

Chapter 22
Mrs. Millet: A Winter Garden

Margaret Millet drove home from the police station feeling bushed, beat, fagged, tuckered. Her sore throat was worse and another day of dry air and east wind would probably bring on a full-fledged cold. Monday morning after the weekend before.

Judy had gone to BFK to put in a full day's work! Once again, she envied Judy Hark's inexhaustible energy, the metabolism that kept her going when Margaret was ready to crawl in a hole. Judy was eleven years the elder; how on earth did she do it?

Thank goodness it was Monday, though; Laura and Tiny had gone to work so she didn't have to face questions at home. The night before she had checked in by telephone, but postponed a chat about the Retreat, saying she was tired, and would tell them all about it later.

Home. Make a cup of tea. Gargle Listerine for the sore throat. Take a nap. The Repose Retreat had truly used her up, even before the discovery of Glenda's body and the police station visit. Her unmade couch/bed had never looked more inviting.

The clock said five minutes past two when Margaret came fully awake. She had dozed in and out of sleep for half an hour, her mind playing a fantasy game with the scenes her eyes had recorded. She had floated through the Shrine of the Dunes, chasing a wisp of song, "I've seen fire and I've seen rain..." and watched the ocean rush onto the sand behind a flaming bonfire. Something in the water rolled back out to sea before she could identify it. Jason thumped his bongos, thump, thump.

The thumps woke her. There it went again; thump, thump. Laura's height-loving cat Boris, bounding across the roof above her head.

Margaret felt better. Rested, able to think again—and there was plenty to think about. The interrogation at Chief Belgrave's office—she gave it a "U" for unsatisfactory. The Chief seemed to believe what they told him, but he showed no urgency. He and Detective Soong had thrown Glenda's murder into the pot of routine along with Cassandra's disappearance and the truck driver's death. The pot simmered and the Chief expected to solve the case in time—but did they have time?

Too many people are dying, she thought. All people who could have known about, or been involved in, the embezzlement of beef steaks. How could a load of steaks equate with a human life? On her tight budget, she hadn't eaten filet mignon in years.

Now, of course, it wasn't really a matter of money. For the murderer, it was a matter of staying out of jail—even staying off death row! Crime started small and escalated. The tune from Oliver! hummed through her head: "After all, he started small—you've got to pick a pocket or two, boys—you've got to pick a pocket or two." Picking pockets had led to murder in the Dickens story, too.

Glenda had been killed, and others might be in danger. Especially Darlene—Darlene might know a good deal more than she had ever revealed. Darlene was at risk. And Frank Slee, if he wasn't the killer. Julius Portera? Likewise. Even Venus Valentine could be in danger— she might know things without realizing she knew. But mainly Darlene, who answered the phones at BFK and lived in Repose—where people disappeared and bodies were found and lost again.

She wondered if Mbyrna Gates knew that Glenda was "missing." Should she call? Probably, but she didn't want to. When she had called about Clumber's death, Mbyrna wouldn't talk to her and Glenda was closer to Cassandra than the truck driver. Was Cassandra still alive? The longer she stayed lost, the more unlikely it seemed. Margaret thought of the grief that might be coming to Mbyrna. What it was to be a mother.

Here, no use dwelling on that. The question was, what could be done?

She shed her warm robe and donned blue jeans and a sweat shirt. At least, she could check on Darlene, who hadn't gone to work this morning, according to Detective Soong. She had Darlene's street address; Judy had copied it from the BFK personnel files for her, "just in case." She could drop by unannounced and talk to Darlene and Jason, if they were at home. She'd stop at Repose Store, too. If the police search party had found Glenda's body, Martha might know. Anything was better than sitting at home, wondering who would be next.

Darlene's residence was a clapboard bungalow in the "craftsman" style of the 1930s, painted yellow and fronted by tall Eucalyptus trees. It stood at the dead end of a street with no sidewalks, deep in the residential part of Repose.

Margaret parked on the street. A gravel driveway led past the house to a one-car garage, and she could see a corner of Jason's trailer behind that. She stepped up to the roomy, old-fashioned porch, half walled and furnished with lawn chairs and a swing. The steps creaked underfoot but the porch felt solid. When Darlene failed to answer her knock, Margaret went around back.

She saw a large vegetable garden, now autumnal with dried-up tomato and pea vines. Yellow squash lay ripening among the weeds. Jason knelt in a freshly cultivated patch of earth about eight feet long by four wide.

"Hello, Jason."

He jumped and stiffened, but did not immediately turn. Instead, he waved the trowel in his right hand and applied it to something directly before him.

Margaret moved closer and saw a flat of green shoots, a few of which had already been transplanted into the rich, dark earth. "Kind of late in the year to plant a garden, isn't it?"

Jason raised his head. "Hi, there, Dunes Lady. I'm planting my winter garden—snow peas, cabbage, onions and brussels sprouts, all great winter crops. What you see here is the healthy, invigorating cabbage, a fine source of vitamin C." His lazy grin was infectious as ever.

"You really do provide the necessities, don't you. What a nice place—lots of room to grow food. Not many of these big lots left—you're lucky to have it."

"Well, we only rent. Nobody owns the land, but the Colony has possession, and they like us to make it productive."

"Nobody owns it? I don't understand."

"Of course not. The land is here throughout all time and we are only temporary, you know."

He had a point. "Don't let me interrupt your work. I'm looking for Darlene—or Thalia, whichever."

Margaret looked around. Behind Jason's travel trailer, fruit trees grew along both sides of the lot. At the back, a high mesh fence topped with barbed-wire enclosed the goat pen. A billy goat pulled up a clump of grass and peered through the fence at her, his chin whiskers wagging as he chewed.

"Darlene," Jason said. "She's gone to work. Monday, you know."

"Oh? Do you know what time she went in?"

"Late, I expect. She usually is. Why, is something wrong?" Jason pressed the soil around a seedling and rose.

"I'm not sure." Margaret realized she should have called BFK. The fact that Darlene wasn't there first thing didn't mean she hadn't gone to work at all.

"Jason, I'm worried about Darlene. Cassandra is still missing, and now—I think it's okay to tell you this— Glenda Ravenet, the Office Manager at BFK, is missing, too. Her car was found here in Repose. If Darlene has any knowledge about the BFK crimes—the theft and the murder—she could be in terrible danger."

"Glenda missing? How do you know that, Mrs. Millet?" Jason did remember her name.

"I'm sorry, Jason, I can't tell you. The police are looking into it, and they asked me not to say."

"That's serious, of course. I don't think my sister knows anything, but I'll talk to her tonight, ask her to be careful. Thank you for being concerned. It's nice of you."

"Could you call her now and make sure she got to work?"

"We don't have a telephone. Don't worry, if anything was wrong with Darlene, I'd know." Jason folded himself back to the ground and planted another cabbage.

A whiff of goat reached Margaret's nostrils. It crossed her mind that a "winter garden" would be just the thing to cover a grave. Could a young man with Jason's shining philosophy be mixed up in murder? She most sincerely hoped not.

She backed away. "Goodbye, Jason. It was nice to see you. When I get home, I'll call and make sure Darlene is all right."

He waved a hand. "Thank you, Dunes Lady. Come again."

Jason hadn't seemed the least concerned about Darlene's safety. Did he ever worry? Philosophy was all very well, but shouldn't a loving brother feel some anxiety when crime and violence came so close to his sister?

Back on the main road, she drove past Temple Hall and pulled into the graveled area in front of the Repose Store. There were no police vehicles in sight, so perhaps the search party had finished and gone away.

She fished for a quarter and stepped into the phone booth. She had to know about Darlene.

"BFK Restaurant Supply. How may I direct your call?" It was Darlene's voice, and Margaret felt so relieved, for a moment she couldn't speak. Darlene repeated, "BFK Restaurant Supply...."

"Hi, Darlene. This is Margaret Millet. Can I talk to Judy Hark?"

"Is it reely important? She's in Julius's office. They're interviewing somebody." Darlene spoke impatiently and very fast.

"Oh. No, it's not important. Just ask her to call me at home when she gets a chance. Uh—is anything wrong?"

"Is anything wrong? Golly, I wouldn't know where to start! We're short handed here, Mrs. M. I don't have time to talk. Bye-ee!" The phone went dead.

Margaret entered the store. Martha was busy at the counter, so she browsed the corner where a rack of greeting cards flanked several shelves of books. The works of Kahlil Gibran were prominently featured.

She chose a birthday card with a Kliban cat pictured on the front and took it to the cash register.

"Isn't that cute," Martha said. "Let's see, with the tax that comes to $1.68."

Margaret produced two one-dollar bills. "Hear you had some excitement around here this morning," she ventured.

"Oh my, yes! Police cars and dogs and I don't know what all. Searching the woods for some missing person, one of the deputies told me."

"Did they find her—or him?" Margaret scrambled to cover her inside knowledge.

"I don't think so. A bunch of them came in here for a snack a little while ago, and they sure seemed tired and disgusted. Then they all packed up and left. Guess we'll read about it in the paper."

"Oh, were there reporters?"

"Uh-huh. And TV, too. The Police Chief spoke on camera right out in front of the store." She slipped the card into a small sack and handed it over. "Seems strange to see policemen in Repose, doesn't it? We don't have any crime. The police don't even bother to come through here, as a rule."

On her way home, Margaret rehearsed what she would tell her daughter and son-in-law. She'd start with her cabin-mates and the poker game (that should amuse them), then Jason's triangle lecture and Venus's three ages of woman. Yes, there had been a disappearance—or so she'd heard. Yes, somebody who worked where her friend Judy was working. Odd, wasn't it? She would not mention finding Glenda's body—at least, not yet. With luck, that news would not be released until the body was re-found.

Chapter 23
Mrs. Hark: Another Day at BFK

When Judy Hark entered the BFK building that Monday morning, she felt as though she had walked into a migrating flock of geese. Julius Portera had called the employment agency, and half a dozen job applicants flapped around the tiny area in front of the reception desk, honking for attention.

Darlene had made it to work after all and was handing out application forms. "Please fill this out and bring it back later. Yes, the job is open right now—we'll interview today." The telephone console buzzed in the background.

Darlene greeted her as she rounded the counter. "Thank God! Where have you been? Never mind—get to your desk and start taking these calls. I'm going crazy out here and the customers want their deliveries. Do you know how to take an order?"

"Doesn't Frank Slee do that?"

"The cops have got him tied up back in the warehouse."

Judy pictured Frank Slee in his brown suit, bound hand and foot and laid out on a stack of cauliflower crates. She shook the image out of her head. "I haven't done it, but I'll try."

"Good. The order forms should be on Frank's desk—or Glenda's." Darlene handed her a fistful of pink telephone message slips. "There are three people on hold, but I'll take their numbers. Call these guys back, for starters."

"Where's Julius?"

"Back there. More cops."

Judy had seen all the policemen she needed that morning. She took the messages into her office and shut the door. When snooping, she had seen a pad of order forms in Glenda's desk drawer. She got the pad and began to return the calls. The customers knew what they wanted and how to order it, which helped. She couldn't quote prices, and explained that she was just filling in so their orders could be delivered; the Sales Manager would get back to them with figures.

Darlene came in with more message slips. "Let me know when you get caught up and I'll start transferring calls instead." Darlene wore full war paint, her hair teased to a golden haystack and her eyes wild with blue shadow and black eyeliner.

"Where's Glenda?" Judy watched for her reaction.

"Burning in Hell, I hope!" Darlene dashed away, her heels quick-timing down the hall.

During a lull between calls, Julius entered, nodded and picked up the orders from the "out" tray. "Darlene said you were handling these. Bless you, Mrs. Hark. Glenda hasn't come in, and the police...but I guess you know. That Detective said that was why you were late—you reported her missing?"

"Not exactly. I've been at the Gambol Beach Police Station, answering questions."

"Umm. Here, too. What are they saying—the police, I mean? Why do they think she's missing?"

Glenda was dead but she wasn't supposed to say, so how could she explain? "I'm not sure, Julius. They said her car turned up in Repose and they were searching for her."

"But why question you, Mrs. Hark?" Julius asked, then offered a possible answer. "I guess they're questioning everybody who works here, since Darius Clumber was killed. I wish I knew what's going on." He seemed bewildered, but his deep blue eyes still carried some of the glow she had seen the day before, when he was with Venus. It was as though he acknowledged the troubles at BFK, but they didn't really reach him at his present altitude. Margaret had it right; cloud nine.

Impulsively, she said, "Yesterday—wasn't Venus's talk wonderful? I enjoyed it so much!"

"Venus is altogether wonderful. Were you there? I didn't see you." He ran a hand through his black curls and smiled warmly.

"Yes, I was there. I saw you. You looked so happy—are congratulations in order?"

The man blushed to his hair roots. "Could be. I'll let you know. Thanks for pitching in, Mrs. Hark. I don't know how we'd manage without you."

"Yes, but I can't work here much longer. I was only helping until Cassandra Gates...My husband wants me at home."

"Don't desert us now; we need you! I'll interview the applicants today. Will you help with that? You can stay long enough to train somebody, can't you?"

"I don't know the job very well myself, but I'll try." She was touched by Julius' appeal.

"Good." He started out, orders in hand. "I'll get these back to the warehouse and see the trucks loaded. Is Frank still back there?" He didn't wait for an answer, but went off down the hall, leaving her door ajar.

She sighed and rose to close it and was forestalled by Detective Soong, who entered on noiseless feet. How long had he been in the hall, listening?

"Mrs. Hark. We meet again. Don't disturb yourself—I'm

just going to Ms. Ravenet's office. Thought I'd tell you, so you wouldn't be alarmed." His head swiveled and his hooded eyes took in everything; the papers on her desk, the humming copy machine, the filing cabinets. "Ah, I thought I remembered a connecting door."

He crossed the room and entered Glenda's office, closing the door behind him. Judy heard drawers opened and furniture moved. A few minutes later, he called, "Mrs. Hark—do you have keys to these filing cabinets?"

"No. Aren't they in Glenda's desk?"

He opened the connecting door. "Actually, only the small one is locked."

Judy knew which filing cabinet he meant—the cheapie she had burgled with a letter opener. Well, this was her chance to get another look at those unlabeled file folders. "Maybe I can open it. Sometimes—there's a knack, you know."

The letter opener still worked. She opened the bottom drawer. "Remember I mentioned Wineena Packing Company? The company that wasn't on the computer? Well, there's a file here with their papers in it."

Only there wasn't. The three unlabeled folders she had seen on Saturday morning were no longer there. Neither was the green notebook. Only computer printouts remained in the drawer. "It's gone. Every time I find something, it disappears."

Detective Soong listened to her explanation and took notes, but she wasn't sure he believed her. She returned to her office. He stayed in Glenda's a few minutes longer, then went out the hall door.

A little later, Judy pressed a lighted button on her telephone to take another customer call. Someone was talking on the line. She heard, "...need it right away!" The voice was loud and male. Then Darlene said, "It's off. No more, not now—not ever. I'll get back to you—don't call here again." The connection was broken.

Judy realized she had pressed the wrong button; her customer was on the other line. She pressed the blinking light. Her mind wasn't on the customer's order.

That evening, Judy entered her kitchen from the garage. "Hi, Willy, I'm home."

Willy rose from his recliner. "About time. Those people work you too hard."

"I know. It won't be much longer, Willy. We hired my replacement today. She's young and smart—shouldn't be hard to show her what's what."

Willy grunted. "Supper's in the oven. Margaret Millet wants you to call her, but let's eat first."

"Bless you, dear. What are we having? I'm empty as a hollow log."

Willy had watched the news, so dinner (baked potatoes and warmed-over chicken) was served with the TV version of the missing person search. "The Chief asked for help from the public," Willy said. "That woman's car was found on a side street in Repose and 'foul play is suspected.' When the reporter asked if the disappearance was connected with the truck driver's murder, Chief Belgrave said he couldn't discuss an on-going investigation."

Judy listened with interest—Willy was an accurate reporter. Mbyrna Gates and Clark Atherton must have seen the news, too. She wondered how they were taking it.

When Willy went back to his chair, she stacked the dishes and took her portable telephone into the bedroom, the better to have a heart-to-heart with Margaret Millet.

"What are you doing?" Margaret asked.

"Talking to you—but I'll have to do the dishes and some housekeeping before I can rest. This place is a mess."

"Oh, ugh!" Margaret said. "Can you catch that disease over the telephone? Housekeeping, I mean."

"Maybe—but I think you're immune."

Margaret laughed. "I think you're right. How did things go at BFK today?"

Judy told her, starting with the exchange she had overheard on the telephone between Darlene and some man.

Margaret said, "Could it be the one who called Cassandra on my phone? Did he sound nasty and threatening?"

"Not really. Just eager to get something—said he needed it right away. Darlene said 'It's off. No more, not now, not ever,' just like that. Then she said she'd get back to him and hung up. I only heard a few words."

"Wow. What do you think? A customer for stolen beef? If so, Darlene is in it, right up to her painted eyes!"

"And Frank Slee, I think. He normally checks the orders and prices them, but I barely saw him today—he avoided me, even after the police left."

"Highly suspicious, when you were doing all the office work."

"That's not all. Remember the file folders I saw in Glenda's office? I opened that cabinet for Detective Soong today, but the folders and the notebook I saw there..."

"Were gone? Good grief!"

"Exactly. I've been thinking about it ever since. Glenda most likely took them out. She was the only one who had the key, I'm sure."

"Of course, if you could pop that lock, so could some-body else. But you're right; it was probably Glenda. She could have destroyed all records of those transactions. How much money was involved, I wonder?"

"Not all records. I still have Cassandra's little black book. I think I've decoded some of it, too—it came to me while I was taking orders today. Here's the first line on the page marked 'BB:' 0911—September 11. D—delivered. 50—fifty cases (and that's a lot!). 7OZFM—seven-ounce filet mignon (each steak weighs seven ounces). CH—charge. 3750—three thousand, seven hundred fifty dollars. At $75 a case, that's the total for fifty cases. Then, NOET—no electronic transfer; the order went C.O.D."

"That's terrific! So Cassy saw that letter giving Bully Beef Steak Houses such a special price and began to keep track of their orders."

"The items are in the same sequence as on BFK's order forms. That's what tipped me off."

"Judy, you're wonderful! That black book..."

"Yes, I know. I'll have to give it to the police. Will I go to jail for suppressing evidence?"

"It wouldn't have meant a thing to them if you hadn't deciphered it!"

"So, how did your day go?" Judy felt sure Margaret had also been active.

"I went home and took a nap; don't know how you keep going like you do. I worried about Darlene and went back to Repose this afternoon, but she had gone to work, after all. I saw Jason, though. He was planting a garden."

"Planting a garden! In October?"

"That's what I said. He said it was a winter garden. Cab-bages. He was setting out cabbages."

"Yes, cabbages do grow here in the winter. The truck gardens are full of them."

"And snow peas and brussels sprouts, he said. All the same, any patch of fresh-dug earth looks suspicious to me, just now. Surely, though, the police have seen his garden along with everything else in Repose. They've searched the area twice."

Margaret went on to describe her visit to Repose Store and what Martha had said about the police search.

"Willy saw it on the news. Have you heard from Mbyrna Gates? I hate to call her—and I'm not sure I could talk to her about Glenda without spilling the beans—but she must be hurting if she's seen the TV."

"Haven't heard a word from her or Clark Atherton."

"There are so many questions," Judy said. "My replacement was hired today, so I'll be out of BFK before long."

"And the retreat is over. What else can we do? I'm not ready to give up, are you?"

"Tomorrow's Tuesday. You can see Venus at Yoga class."

"Yes, there's that. I'd like to talk to Cassandra's roommates, too. Do you have the address?"

"I do. They probably work during the day, though. And what about Darius Clumber's landlady? I got her address out of the files, too."

Between them, they planned the next moves in their investigation. We're getting good at this, Judy thought. On Tuesday evening, Margaret would tackle Cassy's roommates. Judy would visit Clumber's landlady on her way to work in the morning. She would observe Frank Slee and Darlene closely during the day and talk to them both, if the opportunity arose. She must make the most of her remaining days at BFK.

Chapter 24
Mrs. Millet: Money to Help Repose?

On Tuesday morning when Margaret Millet entered the Veteran's Hall, it seemed strange to carry her exercise mat into the large, echoing community room and not find Judy Hark among those present. The other Yoga devotees missed her, too and waylaid Margaret with questions as to Judy's health and whereabouts.

"No, she won't be here today. Other commitments. Yes, too bad. You know how busy she always is..."

Venus Valentine called them to order and the ninety minute session began. Deep breathing, gentle stretching, then more strenuous positions and movements. The wind-chime music tinkled from Venus' tape player and Margaret's muscles relaxed, her lungs fed oxygen into her system, her mind begin to clear and float above the everyday concerns of life. It did her good.

During the intermission, she approached Venus, who looked fit and glowing in purple leotards and a silver and purple top. "Venus, your talk on the ages of women was a real eye-opener; made me look at getting old in a whole new way. I enjoyed the Retreat so much."

Venus wiped her forehead with a towel, draped the towel around her neck and pulled her dark braid free with one hand. She turned her back to the others and spoke in a low voice. "I'm glad you still feel that way, after what happened."

"Do you mean Glenda Ravenet?" Margaret kept her voice down, too. "Did the police question you?"

"Yes! They questioned everybody and searched the entire Colony, looking for her. Her car was parked on the side street close to the Shrine and they wanted to know who'd seen her and what she was doing in Repose. Did you see her there? I've never met the woman, so I couldn't help them."

"I met her once at BFK, but no—I didn't see her during the Retreat." This much was true. It was hard not to add, "but I saw her dead body afterward." Instead she said, "Glenda's disappearance may be linked to the murder of that BFK truck driver—and to Cassandra Gates. I do wish we could find Cassandra! And I'm worried about Darlene—Thalia, that is. She works at BFK, and she may be in serious danger."

"Oh, Mrs. Millet—do you think so?" Venus stepped back and her eyes widened in alarm.

"Yes! I've talked to her brother, but he seems to think everything is fated, predestined, or something—he didn't seem worried. Do keep an eye on her if you can."

The intermission ended and the Yoga students returned to their mats. Venus said, "Thank you, Mrs. Millet. I'll talk to Thalia," and turned back into a teacher. When the class ended, she gathered up her equipment and made a speedy exit, so Margaret had no chance to talk to her again.

Back in her granny pad, Margaret found her cupboard (or rather, her refrigerator) nearly bare; she was even out of graham crackers and peanut butter. After a meager lunch, she drove her trusty pickup to the local supermarket for a thorough re-stocking. Nearly out of granola, she bought old-fashioned rolled oats, shelled walnuts, sunflower seeds and raisins. The corn oil, honey, and grapefruit juice to complete the recipe were still on hand in her cupboards. She bought a piece of beef chuck (on

sale) and wistfully eyed the packages of T-bones and filet mignon. Oh, well. The beef chuck would make two
batches of stew meat for the freezer and a small pot
roast for immediate use; it would last for weeks, while a
steak would be gone in one meal.

Her cart was nearly full. Cottage cheese, bananas, car-
rots, jugs of drinking water, the "new and improved"
laundry detergent—how she hated to see "new and
improved" on a product she regularly used! It always
meant "spoiled and cheapened." The "now creamier"
peanut butter, for instance—so softened (diluted) it had
to be refrigerated to the proper consistency. And her
favorite brand of tea bags, now labeled "a bright new
blend specially formulated for iced tea," bagged in such
stingy quantities it took two bags to make a mug of righ-
teous tea.

The check she wrote at the cash register left her bank
account in shreds, but her Oregon rents were due, so it
should be all right.

At home, Margaret stowed the groceries, turned the
radio to the "oldies" station and assembled a batch of
granola to the tunes of her girlhood. Some recordings
were the originals, played just as she remembered them,
and they made her feet dance. Others were later ver-
sions, usually played too fast or minus the saxophones,
and these she could have done without.

With the granola in the oven, Margaret made a mug of
tea and relaxed in her rattan chair. The smell of toasted
oats came from the oven and the soothing cadences
of "Blue Champagne" slid from the radio speaker. The
original recording by Freddy Martin's Orchestra, led
by Freddy's mellow tenor sax. She shut her eyes and
remembered dancing at the Trianon Ballroom in Seat-

tle...with a tall sailor in dress blues...The aircrew wings pinned above his jumper pocket had three stars and they scratched her cheek as he whirled her about in the crowd that circled the huge, polished, dance floor. "Blue Champagne, purple shadows and blue champagne..."

Her kitchen timer dinged a loud, inconsiderate ding and called her back over half a century—time to stir the granola.

At 5:30, Laura tapped on the door. "Tiny made a pot of his famous beans and I brought you some." She had a soup bowl in her hands and hastened to set it on the table. "Hot, hot! Eat 'em while they're hot."

"Thanks, honey. Tiny's beans are good. They'll make me a nice supper."

"How did they feed you at Repose? And what's this on the news about a missing person down there?" Laura's attempt to be casual didn't hide her concern.

"Sit down and I'll tell you about it while I eat these yummy beans. Care for a beer?" Poor Laura, she did worry so—and maybe I give her cause, Margaret thought. She opened two beers, got out a spoon and dipped into the beans.

It was six-thirty before Laura left her and Margaret felt better for having shared the enjoyable parts of the Retreat (not the finding of Glenda's body), and the interview with Chief Belgrave at the police station the previous morning. After all, this was her beloved daughter, the prop of her declining years, who deserved to be informed and consulted.

And now it was time for more detecting.

Casandra's roommates lived in the north end of Gambol

Beach, an area wedged between the coast freeway and the ocean. Considered a "good" part of town, its ocean-front cliffs boasted expensive homes. Behind them, more modest housing prevailed and the frontage road along the freeway was lined with touristy gift and antique shoppes, mini markets, service stations and a branch post office.

The girls' apartment on Catalina Avenue was near the shopping street. An elderly, white stucco building nestled in semi tropical shrubbery, flood-lights illuminated its two story facade. Each apartment had its own front door, painted coral, and those on the second floor opened onto a wide balcony. Each door had a peep-hole and a card holder for the occupant's name. The building faced away from the freeway and, had the intervening structures been removed, would have enjoyed an ocean view.

Cassandra's apartment was on the ground floor, its door beneath the overhanging balcony. Margaret knocked, heard footsteps, and the porch light came on. She smiled pleasantly at the peep-hole. The door opened. A dark-haired girl wearing something long and soft said, "Hello?"

"Hello. Is this where Cassandra Gates lives? I'm a friend of hers, Margaret Millet. May I come in?"

"Cassy isn't here...maybe you know..."

"Yes, I know. That's why I came."

The girl held the door wide. "Come on in. I'm June. June Stratton." She led the way into the narrow living room and waved a hand at a hard-used couch. "Have you heard from Cassy?"

June's garment, now that Margaret could see it, was a floor-length, yellow sweat shirt with a cuddly panda pictured on the front. The back side of the panda decorated the back of the shirt. The girl had curly dark brown hair, warm brown eyes and smooth tanned skin. She looked as cuddly as her Panda bear.

"I wish I could say I had," Margaret replied. "How about you? Any news?"

June shook her head sadly. "No news."

"I'm sorry. Her mother must be frantic. And now another woman who works at BFK is missing, too—I expect you've seen it on TV."

June had. They discussed Glenda's disappearance for several minutes, Margaret taking care to reveal as little as possible.

"It's good of you to come and see us," June said. "We haven't heard a thing since that policeman was here."

"I hope you were able to help. Cassy stayed at Repose with Darlene Evans—her co worker, you know—for a while. Then she just vanished into thin air."

"Well, Frances—that's my other roommate—didn't think we should tell the police..." June paused, confused and blushing. "Personal things, you know."

Yes! I'm on to something! Margaret tried to do as Judy Hark would have done—be sympathetic—and wished fervently that Judy had taken this assignment. Judy was so good at getting people to unburden themselves. Careful, now. "Oh, I quite agree. I mean, the police are so nosy and they ask about things that probably have nothing to do with Cassy's disappearance at all. I'm sure you did the right thing."

"Do you think so? Oh, I hope so! They wanted to know why she had her phone taken out, and that was weeks before she left. That wouldn't have anything to do with it, would it? We said we didn't know 'cause we didn't want to talk about Cassy's troubles with...well, you know what I mean."

"With her family?"

"Them, too—her mother wanted her to come back home, for Pete's sake—but mostly that Clark whatshis-name, you know. The one who wanted to get married."

Margaret laughed. "And Cassy was doing just fine on her own, wasn't she—the three of you to share the rent, and this nice apartment near the beach..."

June nodded vigorously. "You do understand! He was here again yesterday with Cassy's mother, about the car."

With intense interest, Margaret put a question in her eyes and waited for more. Once started, June spoke freely, as though she welcomed the opportunity.

"The finance company sent a man to repossess Cassy's car, so we called Mrs. Gates." Mbyrna and Clark had come to Gambol Beach with a locksmith to open the car and had taken it away. June didn't know if they paid up the auto loan, but supposed they had, as no further minions of the finance company had shown up to bother them.

"Did Mrs. Gates take any of Cassy things?"

"No. We told her she could, but she said no. We didn't have the heart to ask her for the rent."

"Yes, that's a problem, isn't it. Maybe I can mention that to her—I'll see what I can do."

"Wow, we'd sure appreciate that, Mrs. um..."

"Millet. You say Cassy had her phone disconnected some time ago?"

"That's right. Way back in September. We got a new number, unlisted and we're not giving it out. We split the phone bill, too—except I paid Cassy's share this month. Frances has a budget—figures her expenses to the penny and she was so mad about Cassy's share of the rent that I just paid the phone bill when it came. Cassy will pay me back when she can."

"That was good of you. What was the amount you paid? I'm sure Mbyrna Gates wouldn't want you to be out of pocket."

June was obviously grateful. "We love Cassy," she said, "but it's hard enough to pay the expenses when there are three of us. We don't know what to do—is Cassy going to come back?"

Margaret said she certainly hoped so. "Do you know Darlene, the girl who lives in Repose?"

"That Darlene! Cassy thought she was really something. I'll bet she could tell you where Cassy is, for that matter. But please, a make-up expert? She went around looking like a hooker! Cassy said she didn't wear make-up at Repose, though; said she was entirely different off the job. I think they had a fight—something about what was happening at work—and then, Cassy said it was okay, that Darlene was doing it for Repose, and Repose was such a worthy cause. It didn't make sense to me, but they patched it up and everything was roses again."

"Did you ever meet Darlene's brother—Jason?"

"No. Frances said he came by once; right after Cassy left, as a matter of fact. He said not to worry and Frances said he was a real Hunk, and he seemed crazy about Cassy, too. That's why we thought it was okay."

"Did you tell the police about this? That Jason said Cassy was all right?"

"No. By the time they asked, Cassy wasn't there any more."

"Did Cassy seem frightened when you last saw her?"

"Yes she did, and I did tell the police that."

"Do you know what she was afraid of?"

"No, not really. She said Darlene was scared, too. Something about money that was coming into the company and going out to help Repose. She said some scary people had got on to the plan."

At this point, Margaret heard a key turn the front door and the door opened. A young woman stopped in her tracks when she saw Margaret and gave June a look that would have curdled fresh cream.

June said, "Hi, Frances! Mrs. Millet, Frances Lenger, my other roomie."

Frances was older than June, and so fair she was almost albino. She had short tufts of ash-blonde hair, sticky with hair-spray, around a pale, pouty face and wore orange lipstick, inaccurately applied. "And who is Mrs. Millet—the Avon lady? We don't want any."

Chapter 25
Mrs. Hark: The Landlady

According to his personnel record, Darius Clumber had lived at 664 B Sander Street in "old town" Santa Porta. Judy Hark reached that address at 7:00 A.M., allowing herself a full hour to interview his landlady.

Clumber's former abode was an ex-garage, probably converted during World War II when the town was packed with service families and even chicken coops were turned into apartments. It stood behind a stucco bungalow in the "California Mission" style.

Judy approached, rehearsing her lines as an apartment seeker.

The landlady with the colorful name, Rose Aurora, took her time coming to the door. "Yes?" Her manner said she had seen and heard everything and nothing could surprise her.

"Good morning, Mrs. Aurora. My name is Judy Hark. Please excuse such an early visit, but I'm on my way to work. I understand you have a studio apartment for rent?"

Rose Aurora's world-weary expression changed to one of mild interest. Her hair was too black to be true and her "Spanish eyes," showed remnants of yesterday's eye liner. She wore a shabby pink rayon wrapper and satin mules with run over heels, but something in the turn of her head and the lift of her eyebrows spoke of better, more dashing days. She looked Judy over and said, "Judy Hark. Just call me Rose, everybody does. Where do you work?"

"Oh, the work is temporary. In fact, it should be over

by the end of this week. I have my Social Security. I need a small place with reasonable rent because I don't normally work." Judy knew if she was truly seeking an apartment, she would be the ideal tenant, a female Senior Citizen with a steady income. Compared to college students, bachelors, and party-loving working girls, she was a landlady's dream.

"Well, Judy, I do have the studio in the back. I lost my last tenant—such a tragedy. Maybe you heard about it? Poor boy, he was murdered! Oh, not here—not here in the apartment! He'd been with me for years—my tenants always stay for a long time; I treat them right, you know."

Mrs. Hark shuddered. "I'm glad it didn't happen in the apartment. I don't think I could..."

"Oh, I know! Gives me the horrors to think about it. He was so good to me—almost like a son. But his stuff is still in there and I'm not supposed to go in. The police..."

"That's too bad. I did want to see it. I've already given notice; I need to move by the end of the month." Judy tried to look like someone who would take her rent money elsewhere if not immediately accommodated. She wished Margaret Millet had taken this assignment— Margaret was such a good actress; bluffing a landlady would have been child's play for her.

Rose said, "The police don't care if I starve, do they? I have to do what I have to do. Just come through the house, Judy, and we'll go out the back way."

Judy carefully negotiated Rose Aurora's living room, a maze of overstuffed furniture and toe-tripping rugs. The dining room and kitchen were easier. The kitchen opened to a glassed-in porch and steep wooden stairs to the back yard, a challenge for high heeled shoes.

"How did you hear about my vacancy?" Rose asked.

"At work. You see, I'm helping out at BFK."

"Where Darius worked? Did you know him?" Animation lifted Rose's features and her smile was fond.

Judy was glad somebody had loved Darius Clumber. Certainly no one at BFK seemed to regret his loss. "I had seen him, but we never met." She remembered Clumber in the BFK truck, following her car and leering down at her as he passed. "I started work there after he was killed. Do you think they'll catch the murderer?"

"Who knows? Such a weird thing! His load stolen, the truck left at BFK and poor Darius shot and dumped in Gambol State Park. You know what I think—I think it's organized crime. The Mafia. I don't think the police will ever catch anybody. A hit man, that's what I think." Rose shuddered.

"Here we are."

Most of the garage had been left open as one big room about the size of Margaret Millet's granny pad—but what a difference! No raised beam ceiling, skylight, or mirrored walls here. A king-size bed took up half the floor space. The walls were painted a dingy forest green and lined with crowded trophy shelves. At the back, half the garage width had been enclosed for the bathroom and the other half fitted out as a kitchenette. A small table, a kitchen chair, a TV set, and a battered recliner completed the furnishings. The place was dark, cold, and cluttered. It smelled of tobacco and unwashed socks.

Rose crossed the room and opened a sliding window. "What a fug! All this stuff will be cleared out—the place would be real cute if you fixed it up with your own things."

"I'm sure a little fresh paint would do wonders." Judy

mentally thanked her stars that she didn't have to live in such quarters.

"You can paint it any color you like and I'll pay for the paint! This green, now—it's dark. Real dark. A nice cream color..."

"What are all the trophies for?"

"Oh, that was Darius's big thing! He was a champion at darts. Beat all comers. Even had his picture in the paper. I figure, if his folks don't take them, I'll give his trophies to his pals down at the Parti-Timer, to remember him by. I'm going to keep this one, though." Rose hefted a bronze loving cup engraved with Darius Clumber's name and the date of his winning. It looked like the trophy pictured in the newspaper report of Clumber's murder.

"Darius had family? Will they take away his furniture and things?"

"That, or give 'em to the Good Will, his mother said. He didn't have anything but what you see, nothing nice. Even his car was an old heap. The cops took that—going over it for clues, I guess."

Judy pivoted to see it all. "He made good wages; what did he do with them?" Truck drivers got union wages and BFK gave bonuses, as well. Men lived in nice homes and sent their children to college on trucker's wages.

"Darius said he wanted to make it big or not at all. Every week he put three quarters of his pay into lottery tickets. He never won much—five hundred dollars was the most he ever got back."

What a waste. Margaret Millet had once told her the mathematical odds against a big win from the lottery were greater than the odds of being struck by lightning!

Rose Aurora pulled a tissue out of her pocket and

dabbed her eyes. Some of the leftover eye-liner smeared her cheek. "A week ago tonight they found his body. Oh, I still can't believe he's gone. We never know, do we? You see someone and talk to them and never know it's the last time."

"I'm so sorry," Judy said.

"He came home late that day—must have been about seven o'clock—and he bounced in the back door and said, 'Hey, Rosie' (he always called me Rosie) 'hey Rosie,' he said, 'how would you like a diamond bracelet?'

"I thought he must have finally won the lottery. He said no, not yet, but he was going to have money from now on. And they killed him the same night. Oh-h-h." Rose broke down and sobbed into her tissue.

"Here dear, sit in the chair." Judy guided Rose to the recliner and hovered sympathetically. "What a pity. What he said about having money—is that why you think it was the Mafia? Did you tell the police about it?"

"They didn't ask me. They wanted to know what time he went out again, but I was asleep; I don't know. He was just gone and there it was in the morning paper, 'Body Found in State Park.' His folks didn't even have a funeral! They cremated him and scattered the ashes."

"When did you go to bed that night, Rose?"

Rose wiped her eyes again. "I stayed up and watched David Letterman, or part of it. He got pretty silly, so I went to bed—about 11:30, I guess."

Yes, David Letterman was pretty silly. Having been raised on Jack Benny and Burns and Allen, Judy had never thought David Letterman was funny. "And Darius was still in his apartment then?"

Rose nodded and got up. "I shouldn't be going on about Darius; you're on your way to work. The rent is three-fifty and that includes all the utilities, except your telephone. I do like to take a deposit, but in your case..." The reversion to landlady-mode was sudden and complete.

Rose opened the bathroom door. "You might want to look in here before you go."

Judy inspected the bathroom, very small with a shower but no tub. She opened the kitchen cupboards, all two of them. She would have liked to search the place for something to connect Clumber with the meat thefts, but the police surely had done that.

"It would take a lot of work to fix it up," she said, "and it may not be available soon enough for me. When do you think I could get in?"

"I can't say; it all depends on those cops. Can I call you?"

"Give me your number and I'll call you. Thanks so much for the showing. I'm so sorry about Darius. I don't think the people at BFK have any idea how much he meant to you."

Judy noted Rose's phone number, declined a cup of coffee and walked out by the driveway.

She made it to BFK with ten minutes to spare, stowed her purse under the front counter and fetched a cup of coffee from the lunch room. Darlene was not in, so her immediate duty was to cover the phones. She set her mug on the counter and turned off the answering machine that handled off-hours telephone calls. Frank Slee's extension was lit; he must be calling out, since the machine took the incoming calls. Julius was in his office with the door closed; she had heard his voice as she passed. Wasn't the new girl supposed to come in today?

The front door opened and Detective Soong made one of his silent, slippery entrances. "Good morning,

Mrs. Hark," he said softly. "Just the lady I want to see."

Judy wanted to see Detective Soong too, and she told him so. He apparently was in charge of the investigations at the BFK end and she wanted to give him Cassandra's little black book. This was as good a time as any.

"I found something that belonged to Cassandra Gates and it may have a bearing on the meat thefts." She got the book out of her purse and handed it to him. Her translation was on a bit of paper folded into the book.

The phone interrupted, so she let Soong inspect the book while she answered it. The call was for Julius and she buzzed his extension.

"Where and when did you find this?" Soong asked.

"In Cassandra's desk. It was jammed behind the center drawer and I only found it because the drawer wouldn't close. My translation is on that paper—it was easy enough, after I had taken some orders for steaks."

"And you think this is something important—why?"

"Well, the prices! These people were getting restaurant steaks for half the going price. Cassandra thought it was important or she wouldn't have kept this record."

"You're sure it was Cassandra?"

"Yes, I am. I've seen samples of her handwriting in the files. She wrote it, I'm quite sure."

Through the glass door, Judy saw Darlene approach from the parking area. "Nobody else knows about that book and here comes Darlene! Put it in your pocket, quick!"

Detective Soong looked startled and took her advice. "I'll talk to you later," he said and stepped away from the counter. When Darlene burst through the door in her usual helter-skelter fashion, he was strolling down the corridor toward the lunch room.

Chapter 26
Mrs. Millet: Pizza and Beer

On Wednesday morning, Margaret Millet was nagged by a feeling that she had omitted something when she and Judy compared notes the night before—there was some detail she had forgotten to mention. What was it?

These unsatisfactory telephone pow-wows! They had to hint at things that shouldn't be said on the phone, and they didn't put things down on paper. Margaret always thought better when she could write things down and so far in this case (these cases?) they hadn't done that.

What had she left out? Was it something about Mbyrna Gates? She had told Judy how Mbyrna and Clark Atherton picked up Cassandra's car before it could be repossessed. Query: why weren't the police interested in that car? And since the car had been left at the apartment, who took Cassandra to Repose? Probably Darlene or Jason. She should have asked June Stratton, the nice roommate.

As for the other roommate, Frances Lenger...Oh my, that was one tough cookie. Frances had refused to believe Margaret was Cassandra's friend. "How come we've never heard of you before? How many old white ladies are friends with a black kid like Cassandra?" And, "What have you spilled, June? Can't you see she's a snoop? Everything you told her will show up in the papers!"

June had protested, "She knows Cassy's mother, Frances. She's going to ask her to pay Cassy's rent."

Frances didn't believe that, either. It was all a ploy to

get information. Under her sneering skepticism, June wilted like a violet in a vase gone dry.

Margaret had done her best to win Frances over, with no joy. At last she said, "You're wrong, I assure you. I'm only interested in finding Cassandra," and made a dignified departure.

Perhaps if Mbyrna Gates paid her daughter's rent, the situation might still be mended. Frances was adamant about not telling anything—what did she know? Maybe Mbyrna could find out. Or not; Mbyrna Gates and Clark Atherton were not popular with Cassandra's roommates.

Poor Mbyrna. The thought of her pain made Margaret's eyes fill as she washed her breakfast dishes, and salty drops fell into the suds.

She was drying the last spoon when the phone rang. "Mrs. Millet, it's Mbyrna Gates. I'm glad I caught you at home. Can I talk to you? If I don't talk to somebody soon, I'll go crazy."

"I was thinking about you, Mbyrna. Of course you can talk to me."

"Can you come for lunch? At my house—come early, about eleven. I'm at the college now. I have one more class and I'll be through for the day."

Margaret could and the invitation lightened her spirits so much that she realized afresh how Mbyrna's sorrows weighed her down. She made the bed, picked up scattered clothes and newspapers, swept the floor. She called Judy at work to tell her of the lunch meeting and pulled out her "Cassandra Gates" file folder; she would take it along, incomplete as it was. She had added notes on the Retreat and her visit to Cassandra's roommates. There might be something helpful there, something that would comfort Mbyrna.

Margaret's pickup was almost out of gas. At her Chevron station, the young man who was supposed to help the helpless was helping a pretty girl, so she wrestled with the gas hose herself and left her windshield dirty. She paid by credit card (the bill wouldn't come until after her Oregon rents had been deposited) and headed for Santa Porta.

Mbyrna's door opened before she had a chance to ring. "You came! Thank you so much, Mrs. Millet. Come in, come in!" Still well dressed, Mbyrna's eyes were swollen and her warm brown skin had faded to a dismal gray under her makeup. The corners of her mouth drooped as though she would never smile again.

She led the way to the kitchen. Like the rest of the house, it was extravagantly modern, equipped with every known appliance and gadget. The breakfast booth had a bow window overlooking Poppy Valley, aglow in the midday sun.

Mbyrna had picked up a pizza on her way home. The box on the kitchen counter smelled good. "Shall I heat this a little more? Yes, I'll pop it in the microwave, it will only take a minute." She laid out pottery plates and took a bowl of green salad from the refrigerator. "What would you like to drink? Coffee? Tea? Cola?"

"You wouldn't happen to have a beer, would you? It goes good with pizza."

Mbyrna had beer—delicious imported Mexican beer. She opened a pair of brown bottles. "This is just what I need. I'm glad you're not narrow minded about alcohol." The stiffness in her shoulders loosened visibly and she almost smiled as she served the pizza.

"Too right. Beer pads the ends of the nerves." Margaret parked her purse and file folder on the bench seat and helped herself to the salad. She would eat and listen. Mbyrna seemed ready and eager to talk, and besides padding the nerves, beer was a great tongue lubricator.

"What do you know about Glenda Ravenet?" Mbyrna spoke through a mouthful of pizza and then took a generous swig of beer. Polite manners discarded, she ate as though she hadn't done it lately.

"Well, she's missing and the police 'suspect foul play,' as they so politely put it. What have you heard?"

"The TV, of course. And that Chinese detective was here." Was that a note of racial prejudice in Mbyrna's voice?

"Oh? What did he have to say?"

This was what Mbyrna wanted to talk about. She gave Margaret a question by question account of Soong's visit. "He asked such personal things. Did Cassy have a boy friend? Did she get along with her co-workers? What did she think of Glenda Ravenet, of Darlene Evans, of her boss? And how well did she know that truck driver before he was killed? As if she had anything to do with that truck driver!"

Margaret listened attentively. As Mbyrna got all this off her chest, she caught the line the Santa Porta police were taking, how they saw the investigation. By the questions Soong had asked, he thought Cassandra was dead. He was seeking her killer.

When Mbyrna finally ran down, Margaret said, "Judy has been working at BFK, as you know. She says the beef hi-jacking was not a one-time thing and some sort of under-the-counter theft might have been going on for some time. There are indications that Glenda was mixed up in it, too. Judy thinks the whole scheme began to come apart when either Cassandra or Darlene—or both of them—caught on. The truck driver was killed, Cassandra got scared and hid out, and now Glenda is gone, too."

Mbyrna attacked her salad fiercely. "Cassandra wouldn't have got mixed up in stealing meat. She was the most honest child in the world. She often didn't tell me things, but she never lied. As long as she was here at home, I knew everything—all I had to do was ask her. If only she hadn't moved out! All the trouble started when she moved out!"

Margaret consulted her file folder. "I talked to her roommates. They seem like nice girls and they were both very protective toward Cassy. You know Mbyrna, a girl needs to go out and try her wings before she settles down. You did that, didn't you?"

"Yes, I did, but I didn't get mixed up in a murder!"

"The murder didn't happen because Cassy left home."

"No, but she got into it because she got a job instead of sticking to her college education. She took the wrong fork in the road, Mrs. Millet—the wrong fork in the road. Where is she? What's happened to her? It's driving me crazy!" Indeed, Mbyrna had a wild look in her eye. She coughed and pushed her plate away as though the food had begun to choke her.

"Are you okay? Drink your beer, dear."

Mbyrna took the advice. Margaret thoughtfully munched a bit of pepperoni. "Cassy's roommates said you and Clark came and got her car."

"That's another headache. We had to pay off the loan so they wouldn't repossess it. That child..."

"And it's Mother who fixes everything, isn't it? But

what can you do, when she's missing?" Margaret sympathized. If Mbyrna didn't pay Cassy's bills, it was like admitting her daughter wouldn't come back.

"The girls have another problem, too. They didn't like to bother you with it, but it's a hardship for them to pay Cassy's share of the rent and expenses."

Mbyrna looked stricken. "So that's why—why they wanted me to take Cassy's things. Oh God, what shall I do?"

Margaret shook her head. "No, they're not looking for another roommate. You could pay the rent; those girls need the money. I gathered there was a telephone bill, too."

"Telephone bill? Cassy didn't have a phone any more; you know that, Mrs. Millet."

"After Cassy had her phone taken out, the three of them shared one phone. Have you got another beer—and do you think you could call me Margaret?"

Mbyrna had more beer. They were both silent as she opened two more bottles.

"Thank you. I do like my beer in glass bottles, don't you? No matter how well they line the cans, you always get a metallic taste from the fresh-cut edge where you pull open the tab." A neutral subject, while Mbyrna considered the practical aspects of Cassy's absence.

"Those girls don't like me, Margaret. They don't like me one bit. Clark had to be very firm with them when we took the car. The blonde one was really nasty."

Yes, the blonde one was nasty. "I liked June, the dark one. She seemed truly concerned about Cassy. I think they may have gotten a wrong impression of you and Clark, but I don't know why. If you talk to them, you might be able to clear it up."

Mbyrna sighed. "And if I pay Cassy's rent. Yes, I'll do that. And if they want her things out of there, I'll have to deal with that, too. Unless..." She looked at Margaret in a speculative way.

Oh no, not me. "June paid the telephone bill. She said Frances was so unpleasant about the rent that she didn't even mention it to her. You know, you should try to get June alone when you pay her back. Ask to see that phone bill. If Cassy made any long distance calls, the numbers she called would be on it. If you could bring it away with you..."

"I didn't even have their telephone number. I can't believe it."

"June said they didn't give it out because Cassy wanted to avoid Clark Atherton. He went to Repose looking for her, too—did you know that? Cassy stayed with Darlene until Clark showed up. Then she went off on her own and Darlene didn't know where. At least, that's what Darlene's brother said."

"But why did she go to Repose in the first place and why didn't she tell me?"

That was it! Something clicked over in Margaret's brain and she realized this was the thing she had failed to tell Judy Hark. "I'm not sure, but June said Cassy and Darlene quarreled about money coming from BFK. Then they made up—because Darlene said the money was to help Repose."

"Money to help Repose? But they're rich, aren't they?"

"It looks that way, with all that crop land and the rental houses. It's a fascinating place." Margaret took another slice of pizza. "I'll tell you about the Retreat, last weekend."

She told Mbyrna about the lectures, the bonfire on

the beach, the blooming romance between Julius Portera and Venus Valentine. And the evidence, inconclusive though it was, that Cassy might have obtained food from the Repose kitchen in the middle of the night.

"You do think we'll find her, don't you?" Mbyrna finished her second beer.

"We have to find her. Tell me, what did you do over the weekend? Was Clark with you? I thought of you, all the time I was snooping around in Repose."

"My children kept me busy. Clark didn't come near us—I was a little hurt, in fact. I didn't see him until Monday, at the college."

"Really? That's odd."

"He said his car had been in the shop, so he couldn't come to see me. He was at home all weekend, he said, grading exams."

Another note for Margaret's file. Where was Clark Atherton while Glenda Ravenet was getting herself murdered? Not that he had any known motive for the crime. She really must get together with Judy Hark and work out who had opportunity—and motive—for the killings. The suspect list was too long and too vague. If they put their heads together, they might be able to pare it down.

Chapter 27
Mrs. Hark: Button, Button

How did it get to be Friday? Judy Hark's last day on the job. Well, BFK would manage without her. The "new girl" (actually a college graduate in business administration) had caught on quickly and was now ensconced in Glenda Ravenet's office. And Darlene knew a lot about the company's accounting procedures—a surprising amount, for a humble receptionist. As far as the office work was concerned, Judy could leave without guilt, her job well done. She wished she felt the same satisfaction with her detecting.

Julius had brought in a CPA to audit the books, an inventory would be taken and the losses to fraud and theft would come to light. Judy expected large ones, but she didn't think they would sink the company. All in all, it had been a sneaking, petty business, aside from the murders. She wondered how much of this sort of thievery went on in the business world, undetected.

The police still hung around. Louis Soong made BFK his first stop every morning and every morning, Judy asked the same question; "Have you found Cassandra?" Every morning he shook his head and asked, "Have you noticed anything?" She too, shook her head and Soong made the rounds, watching everyone, keeping everyone off balance.

Eight thirty. Soong was about due.

Judy's office door opened and she looked up from the invoice she was checking. Her visitor was not Detective Soong. Frank Slee stepped in, smiling his permanent, ingratiating smile. "Judy—by any chance, have you got a needle?"

"Oh, hello Frank. No, I don't think so. Maybe Darlene has one; did you ask her?"

He laughed. "Who, Darlene? Not likely. Darn it, that button came off last week and I didn't get a chance to fix it—and this is my Friday jacket. I put it on this morning without thinking. Now where can I find a needle? Do you think...in Glenda's desk?"

He showed her the sleeve of his plaid sport coat. A raveled thread hung beside the remaining button—a brown button in the shape of a football. It looked identical to the one Chief Belgrave had showed her at the police station; the one found near the shelter hut in Repose; the one...

Judy controlled her voice with an effort. "Did you save the button, Frank? That might be hard to match."

"Oh, yeah. It came off right at my desk and I put it in the drawer. All's I need is a needle and thread. Unless you'd like to sew it on for me? I'm not very good at sewing." His permanent smile remained fixed. Frank's eyes met hers with a wide, innocent gaze. I'm a little stupid, they seemed to say, but I'm friendly as a puppy and just as harmless.

Frank had left the door open and Louis Soong slipped through it in his noiseless, listening way. He laid a hand on Frank's wrist. "Mr. Slee. I know where your button is."

Frank jumped and tried to pull away. "Gee, you shouldn't sneak up on a feller like that! Give a guy a heart attack!"

Soong repeated, "I know where your button is."

"Well, so do I. The problem is the nee..."

Soong tightened his grip. "Mr. Slee, we're going to the

Police Station. You have some questions to answer."

Frank's jaw dropped so far Judy could see his tonsils, red and unhealthy looking; he should have had them out years ago. She said, "Mr. Soong, wait a minute. Frank says his button is in his desk drawer. Couldn't you look and see? I'm sure you wouldn't want to make a mistake about this."

Soong thought it over and said, "All right, show me your button, Mr. Slee." He marched Frank into the hall without releasing his wrist. Judy followed them into Frank's office and closed the door behind her.

Frank gave her a bewildered look as he and Soong, joined like Siamese twins, stepped behind his desk. With his free hand, Frank opened the shallow middle drawer and rummaged among the rubber bands, paper clips and felt pens it contained. His eyes lifted in panic. "It was right in this corner. Where could it have gone?"

Soong showed a smug, I-told-you-so face. "Okay. We looked. Let's go, Slee."

"Wait! Are you arresting me? What's the charge? I haven't..."

"You can call a lawyer when we get to the station." Soong propelled Frank toward the hall.

"Wait! I didn't do it! It was Glenda! My God, I didn't kill Doofus, it was Glenda! I helped her sell the steaks, but I didn't kill anybody! Not me! She's split with all the money and I won't get anything! I'm not going to take the rap. I'll tell you all about it. I didn't kill anybody!"

The man fairly babbled. He dug in his heels and balked. Soong pulled hard, but Frank outweighed him by fifty pounds. They looked like two kids playing "Statue."

Judy said, "Let's listen to him, Mr. Soong. I'll be your witness. If he's willing to tell us what happened, I think we should listen."

Soong released Frank and reached for the gun in his shoulder holster. Frank did a classic pratfall on the office floor and stayed there, waving his hands and feet like an over-turned turtle, still babbling that he wasn't a murderer, he would tell them everything. He looked so funny, Soong couldn't help laughing—and he didn't draw his gun.

"You, Mrs. Hark, are obstructing justice." Soong chuckled. "You may have a point, though. Slee, I'm going to let you talk if you want to. It may mean my hide, but Mrs. Hark will perish from curiosity if she can't hear you and we don't want that. Then you're going to come quietly, understand? Mrs. Hark, you are my witness that talking was his own idea."

"Yes, indeed. Frank, get up off the floor and sit down. I don't think you killed anybody. I'm going to get you a cup of coffee and then you can tell us all about it."

Judy met Julius in the hall. She beckoned him into the lunch room and said, "Julius, help me carry some coffee to Frank's office. Get a cup for yourself. Detective Soong is there and Frank's going to do some explaining."

"About what?"

"Embezzlement, hi-jacking, murder...We'll see, won't we."

They carried the coffee mugs back toward Frank's office. Judy looked up the hall, saw Darlene's back, the telephone grafted to her left ear. Apparently, she hadn't heard the commotion. Good. The fewer who heard Frank's story, the better.

"Here you are. Coffee for all."

Frank's office was large and well furnished for the benefit of visiting clients. Detective Soong had parked Frank in the swivel chair behind the desk and then taken one of the customer chairs for himself. Judy sat beside him and Julius took up an observer's post against the wall.

Frank pulled a gingham handkerchief out of his breast pocket and wiped his dripping forehead. "You, too, Julius. Well you might as well hear it now as later, I guess." His face was still scarlet, but his breathing had subsided to near normal. He gulped some of the hot coffee and began.

"Glenda knew somebody who had contacts in the restaurant business down south—Santa Barbara and Los Angeles. They were willing to pay cash and arrange deliveries. All's we had to do was get our driver to fake an order, load the truck, and then transfer it to this Wineena Packing van.

"It worked. We started small and Glenda ran the bookkeeping angle to account for the meat—this guy wanted nothing but the best filet mignon—and she changed the cash to gold coins, so if we had to split, we could each take a share and make for Mexico. She said it was the chance of a lifetime and we could live easy the rest of our lives.

"Then that little black girl, Cassy Gates, started to ask questions. Glenda said she'd handle it and first thing I knew, Cassy was out of here and even her pal, Darlene, didn't know where she was. Real weird." Frank's eyes slipped back and forth between their faces, bewildered and shifty.

Soong asked, "What did Glenda tell you about the black girl?"

"Oh, she said not to worry. She said we'd have to hold off until things quieted down. Then Doofus Clumber got antsy and branched out on his own. He sold a whole shipment to somebody else, not our guy at all, and turned up dead! Honest, I don't know who killed him. It could have been Glenda, or the Wineena Packing guy, or even the guy he sold the meat to—but it wasn't me! That's the one thing I'm sure of—it wasn't me!"

"Do you think Glenda killed Cassandra Gates?"

"Hell, I don't know. After Doofus got shot, I asked for my share of the money we already had, but she said just lay cool, not now, and like that. That made me nervous. It was already quite a lot, you know and I figured she could take it and split. And that's just what she did. She's gone and you can bet she took the money with her!"

She was gone, all right. The sight of Glenda's contorted body lying in that makeshift hut rose in Judy's mind; an image she would never forget.

"Where was the gold kept?" Soong asked.

"Glenda wouldn't tell me. Hell, if I knew that, I wouldn't be here!" This remark had the authentic ring of truth.

Judy watched Julius as he watched Frank Slee. His astonishment turned to resentment and red anger, surging up his neck and face. As each question was asked and answered, his jaws clamped tighter and his hands gripped his coffee mug until she thought it would shatter. Was this the reaction of a man about to give up worldly endeavor and enter a spiritual life?

"How long did this thievery go on?" Julius ground out the words between clenched teeth.

"Let's see, the first I knew about was right after Clumber got hired—about five years ago? It was small, at first. The whole truck-loads didn't start until just before Christmas, last winter."

Soong asked, "Have you ever been in Repose?"

"Repose? Oh, that bunch of loonies in Gambol Beach?

Hey, I don't know anything about that place."

"Okay. I'm taking you in. The charge is grand theft and resisting an officer, for now—and give me that jacket. I'm putting it in evidence. We'll see what the District Attorney wants to do about other charges. You sure you can't think of someplace else where you might have lost that button?"

"What's all this about my button? Honest, I lost it right here."

Judy said, "Frank, who else was in on this? You and Glenda and Darius Clumber—was that all? Does Darlene know what you were doing? Was there someone else working with Glenda—maybe someone outside the Company? And was there someone who knew you had lost that button? It's important, Frank, believe me."

Frank met her gaze with frightened eyes. "I don't know. I swear I don't know. I don't remember. Sometimes I thought Glenda was taking orders from somebody—maybe it was you, Julius! Maybe you were the boss, all the time! I don't know. I've told you everything I know." He slumped in the chair, a picture of defeat.

Julius raised his fists and looked ready to explode. "You slime! Do you think everybody is as rotten as you? I'd take you apart, but you're too filthy to touch! You..." Words failed him.

Soong said, "Okay, Slee, that's enough. Come on." He pulled Frank out of the chair, cuffed his wrists and propelled him out the door, turning him toward the lunch room and the rear exit. Frank hung his head and stumbled down the hall. Julius and Judy stood in the hallway and watched them go.

"What's going on? Where's Frank going with that detective?"

Judy flinched and whirled. Darlene had come up behind them. "Oh, you startled me!"

Darlene raised a languid hand to cover a yawn. "Sorry. Just wondered." Her eyes were hidden under the long, false eyelashes, her face showed idle curiosity, no more. She gave Julius an adoring smile and waited for him to speak.

"It seems Frank has had his hand in the till," Julius said, still furious. "He's been arrested. Do you know anything about this scam? Stealing our beef and selling it?"

"Who—me? Stealing? I guess not, Julius. What an idea!"

Was the girl as calm and detached as she seemed? Or was she a very clever actress?

Chapter 28
Mrs. Millet: Sea-Wrack

On Saturday, Margaret Millet rose and dressed early. Although her granny-pad was chilly, she didn't turn on the heater; that would add to the gas bill. Instead, she put on a warm, hand-knit vest over her tee shirt and jeans—a vest Judy Hark had made for her.

At nine o'clock, after making up her couch/bed and washing the breakfast dishes, she could wait no longer to contact Judy. She reached for the telephone—only to have it ring under her hand. She picked up the receiver. "Good morning, Judy. I was just going to call you."

Judy sounded annoyed. "I'd have called sooner, but I've already had company this morning—Myrtle Farrini—wouldn't you know! I hate the way she shows up without calling. And she drives right up in my driveway, like she owned the place. You wouldn't dream of doing that and we've been friends for years."

Margaret grinned. She knew Myrtle slightly and had heard a great deal about Judy's social rival. "What did Myrtle want, so early on a Saturday?"

"Oh, the Trunk, of course. I told her I had an important meeting this morning and couldn't possibly sell raffle tickets—at least not until after lunch. She went away mad."

"Just so she went away. Your important meeting is with me, right? There's something I forgot to tell you and we need to sort things out."

"Right. Willy's watching an old Marx Brothers thing on the movie channel." She raised her voice. "You won't even know I'm gone, will you, Willy?"

Margaret heard Willy's answering grunt. "Come on over. I'll put on the kettle."

There was little chance of interruption at her granny-pad. Laura and Tiny both liked to sleep in when they could and seldom appeared before noon on Saturdays. Even then, it was catch-up day for Laura—laundry, shopping, yard work—and Margaret could count on her privacy.

She opened the drop-leaf table to its full length and laid out her case notes and a pad of lined, yellow paper under the skylight's good north light. She set up a folding chair beside the secretary chair, put the kettle on to boil and listened for the clang of the back yard gate.

"Come in, come in! Your timing is perfect." Margaret poured boiling water over "English Breakfast" teabags in a pair of heavy mugs.

"You're all ready for me. Wonderful!" Judy sat in the secretary chair and plunked her purse on the floor. "And you're wearing my vest."

"Coziest thing I own. Nobody else ever knitted a vest for me." Margaret added milk to the tea, brought it to the table and sat in the folding chair.

"First, before I forget again, the thing I forgot to tell you..." The telephone pealed and they both jumped several inches. "Blast that thing! Let the answering machine take it; darn telephones, anyway!"

In far sweeter tones than Margaret had just used, the answering machine told the caller to leave a message.

"Mrs. Millet, this is Chief Belgrave. I just called to let you know the item we lost the other night has washed up on the beach, down by the Air Base. It's not in very good condition, but from what we can tell by prelim..."

Margaret snatched up the phone. "Chief Belgrave—I'm

here. Are you saying Glenda's body has been found?"

"Please, Mrs. Millet, not on the telephone. I just wanted to let you know—it seems everything you and Mrs. Hark reported was accurate. That's all I can say, right now. And I expect you've heard we have the prime suspect in custody—Mrs. Hark will have told you."

"What? Who!? Mrs. Hark's right here—who's in custody, Judy?"

Judy said, "I was about to tell you." Chief Belgrave said, "Good—I won't have to call her then. 'Bye, Mrs. Millet." Margaret gaped at Judy until the dial tone attacked her eardrum, then replaced the receiver. "Well!"

"Did he say Glenda's body washed up on the beach?"

"Was somebody arrested? Who was it?"

They stared at each other until Margaret realized they would have to take turns. "Yes, Glenda's body washed up on the beach, down by the air base. He said our report was accurate and he just wanted to let us know. Then he said 'goodbye' and hung up."

For the space of a mug of tea they re-lived finding Glenda's body at the shelter in Repose, its subsequent disappearance, the police search that had yielded drag marks and a button. "So that's what happened," Judy said. "Somebody lugged her body to the beach and sent it out with the tide."

"Or put it in a car and dumped it later. Was the tide going out then? We can check."

Judy said, "Oh, dear—now I suppose the District Attorney will file murder charges. Poor Frank! They arrested him yesterday at work, on charges of grand theft and so on, but they didn't have a murder case without the body."

"Frank Slee? They arrested Frank Slee?"

"Yes. That was his button, where we found Glenda's body. The football button. He came to me and asked for a needle to sew it back on."

Margaret shook her head to clear the mists. How could Frank Slee sew on a button that was in the hands of the police?

Judy saw her confusion. "Maybe I'd better start at the beginning."

"Please."

Judy told her tale; Frank's obvious ignorance of Glenda's death and the whereabouts of his button, his confession of theft, and his implication of Glenda and Darius Clumber in the stolen beef racket. "It was so strange to hear him blame Glenda, when I knew she was dead. I could hardly keep from telling him!" She added the details; conversion of the illicit profits to gold coin, Darius Clumber's attempt to go into business for himself and Cassandra Gates' disappearance.

Margaret could hardly express her intense admiration. "Good Work, Judy! Now we have something to go on. And the way you handled that detective! If you hadn't made him stop and listen, he'd have just hauled Frank off to jail and we wouldn't know any of this!"

Judy beamed. "Yes, well...Frank is a mess but I don't think he's gutsy enough to kill anyone. He even tried to throw suspicion on Julius."

"Oh? How did Julius react?"

"He was furious. Called Frank 'slime.'"

"Yes, but he's gutsy enough, I'm thinking."

"I can't see Julius cheating his employers," Judy said. "And as for guts, we aren't dealing with a demented killer here, you know. Just a thief who got in too deep on this stolen beef—and who by now is desperately afraid of getting caught. We could even have more than one killer. Glenda could have killed the driver, and then one of the others killed her."

"Just a thief? I'm not so sure. What if the money was used for something else—something terribly important to that thief? What if Julius, for instance, had a very good reason for wanting money?" Margaret wasn't quite so ready to eliminate a suspect. "He made a good salary and all that, but suppose he was planning to make a big change in his life—to leave the commercial world and join the colony at Repose, for example? And just suppose the colony needed money badly and he offered to provide it—in order to get in solid with Venus Valentine. I agree he's not the petty criminal type, but with sufficient motive..."

Judy sipped her tea. "Why would Repose need money? Besides, Frank said the beef thefts had been going on for more than five years. How long has Julius been hankering for Venus? Oh, put him down on your list if you like."

"Our list." Margaret wrote "Julius Portera" on the yellow pad. She skipped five lines and wrote "Frank Slee."

"Frank certainly fits the profile of a thief who got in too deep, like you said. I don't think we can eliminate him. He's strong enough to have moved Glenda's body, too. And there's the button—if he didn't lose it, how did it get there?"

"Obviously, it was planted—by someone who wanted to put the blame on Frank."

"And someone who could have taken it out of Frank's desk at BFK, if that's what happened."

"Right. I see that, Margaret. And that's Julius or Darlene or some unknown party we haven't tumbled to, yet.

Put down Darlene Evans—and her brother Jason—and Clark Atherton, all connected to Cassandra Gates. Come to think of it, put down Cassandra Gates."

Margaret wrote the names. She thought of gentle Jason singing in the moonlight. "Jason? Surely not. Who's your pick so far?"

Judy pushed back the secretary chair, its wheels squeaking in protest and took her tea mug to the sink. "I honestly don't know. I suspected Glenda from the first, but she's dead. Except for Frank, the only people we're sure were involved in the racket are Glenda and Darius Clumber and he's dead, too. Cassandra knew about it—and maybe Darlene, too—and Cassy is missing or dead, while Darlene comes to work as usual and shows no change in behavior that I can detect. She's so cool it's hard to suspect her of anything. I keep looking for someone else. If Julius could be involved, what about Venus Valentine?"

Margaret remembered Venus as she had seen her during the Repose Retreat. Could anyone with that kind of poise and serenity, that philosophy, possibly be connected with crime? "No. Not Venus. You know how sensitive I am to phonies and Venus is not a phony. She absolutely rings true. I have this nibbling fear that she may get hurt—that she might be in some sort of danger—but that's all."

She ran her fingers through her shaggy hair—badly in need of a trim (she just hadn't had time, what with all this detecting) and it stood on end worse than before. "I agree, another hand could be at work here. Who started this stolen beef thing, anyway? Who provided the market for it? "X" the Mastermind who pulls all the strings, keeps out of sight him or herself and tells the others what to do."

"And kills when things go wrong. It could be like that. The police will get names from Frank and question the people who bought the meat. Maybe they'll get onto him that way."

Margaret added "X, the Unknown" to her suspect list.

"You were going to tell me something you forgot—what was it?" Judy asked.

Margaret looked at the telephone. "Yes, well if that thing doesn't ring again, maybe I can. It's something Cassy's roommate told me, the day I visited them. June, the nice one, said Cassy and Darlene had a serious quarrel over money coming from BFK, but they made it up when Darlene explained that the money was for Repose. June didn't know the ins and outs of it, but if that money was from our beef scam..."

Judy said, "I overheard something on the phone one day, too. Darlene said, 'It's off. No more.' to somebody. She might have been talking to one of the buyers. Write it down, Margaret—write it down." Judy looked serious and thoughtful, as Margaret listed, "Money from BFK for Repose?" and "Phone conv. o/heard, 'It's off, no more.'" under Darlene's name.

"There's Darlene's feeling for Julius to consider here, too. I won't forget the fit she threw on the beach, the night she saw Julius and Venus together." Margaret wrote, "In love with Julius, jealous of Venus."

"Yes, it could matter," Judy said. "And why does she go to work looking like a hooker?"

"When she wears moccasins and calico at home. A split personality? Where was she when Glenda was killed, I wonder?"

"That's something the police should have checked.

She was in Repose that night, wasn't she?" Judy studied the list of seven names. "Who can we positively eliminate? What about Clark Atherton?"

Margaret shook her head. "I told you what Jason said. Clark wanted to push Cassy into marriage and when he came looking for her at Repose, that was when she vanished."

"Okay, could he be Mr. X? Can we make a case for that? Where was he when people were getting killed?"

"Good question. Mbyrna said he didn't come near her the weekend of the Retreat, when Glenda was killed. When she asked about it later, he said he spent the entire weekend at home, grading papers. Mbyrna thought he should have given her comfort and support. She felt quite deserted. I don't know about when Doofus was killed—do we have a time for that?"

Judy took a sheaf of folded paper from her purse. "I made some notes, too, after I talked to Clumber's landlady. Let's see...Doofus came home happy that night, said he was "in the money" at last. He played the lottery heavily, she said, and she asked if he'd finally won, but he said no, not that. She heard him drive out again after 11:30 and his body was found early the next morning. That puts his murder roughly between midnight and... and when?"

"The police should know about how long he'd been dead." Under Clark Atherton's name, Margaret wrote, "Whereabouts when Glenda killed? when Clumber killed?" and "Did he see Cassy before she vanished?"

"About those gold coins," Judy said. "Frank said they were hidden and he doesn't know where. We haven't come up with a reason for Glenda to be in Repose. Could those two items be connected?"

"Hmmm." Margaret once again considered Repose as a hiding place. "Unlike young girls, gold doesn't need to be fed. Repose abounds in places where it could be safely hidden. Not the shelter—the police would have found it there. Nearby? How about the shrine?"

Chapter 29
Mrs. Hark: Sunday Service

"So, you see, Willy," Judy Hark told her husband, "Margaret and I agree that the key to everything is in Repose. Not the restaurant supply company—the steak thefts are over and the search moves on. Repose is where Glenda Ravenet was killed, where Cassandra Gates disappeared, where the lives and loves of the people involved are focused. Even the truck driver—his body was found only a couple of miles away."

Willy shook his head solemnly. "You girls have done quite a piece of work. Couldn't you leave the rest to the police?" He held up his hand against Judy's protest. "I'm not saying you should just drop it—of course not. You should write up a complete report and hand it over to Chief Belgrave. All the things you've found out and the deductions you've made. The Chief's a smart man, and he'll appreciate it."

They sat side by side in two chairs facing their living room TV set. Willy's recliner was tilted, his feet elevated, his back comfortably supported. Judy sat upright in her upholstered rocker, her slippered feet on the footstool. As she spoke, her knitting needles shaped one of the soft, fleecy, infant caps she often created. Her daughter was a nurse-midwife in chilly Oregon, and the caps were for new babies. The TV set, for once, was turned off, since Sunday morning television offered nothing but preachers and infomercials.

"Margaret wants to see Venus and sound her out about the financial situation there. She thinks some of the money from the stolen steaks might have been earmarked for

Repose. She's also afraid Venus may be in danger. She doesn't know why, but she's afraid."

"Doesn't know why? Isn't a murderer running around loose a good enough reason to be scared? Heck, I'm scared—aren't you?"

"Not now. I was when we found Glenda's body." Judy could never keep things from Willy for very long and she had told him all about finding the shelter and Glenda's remains. He received the story with remarkable calm until she got to the part where the body was gone when they returned with the police. That shook him and this morning he was carefully, reasonably, trying to get her to terminate her investigations.

"We still think Cassandra Gates may be alive, Willy. We want to find her and neither Margaret nor I will give up until we do."

Willy sighed deeply, laid his head back against the chair and closed his eyes. "What happens next?"

"This morning, we'll go to the Sunday service at Repose. Margaret called Mbyrna Gates and asked her to come, too. Afterward, we'll talk to Venus about money and perhaps have a look around for Glenda Ravenet's gold coins."

Willy's eyelids opened a narrow slit. "Hmmm. And what's her name—Darlene? And her singing brother? And the man from BFK—Julius? Are they expected to attend?"

"It's possible. Would you like to come, Willy? Margaret's picking me up in half an hour."

"No thanks." Willy was silent for some minutes. Judy continued to knit. Just when she thought he must have dozed off, he said, "At least that salesman is still in jail."

The doors into Temple Hall stood hospitably wide and

Judy peered into the dim interior. The hall looked quite different inside. Folding chairs now made a double circle around a boxy, white-draped object in the center of the hall. An altar? A pair of tall white candles in silver candlesticks indicated that usage. A carved, high-backed chair of dark wood padded in blue plush stood close to this altar. The drapes were drawn over all the windows but one, where a shaft of light came through to illuminate the carved chair. Perhaps a dozen people were seated in the circle, and there was no talk, only a reverent silence.

Margaret Millet puffed to the top of the staircase and joined her on the landing. Judy whispered, "Are we early? Hardly anybody here."

"I don't think so. Mbyrna said she'd come, but she may be late and not to wait for her. Let's go in."

They quietly entered the hall and sat in the outer circle. Judy spotted Julius, seated on the far side of the altar. Was that Darlene/Thalia behind him? She couldn't be sure. She dropped her purse under the chair and folded her hands, feeling the hush of the room. After a few minutes, soft organ music began to play, although there was no organ. A white-robed man carrying a small tape player approached the altar, bringing the music with him. He lit the candles with a silver igniting wand and retreated to a chair in the circle.

After a rustle of movement, the attendees bowed their heads in expectant stillness. Judy bowed her own head and glanced sideways at Margaret to see how she was taking all this silence. Margaret's eyes were tightly closed and she clutched her purse as though she was walking down a dark alley. No serenity there.

Venus entered, wearing a long, white robe, her hair braided and pinned in a coil around her head. She sat in the carved, illuminated chair, folded her hands and joined in the silence. Were they praying? Meditating? Whatever the process, the results could be felt all around her. Finally Venus rose, approached the altar, and began to speak.

"Welcome to Repose. May the peace of this place give you peace and harmony of soul." She went on in this vein for a minute or two, then read an essay on "devotion to human service" by an author Judy had never heard of and whose name she immediately, comfortably, forgot.

This was the Service. In all, it took twenty minutes. No offering taken, no collection plate passed. The man who had lit the candles stood up and read several announcements: A family had sickness and needed food and comforts. Another member sought help to paint his house. Temple Hall was open at noon daily, for quiet meditation. Herbal tea and cakes were available downstairs on the front porch. Thank you for coming. He snuffed the candles with the snuffer end of the igniting wand.

Released from silence, the little group of worshipers chattered down the stairway. And yes, that was Darlene behind Julius. Judy looked up just in time to see her cross the speakers' platform at the far end of the hall and go out through a door on the right—a door that matched the paneling so well, Judy had never noticed it before.

Only Venus, Julius, Margaret and Judy remained in the hall. Judy gave Margaret a push. "Now's the time."

Julius helped Venus out of her robe. Margaret cleared her throat and squeaked, "Oh, Venus..."

Venus, now in leotards and tunic, folded the robe over her arm. "Why, Mrs. Millet! How nice to see you. And Mrs. Hark, too—welcome back to Repose."

Margaret said, "Could we...that is...do you have time to

talk? We're still trying to find young Cassandra, and..."

Julius said, "Cassandra Gates? The girl who worked for me? Mrs. Hark, what's this about?"

"I should think you'd know by now," Judy said. "This child has been missing for weeks and we're trying to find her. We have found out a good deal and you and Venus may be able to help."

"First let me ask you something. Why did you come to work at BFK? Just to snoop?"

"That's right, just to snoop. And—sorry Venus—we're snooping now. If it won't profane the Temple, could we just sit down and talk about it?"

"A search for the truth could never profane the Temple," Venus said calmly. "Yes, let's sit down and you can ask your questions. I'll do my best to answer." She draped the white robe over the back of the carved chair, then unpinned her hair and let the heavy braid fall over her shoulder. Julius pulled up a folding chair, seated Venus and stood behind her, arms folded, biceps bulging under the jacket of his summer-weight suit.

Judy's eyes had become accustomed to the dim light, even dimmer now that the sun no longer shone through the single undraped window. She scooted two chairs out of the circle and set them opposite Venus. "Go ahead, Margaret. Tell her about the quarrel between Cassy and Darlene."

Before Margaret could speak, they heard someone running lightly up the main staircase. A vigorous male figure in a flowered shirt paused in the doorway. "Is Julius Portera in here?"

"Here," Julius said. "What is it?"

Margaret nudged Judy and muttered, "Jason." Judy eyed the young man with interest. So this was the midnight singer/ philosopher who had so fascinated her friend. Nice looking lad! No wonder...

Jason beckoned and Julius left his guard position to meet him half way. Jason turned his back to the others and said a few quiet words they couldn't hear, then left the hall as quickly as he had come. Julius raised a hand. "Sorry Venus, I'm summoned. I'll come back as soon as I can." He clattered down the stairs.

"Well!" Judy looked at Venus. "I wonder who or what got that kind of response from Julius? Must be something urgent!"

Venus seemed unruffled. "I'm sure he'll take care of it, whatever it is. Julius has been a tower of strength during this business with the police. I don't know what I'd have done without him." She turned to Margaret. "Now, how can I help you, Mrs. Millet?"

Margaret looked around nervously. "Just us. My, this place seems big and empty—do you want to wait for Julius to come back? No? Well, okay."

She cleared her throat and took a deep breath. "Venus, we've been trying from the first to find Cassandra Gates. I talked to her roommates in Gambol Beach and one of the things they told me was that Darlene—that is, Thalia— and Cassandra had a serious quarrel about 'money coming from BFK,' and only made it up when Thalia said the money was to be used for Repose. Can you shed any light on this?" Her voice echoed in the empty hall.

Venus said, "BFK buys our produce. That's the only money we get from them. We can ask Thalia, of course. These roommates—it sounds unlikely."

Judy said, "Forgive me for asking, but is Repose in any trouble, financially? Is there some drastic need for money that Thalia might have known about?"

A cloud seemed to pass over Venus's brow. "Drastic? No, I don't think so. There's a mortgage coming due on a parcel of the farmland—we borrowed on it to build the new packing sheds and get the railroad spur brought in. We plan to refinance the loan, if the lender will go along."

"And will he?"

"Well, he's being a bit awkward. Something about a development he's interested in. But there are other lenders. I'm sure we'll work something out."

"Would Thalia know of this? Could she have used it to worry Cassandra, do you think?"

"Thalia would know; she does our bookkeeping. We make monthly payments on the loan and the due date is no secret."

Judy wondered why Darlene had never mentioned her bookkeeping experience. Why was she content to remain a lowly receptionist at BFK? "Tell me, Venus—how shall I put this—how high is Thalia in your organization here in Repose? Who would be the next leader, if you stepped aside?"

"I don't consider myself the colony's leader, Mrs. Hark. I'm an instructor, acting under Isis, the Earth Mother. We believe there are many paths and each of us follows our chosen prophet among those who have shown the way. Earnest July, who lit the candles for us today, is an instructor under Cronus, for instance. Decisions for the colony are made in council and everyone has a voice. Even our Sunday Services are led by different members in rotation. They are open to the public, since we are always open to new members and to sharing our way of life."

This was enlightening, but not the answer to Judy's question. "Let me put it another way. What future do you see for Thalia, here in Repose?"

Venus frowned. "I have done my best with Thalia, sought to show her our way of living for her own sake and because her brother Jason is so at one with us and so dear to all of us here in Repose. Always, Thalia has shown outward acceptance, helped with our Retreats and other activities...and yet...a future at Repose? I have never felt that Thalia was content here, or was likely to stay. I think she has some other future in mind."

Margaret said, "Venus, are you aware that Thalia cares very deeply for Julius?"

Venus stiffened and drew in her breath.

A movement drew Judy's attention to the far end of the hall. That nearly invisible door at the back of the speakers' platform opened.

Darlene/Thalia came through the door. Her calico granny dress swishing about her shins, she strode to the front of the platform. A taller figure, white eyeballs gleaming in his black face, followed and stood beside her.

"Turn around, Venus," Thalia said. "Don't worry, I have a future at Repose. You are the one with no future."

Clark Atherton. He "had them covered" with a wicked-looking hand gun.

Chapter 30
Mrs. Millet: Kwanza and Cassandra

Margaret Millet rose, her mind racing, unable to believe her eyes. Clark Atherton! That British-educated member of academic society. The protector of Mbyrna Gates and her brood. The man who arranged the meeting with Darlene to ease Judy Hark into her job at BFK. Of course, she saw it now; he had done that to keep track of their investigations. She stared at his lean figure, poised on the platform like a panther ready to spring, his close-cropped head, the glittering eyes. This was no upright Englishman! How could she have been so wrong? The British accent—her anglophilic responses had betrayed her, stifled her instincts. She and Judy had discussed him as a possible "X," an unknown mastermind of the Filet Mignon scam, but had seen no real evidence against him. Until now. That nasty looking hand gun was evidence of the first water.

Darlene Evans? Less surprising. The telephone conversation Judy overheard at BFK, the quarrel reported by Cassandra's roommates, the tantrum in the dunes, all were suspect. Darlene—and her brother Jason. The thought smote her over the heart. Jason! Jason had neatly removed Julius from their company, leaving three women alone in the hall. "Three helpless women" by the standard phrase. Helpless? That remained to be seen.

How were Judy and Venus taking it? Judy, on her feet but pale and shaken, met her eyes with a look that said, "so this is the answer; now we know."

If Judy was pale, Venus was ashen. She had risen and turned to face the platform when Darlene entered and now stared fixedly at the gun in Clark Atherton's hand. She seemed about to collapse.

Margaret took her arm. "Easy, Venus. They wouldn't dare to shoot us—not here. People all over the place. They'd never get away with it."

Venus raised her chin and quavered, "Thalia...what does this mean?"

Darlene was only too ready to tell her. "I'll tell you what it means, my dear Goddess! It means your reign is over. I'm in charge now! And you two old biddies—my God what a pair! Sticking your noses into everything! If you hadn't butted in, we could have done it easy, no strain. Venus would disappear, Clark would foreclose on the mortgage, I'd take charge in Repose, no problem. Now we have to dispose of you two, and it's your own fault, you ____ ____!"

Margaret turned to Venus, "Clark is your mortgage lender?" Venus nodded.

To Darlene, "And the stolen beef? Is that where he got the money?" She could see the truth on their faces; that guess had hit home. "Amazing. The gold coin business—that was for poor old Frank Slee's benefit, then. Would you have killed him, too?"

Clark Atherton spoke for the first time. "That's enough, Darlene. Let's get out of here and get on with it." He stepped down off the platform and approached the circle of chairs.

Margaret still held Venus by the arm. She backed toward the main entrance as Clark approached, pulling Venus along. Judy Hark stayed close to her side.

"Stop right there, or I'll shoot one of you here and now." Clark said. "You." He waved the gun at Judy. "The coppers wouldn't be surprised to find your body, after all you've poked into. I didn't want to hurt you old birds, but I couldn't know you'd get so far, could I? Darlene, shut those doors and lock them!"

As Darlene's moccasins sped toward the double doors, Margaret glimpsed a new figure silhouetted in the doorway. Mbyrna Gates—late to the Sunday Service, but just in time to bumble into danger! Wait—Mbyrna was not alone! And not bumbling, either. Bending over, she hissed, "Get him, Kwanza!" and released her huge black dog.

Kwanza charged across the floor, claws slipping and clattering on the polished wood. Clark raised his arms to defend himself as the eighty-pound dog crashed into his chest. He went down under the impact and the gun flew in a high arc. Darlene, Judy and Margaret all scrambled for the gun.

Darlene was the faster. Margaret grabbed her around the waist as she dashed by and held on—literally—for dear life. Judy got almost to the gun, but not quite. Someone else reached it first, from the other direction. Someone in denim shorts, with long, flashing legs and beaded corn-row braids, who scooped up the gun and held it high in one hand, a white, triumphant grin splitting her black face. "Hold him, Kwanza! Hey Mom! All right!"

Darlene struggled and clawed. Margaret grabbed her wrist and twisted her arm behind her back, a useful armlock she had learned years ago. "Old women are not always helpless," she spat into Darlene's ear.

Kwanza poised his full weight on Clark Atherton's chest and laughed in Clark's face, his tongue lolling from the side of his mouth. The dog seemed to say, "what a romp! Go ahead, move, so I can bite you!" When Clark got his breath back, he let out a scream of terror.

Mbyrna took the gun, embraced her daughter, and cried, "Cassandra! This is my daughter, Cassandra!"

"We figured that out," Judy said. "Where on earth did you come from, Cassandra?"

"Never mind that now," Mbyrna said. "The police are right outside. Go out and tell them I found Mrs. Hark, will you dear? They've been beating the bushes for her."

"Sure, Mom! Watch him!" Cassandra pointed at Clark, who twisted under Kwanza's paws.

"Friend, Kwanza! Friend!" Clark cried, but Kwanza didn't believe him.

Mbyrna stood away from Clark and held the gun steady. "I've been on the stairs for the last five minutes. I heard everything. How could you—after all we've done for you? Helped you come to this country, get a good job, everything! And you wanted my daughter! You're—" Mbyrna used several words from another language and Clark squirmed and yelled at her in the same tongue. Margaret was glad she couldn't understand it.

Julius Portera dashed in through the double doors and, after a quick glance at the scene, headed straight for Venus, who opened her arms wide. Darlene tried again to wrench free, but Margaret wasn't having it. She didn't really care if she broke the girl's arm. Darlene cried out in pain and ceased to struggle.

Chief Belgrave and three uniformed policemen approached cautiously, standing at the sides of the doorway until they could assess the situation. The "uniforms" had drawn guns and showed their training by moving inside one at a time, covering each other as they came.

"All right, folks. What's going on here?" the Chief called. "Mrs. Hark, is that you?"

"Yes, Chief. Am I glad to see you!"

"Willy said you might be in trouble over here. I can see he was right."

"Did Willy call you? Wonderful! Bless his heart!" Judy pointed. "The man on the floor is Clark Atherton, probably your murderer, and the girl Margaret's holding is his accomplice. Please take charge of them and don't let them get away!"

Chief Belgrave waved at his minions and said, "Do it, men. If Mrs. Hark says so, it must be true!"

Mbyrna handed Clark's gun to one of the officers and called Kwanza, who reluctantly released his prize. One policeman rolled Clark over and secured his wrists while another swiftly dealt with Darlene. Cassandra dropped to her knees beside the dog and hugged him hard. Mbyrna joined them to make a pile of joy in the middle of the floor.

As Margaret watched them, her own cup overflowed. Cassandra alive and well, after so much searching, so much fearful heartache! Just one more detail. "Chief Belgrave," she said, "that gun is very likely the murder weapon."

Chapter 31
Mrs. Hark: Cassandra at Home

At breakfast Monday morning, Judy Hark tried to explain things to Willy; things she really didn't understand herself. Chief Belgrave had taken preliminary statements from everyone at Temple Hall and said to make themselves available for longer interviews when called upon. Clark and Darlene had been carried off to the Gambol Beach City Jail. When Judy finally got home, she was exhausted, so Willy told her to take a hot bath and go to bed; she could tell him all about it in the morning.

Now it was morning. Judy buttered a piece of toast and said, "We found the black girl, Cassandra Gates, alive and well! Or rather, she found us. I was terrified until Mbyrna showed up with that wonderful dog—can we get a black Lab, Willy? And Margaret tackled Darlene— you should have seen her! Then Cassandra popped up and grabbed the gun. It was thrilling! Best of all, you had called the police and they were right outside. How did you know, Willy? You never did anything like that before."

"What gun? Who had a gun?"

"Oh, didn't I tell you? Clark Atherton, Mbyrna's supposed friend, the man who said he was waiting for Cassandra to grow up so he could marry her. He and Darlene came in while we were talking to Venus, and he threatened us with a gun. I really think, if...How did you know, Willy?"

"Actually, I didn't," Willy said. "Someone called on the phone and said you and Margaret were in danger at Repose. So I called Chief Belgrave—just caught him as he was going out to play golf. Guess I spoiled his Sunday."

"We seem to make that a practice." Judy remembered the day she and Margaret had found Glenda Ravenet's body. "Who called you? Do you know?"

"I wrote it down on the phone pad. So is this Atherton your murderer?"

"We think so. Margaret and I are going into Santa Porta this afternoon to see Mbyrna and Cassandra. Clark is definitely involved in the Filet Mignon thefts and he loaned the money to Repose as a mortgage. There's still a lot we don't know, but I think Cassandra can tell us."

Judy rose from the table to look at the telephone message pad. "Jason Evans! Oh, Willy, Jason called you! Margaret will be so happy. I have to call her right now."

That afternoon, the welcome mat was out in Abby Lane. Cassandra opened the front door with a sweeping gesture and ushered Margaret and Judy to the sunken living room, where Mbyrna and her two younger children waited. Mbyrna, in a colorful full-length robe, introduced the children as Kareem, age ten, and Della, twelve. "I couldn't make them go to school today; they were too excited. Having Cassandra back—and she hasn't told us a thing! Well, hardly anything. Said she wanted to wait for you ladies and tell us all at once."

She ushered them to the black leather couch and took the chair opposite. Kareem and Della leaned on the back of her chair. Cassandra dashed out of the room and returned carrying a tray of refreshments; three bottles of cola, a decanter of golden sherry, glasses, and a plate of vanilla wafers.

"It's a party!" Judy said.

"A party indeed. How can I ever thank you for all you've done to find my child?" Mbyrna poured sherry into long-stemmed glasses and passed them ceremoniously across the coffee table. "Now, Cassandra, don't keep us waiting."

Cassy, in an oversize man's shirt and well-worn jeans, picked up an open bottle of cola and sat cross-legged on the floor. She took a long pull at the bottle, wiped the top of it with her palm, and looked up at the expectant faces around the coffee table. "Well, it's like this..."

Margaret interrupted. "Before you start, Cassandra, would you satisfy my curiosity first? Just tell us where you were, all that time. I looked for you everywhere, and you had to get food somewhere..."

Cassandra's white smile flashed and her corn-row braids swished about her shoulders. "Most of the time, I was right under your feet. You know the lectern on the stage in Temple Hall? It opens. The side where the speaker stands is really a door with a spring latch—you know, the kind you push to open. There's a ladder down into a little room underneath and the room has a panel that opens into the back of the pantry, where all the food is stored. I had plenty to eat!"

"And how did you find this perfect hiding place?"

"I don't know why it was built that way, but one day when I was fooling around in the hall, I bumped into the lectern and the door opened. I went down the ladder and took a look—and decided it was something I wasn't supposed to know about—but it sure came in handy when I wanted to hide."

"Thank you," Margaret said.

"Mom told me how you got my telephone calls and decided to investigate. That was super! It must have been Doofus Clumber making the nasty calls."

Judy said, "We thought it might be. Now tell us why you had to hide."

"And why you didn't call your mother!" Mbyrna added. "You should have known how worried I'd be!"

"I know, Mom. I'm really sorry—but I just couldn't risk it. Clark would have killed me and he'd have killed you if he thought you knew anything."

"I just can't believe it. Clark Atherton, after all we've done for him..."

Margaret said, "Me too. Educated in England and so helpful to us. I never had a clue."

Judy shook her head. "I'm getting more confused by the minute, Cassandra. Please start at the beginning and tell us exactly what happened."

"Okay. It started five or six years ago, I guess; way before I got into it. Must have been when Clark first came here from South Africa. He met Darlene someplace—I don't know where. Darlene lived in Repose and worked at BFK. She had a big yen for Julius and for lots of money."

"And wasn't a bit particular about how she got what she wanted," Mbyrna said. Judy remembered that Mbyrna had never been fond of Darlene.

"What Clark wanted was a little kingdom of his own, where he could stay behind the scenes and be the big boss." As Cassandra told her tale, Judy marveled at the maturity of her thinking. How had this child figured out the motivations, the quirks, the personal agendas, of the people who played out this bizarre plot?

Clark Atherton and Darlene Evans, each for selfish reasons, had joined forces to accumulate money and gain control of Repose. Darlene knew the money could be had at BFK—if Glenda Ravenet would help. She arranged for Clark and Glenda to meet.

Clark found Glenda a willing tool. Glenda brought in Frank Slee and Darius Clumber. "I'm not sure how Darlene and Clark managed it," Cassandra said, "but Glenda thought the whole Filet Mignon thing was her own idea. She gave the money to Clark to buy South African gold coins and I'm sure she thought the two of them were going to hop a plane, pick up their money and live the good life on the Riviera, leaving poor old Frank Slee and Doofus Clumber holding the bag. Glenda didn't know Darlene was in on the deal."

Clark did not buy gold coins. When Repose needed money, Darlene brought him in as a wealthy lender. He used the BFK money to give Repose a mortgage on a piece of land, the first step to acquiring the property.

"And how did you find out about this, dear?" Mbyrna asked.

"A little at a time. Clark got me the job at BFK about a year ago, through Glenda. He was so curious about everything that happened there, I began to wonder, you know? And Darlene sort of adopted me. She took me to Repose and I got interested in what they do. And Jason was there."

"A lovely young man!" Margaret said, warmly. "He called Willy and said to call the police, even though Darlene, his own sister..."

Judy said, "Clark really intended to take over Repose, the whole time? He and Darlene?"

"Yes, I think so." Cassandra nibbled a cookie. "You heard what Darlene said yesterday—Venus was supposed to 'disappear' so Darlene could take her place."

"Why did you leave your apartment and go to stay in

Repose?" Judy asked.

"Okay, I was getting to that." Cassy explained in detail. She had come across a steak sale at a very low price, to a customer who wasn't on the books. She asked Glenda Ravenet about it and was told not to worry, it was a special, one-time deal. Then she noticed, just as Judy had noticed, that Glenda kept certain envelopes that came in the mail and handled certain accounts personally. She began to look for these transactions and keep track of them in a small black notebook.

"I could see there was a lot of money involved and it seemed like either Frank or Julius had to know about it, so I didn't dare ask either of them. Finally, I talked to Darlene—the stupidest thing I could have done!"

"Don't blame yourself," Judy said. "She had me completely fooled, too. Nothing seemed to affect her, no matter what happened. She never showed a sign of guilt."

"Darlene never felt any guilt. She was so self-centered, nothing touched her. It was like she was wrapped in plastic, or something."

"Teflon," Margaret muttered, "like Ronald Reagan."

"Anyhow, when I told her Glenda was stealing money from BFK, and I was going to the owners or the police or somebody, we had a big row. She said I couldn't do that or Repose would be closed down and all the people who live there would be homeless. She said everybody was in on it, and the whole operation was set up to avoid income tax and provide money for Repose. I should come and stay at her place and she'd let me in on everything."

"And you went? Without telling me anything? Oh, Cassy, why couldn't you come to your mother?" Mbyrna's voice was harsh with pain as she refilled the sherry glasses.

"Oh, Mom, I don't know. There was Jason at Repose, and Venus, and I liked them so much; they are such wonderful people. I couldn't do anything that might hurt them."

Kareem and Della hadn't spoken or stirred from their places behind their mother's chair, and Judy marveled at their good manners. Kareem was as dark as Cassy and wore the current school-boy uniform; pants baggy to the fall-down point, black t-shirt with sports logo in gaudy colors, baseball cap on backward. Della, cute and pert in a tank top and a red mini skirt, had smooth, caramel-colored skin like her mother. They looked at each other now, and moved to the floor, one on each side of their sister. The younger generation presenting a united front.

Judy asked, "So what happened at Repose?"

"Oh, it was wonderful at first. Jason showed me how to milk a goat and Venus told us about the Goddess and we had scrumptious clam chowder and Jason wrote a song about me. Then Clark came and spoiled everything!"

Cassy had been terrorized by Clark's visit to Repose and told of it in disconnected fragments. Judy questioned her carefully and gradually pieced them together. Clark had learned from Darlene that Cassy knew of the Filet Mignon embezzlement. Darlene let him know how cleverly she had handled the matter, convincing Cassy that the money was needed at Repose. Clark took that line too, at first, but when Cassy asked why he was concerned about the welfare of Repose, he revealed his own ambitions.

"Clark said he wanted me to marry him, Mom. He said I'd be the Queen of his country! He meant to get hold

of the land at Repose and build a fabulous resort, or
maybe bring in industry—I'm not sure. Whatever he did,
it would make us—and Darlene—totally rich. Then he
said that about getting married and how he had taken
me into his confidence and I mustn't betray him. Everybody would be rich and happy. He said to just keep going to work and say nothing to anybody, and I and all
my family would be safe and have a glorious future. The
way he said it, the part about being safe—oh, boy! Was
I scared!"

Margaret said, "The Filet Mignon scheme would have
come out sooner or later and Glenda would have talked.
Clark must have planned to kill her, all along."

Judy asked, "What did you do then, Cassandra?"

"Well, I knew Jason was okay, so I told him all about
it. He was pretty unhappy about Darlene, but said she
would have to learn her lesson and she would, too, when
the time was right. Then he said Clark wouldn't dare to
hurt my family if he didn't know where I was, because I
knew everything about him and could tell the police. He
said I should disappear. I said I knew just the place, and
he said not to tell him, so he couldn't give me away. We
fixed it to leave messages for each other at the hut in the
swamp.

"That night, I put some clothes in my backpack and
tied my sleeping bag on top and climbed down the ladder into the secret room. It had been used before; I could
tell. The doors had wooden latches on the inside, so nobody else could open them. There were some old paperback books—I know all about Nero Wolfe and Double-
O-Seven now! There was even a funny old pottie, like
a pail with a lid. At night, I emptied it in the rest-room
toilet. I got wonderful food from the kitchen—gained a

couple of pounds, I think."

Margaret shook her head. "I saw the light when you opened the refrigerator one night. Couldn't get in, or I'd have caught you in the act."

Judy said, "You hid before Darius Clumber was killed. Did Jason write you a message about that?"

"Not right away. I found a newspaper in the kitchen and read about it. I left Jason a note, but he didn't know anything. Do you?"

"Only what Frank Slee said—that he thought Clumber decided to sell a load of steaks on his own, and Glenda killed him."

Cassandra's face remembered horror. "That fits. It fits with what Clark said when he killed Glenda."

In stunned silence, they took in the thought that this child had been an eye-witness to murder. Then they all spoke at once.

"Oh, my poor baby!"

"And what did he say?" Margaret was shocked but not diverted.

"You actually saw him do it?" Judy gasped.

"Bang, bang! You're dead! Co-o-o-o-l, Cassy!" That was Kareem, age ten.

Chapter 32
Mrs. Millet: Tidying Up

On their way home from visiting the Gates family, Margaret and Judy were quiet for several miles. When Margaret turned her pickup onto the Dolliver Canyon road, she broke the silence. "I said Cassandra could clear things up, didn't I?"

"You certainly did."

"What that child went through—it breaks my heart!" Cassandra had gone to the hut that Saturday night to see if Jason had left a message in their "post office," a coffee can with a plastic lid, hidden in the rubble wall of the hut. She heard angry voices, so she ducked into the reeds and crept closer to see who was there. Margaret imagined the dark scene Cassandra had described, her terror as she witnessed Clark Atherton and Glenda Ravenet in their final quarrel. Clark wanted to get rid of Glenda, told her she was of no further use to him and would be prosecuted for theft and murder if she went to the police. Glenda said she had nothing to lose and pulled a gun out of her handbag. She lost the gun to Clark, who said, "One good deed deserves another!" and shot her dead.

Judy said, "And after she saw that cold-blooded killing, to go back to that tiny room under the lectern and stay there, all alone, for another week! How could she?"

"Cassy thought Clark might have found her coffee-can post office, so she was afraid to go near it," Margaret said. "She didn't know we found Glenda's body the next evening, or that Clark dumped it in the ocean while we were calling the police."

"It turned out good for us, though. She sure showed up at the right moment! Even with the police right outside, thanks to Jason and Willy..." Judy's voice trailed away.

Jason, Margaret thought. His sister in such trouble, the choice he made when he called Willy to send the police—what must he be going through with Darlene in jail?

Again, Judy echoed her thoughts. "Margaret, we ought to see Jason and tell him how grateful we are."

"Yes! Let's do it."

"I have to go home first. Willy's anxious to hear what Cassandra had to say. Why don't you go, Margaret? Go to Repose. Jason will need someone to talk to and he likes you. What is it he calls you—Dune Lady?"

Later that day, Margaret did drive to Repose. She parked her pickup in front of Darlene's cottage and walked down the driveway to the back yard.

She found Jason in front of his trailer. He wore jeans and the blue Hawaiian shirt and sat cross-legged with his bongo drums before him, as he had at the Shrine the night they met. He wasn't drumming. He leaned forward, the picture of dejection, forearms on the silent drumheads.

Margaret whistled the first bar of "My Nubian Princess." Jason raised his head and managed a feeble smile. "Hello, Dune Lady. Nice of you to come."

She sat on the trailer steps. "How could I not come? You saved my life, Jason."

The long, sandy lashes swept his cheek and the smile broadened. "Yes, there is that."

Margaret waited for him to speak again. The peace and stillness of Repose were all about them. Even the goats lay down in their pen, enjoying the warm, sunny afternoon under the trees. Jason's cabbages had doubled in size, she noticed. The dead tomato vines had been cleared away and fresh, green snow pea sprouts reached for the lattice.

Finally Margaret said, "We went to see Cassandra this morning, Judy Hark and me. She seems to be all right and her mother is very happy to have her safe at home."

"Yes. Cassandra, my Nubian Princess."

"You knew she was alive, all the time." Margaret couldn't keep the note of reproach out of her voice.

Jason looked up. "Oh, yes, I knew. I told you that in the dunes."

"Yes, you did, and I believed you. It was very comforting to me—but it didn't do much for Mbyrna Gates. She's had a terrible time."

"Couldn't be helped, Dune Lady. Telling Mrs. Gates would have tipped the evil cradle-robber." Jason straightened his back and stretched his shoulders. "A man who had every chance to be good and worthwhile, but whose soul was full of evil and greed. How does that happen? Is it envy? The desire for power over people's lives and the things, the trappings of wealth? I think and think about it, and it doesn't make sense."

"I know. And how could Darlene have chosen Clark's philosophy over yours? A classic case of being led astray, Jason. You must try to forgive her."

"Is that how you see it? I'm not so sure."

His face drooped and Margaret was sorry she had mentioned Darlene. She quickly changed the subject. "I have a confession to make. For a little while, I was afraid you were one of the bad guys. You lured Julius away just before Clark showed up with his gun. I was so relieved when I learned you had called Willy and warned him! I can't tell you..."

She had only made matters more painful. Jason couldn't look at her. "Yes, I called and told him to get the police out here, after I overheard Darlene and the Evil One making their plans. They were going to take Venus to one of the cabins and, as they so politely put it, 'quietly dispose of the Goddess.' Monterey Pine Cabin—they were going to take her there and kill her. My little sister said, 'Just wait until after the service, when Venus is alone in Temple Hall. She always stays to meditate.'" His voice broke and he buried his face in his hands.

"Oh, Jason, I'm so sorry."

When he could speak again, Jason said, "Actually, I called you first. You weren't home, so I tried Mrs. Hark—and got her husband. He said you were here in Repose attending the service and would stay after to talk to Venus. So I said he'd better call the police, you were all in danger of your lives."

"And when the police came?"

"They wanted to catch Atherton in the act, so they waited at Monterey Pine Cabin. Julius was with Venus in Temple Hall and might have spoiled the ambush, so they asked me to get him out."

"And Mbyrna coming in with Kwanza—was that part of the Police strategy?"

"No! Oh no, that was completely unplanned. We saw her walking around, but didn't expect her to go into Temple Hall because she had the dog with her.

"I stayed in the parking lot, and the police waited in the bushes around the cabin until Cassandra came flying down the path and yelled, 'Hey, Cops! Where are you?! Help!!'" Jason chuckled. "The Chief made a dash for Temple Hall. You should have seen his face."

Margaret imagined Chief Belgrave's chagrin at being summoned in such a manner—when he thought he and his men were completely hidden in ambush. "Those blue uniforms were a wonderful sight, all the same. I don't know how much longer I could have held onto..." She bit her tongue. No need to tell Jason she had personally captured Darlene. Talk about rubbing salt in the wounds! "Uh, Clark might have gotten away from the dog and I don't know if Mbyrna could really have shot him."

Jason rose. "Allow me to offer a little hospitality, Dune Lady. Let's move to the lawn chairs and have a cool drink."

He went into the trailer and Margaret sat in one of the folding aluminum chairs. The sun had moved enough to put the chairs in the shade of the trailer awning, but only just; its plastic arm was still warm to the touch. Jason brought out tall glasses, tinkly with ice. The drink, a delicious fruit juice concoction, reminded Margaret of her mother's homemade blackberry shrub.

"Thank you, Jason. Very refreshing. It reminds me of my mother's homemade blackberry shrub."

"Glad you like it. It does have blackberry juice in it—among other things."

"Jason, did I ever tell you how I happened to be in the dunes that night? When we met at the shrine?"

"No, Dune Lady. Why don't you tell me."

So she did. She told him how much she had hoped to find some trace of Cassandra and her idea that he might be the food provider. How she had heard him singing of Fire and Rain—she even told him the song was dear to her because of the man it made her remember—and how she had followed him to the dunes and later, had gone to Temple Hall and seen the refrigerator light come on in the kitchen. "I was so close to Cassandra that night, but still so far."

Jason said, "It wasn't the time for you to find her."

"But I wanted to, so much! I wanted to traipse around Repose calling, 'Cassandra! Cassandra!' like the song about Chloe in the swamp."

A leggy whirlwind flew around the corner of the garage and cried, "Did somebody call my name?" Jason rose and Cassandra charged into his arms. "Oh, Jason, Jason!"

"Well," Margaret said, "If I'd know it would work, I'd have tried it sooner!"

Several weeks later, Margaret got out her file on Cassandra Gates. She added her copy of the statement she had given the police and the more complete report she had written for her own satisfaction. There were newspaper clippings, too, as the case attracted a good deal of attention in the media. Clark Atherton had been charged with the murder of Glenda Ravenet and his lawyer planned to plead self-defense. She wondered if he would get off. It seemed unlikely, considering Cassandra's eyewitness testimony.

Darlene and Frank Slee had confessed to grand theft and would testify against Clark Atherton. Some sort of plea-bargain there, Margaret supposed. It seemed that Glenda Ravenet must have taken Frank's button from his desk and had it with her when she was murdered. If she had shot Clark Atherton instead of the other way around, she might have used it to implicate poor, foolish Frank in the killing. Glenda and Clark—what a murderous pair!

As for Darlene/Thalia, Margaret could not predict the

future of that dual-personality girl. Would Jason ever forgive her? Would Venus? For that matter, why should they?

Another item for the file, and this a happy one—the wedding invitation she had received from Julius and Venus. She planned to be there "with bells on."

Julius had quit BFK to manage the crop-land at Repose. BFK attached everything Clark Atherton owned and Repose wouldn't have to repay the mortgage until a judge decided who should get the money. Since Julius had left the company on friendly terms, it seemed likely that BFK might extend or renew the mortgage.

Cassandra Gates safe and sound—now there was a happy ending! Everybody wanted Cassandra. Her father had come back from South Africa and he and her mother wanted their daughter safe at home. Jason wanted Cassandra in Repose, sharing his simple life. It seemed nobody had asked Cassandra what she wanted—except Margaret Millet and Judy Hark.

Curious to the last, Margaret and Judy had invited Cassandra to lunch at Shelley's Restaurant. Judy insisted on paying and ordered Filet Mignon all 'round. "It's the fitting and proper way to celebrate your safe return!"

Margaret attacked her steak. "Tell us, Cassandra, what are your future plans?"

"As soon as things quiet down at home, I'm going back to live with my roommates at the apartment. Jason is nice, but I want to have lots of dates and fun. I'm going to keep my job at BFK and study bookkeeping in night school, so I can work up to be Office Manager. Then, when I'm about thirty or so, and I can support myself no matter what, I'm going to marry some nice man and have two—that's two—children, a boy and a girl."

"You've got it all figured out."

"I had lots of time to think about it, down in that little room."

At her table with the file before her, Margaret smiled as she remembered Cassandra's words and the confident way she grinned and tossed those corn-row braids.

Another item belonged with this file—the item that started everything. Margaret rose and went into the bathroom, opened a cabinet and took out the small, cardboard soap box. Was that the right one? Yes. The box contained her answering machine tape, the tape with the telephone messages on it. Thank goodness, hiding it so carefully had been an unnecessary precaution!

To think the whole business started with a new telephone number. If she hadn't let the telephone company bamboozle her into giving up her old number, she would never have gotten involved in this strange affair—never have met Cassandra Gates and her family or gone to a Retreat (and played poker) at Repose.

A whole lot of excitement and fright and sorrow and joy would have been avoided. Did she regret the experience? No, she did not.

All the same, she had really liked her old telephone number. She wondered who the telephone company gave it to. Impulsively, she picked up her phone and dialed: 639-3696. All those lovely, lucky, sixes.

One ring. Another ring. Then a prim, recorded voice said, "We're sorry, the number you have dialed is not in service. Please check your directory and dial again."

Not in service!? How could that be? Margaret's ears throbbed with a rush of blood. The very idea! The phone company could perfectly well have given her back her old number! Outrageous!

She paced several lengths of her granny pad. When she could hold still, she pulled out the bulky telephone directory and looked up the phone company's business number. And dialed. After waiting out the voice-mail options and staying on hold for the next available representative, she finally heard a human voice. "How can I help you?"

"You can give me back my telephone number!" Margaret said between clenched teeth. "It's 639-3696. Don't tell me you can't. I just dialed it, and nobody else is using it, and I want it back!"

An ex-chemist, teacher and bookstore owner, Margaret Searles writes (and loves) the traditional mystery. Her stories and articles have appeared in *Whispering Willow*, *Sleuthhound* (contest winner), *Futures Mystery Magazine* (Fire To Fly Award), *Mystery Readers Journal*, the *SLO Death Anthologies*, *New Times*, and other publications. She holds memberships in Sisters in Crime and Mystery Writers of America.